SUPREME THREAT

A LOGAN ALEXANDER THRILLER

T.L. WILLIAMS

First Coast Publishers

Also by T.L. Williams

The Last Caliph

Cooper's Revenge

Unit 400: The Assassins

Zero Day: China's Cyber Wars

www.tl-williams.com

Acknowledgements

I would like to thank my editor, Emily Carmain, at Noteworthy Editing for her fine work to bring out the best in my writing. To my Beta readers, especially fellow author and colleague, Edward Mickolus, whose professional observations and tenacious proofreading made this a better book, and my wife Carol, who has been at my side throughout my writing journey. To the U.S. Department of Energy and Los Alamos National Laboratory for their detailed information on the U.S. Stockpile Stewardship Program. To the Central Intelligence Agency for permission to use the North Korea map from the World Factbook, and the Publications Review Board for expediting their review of my manuscript. To the New Mexico Tourism Department whose True Adventure Guide and plentiful travel resources helped me craft realistic backgrounds for the geographic areas of New Mexico that appear in this book. To my design team at Expert Subjects, who unfailingly bring out the best in my books by packaging them in artful covers and visually pleasing interiors. And to my readers, thank you for supporting me on my writing journey.

T. L. Williams
Ponte Vedra Beach, Florida

To my grandchildren,

Julia Hunter, Holt, Archer, Chipley, Will, Barrett

With love

Printed in the United States of America

Publisher's Note
This is a work of fiction. The people, events, circumstances, and institutions depicted are fictitious and the product of the author's imagination. Any resemblance of any character to any actual person, whether living or dead, is purely coincidental.

Publisher's Cataloging-in-Publication Data

Names: Williams, T.L.
Title: Supreme threat : a Logan Alexander thriller / T.L. Williams.
Description: Ponte Vedra Beach, FL : First Coast Publishers, 2021. Includes 1 b&w map. | Summary: North Korea's President has directed the nation's Intelligence Service to mount an attack, codenamed Operation Supreme Threat, against the U.S. But CIA officer Logan Alexander, working with U.S. law enforcement and international allies, unveils the plot and races against time to neutralize his elusive foes.
Identifiers: LCCN 2021913595 | ISBN 9780988440098 (pbk.) | ISBN 9780988440081 (ebook)
Subjects: LCSH: Intelligence officers -- Fiction. | Nuclear warfare -- Prevention -- Fiction. | Terrorism -- Prevention -- Fiction. | Korea (North) -- Fiction. | Los Alamos Scientific Laboratory -- Fiction. | United States. -- Central Intelligence Agency -- Fiction. | BISAC: FICTION / Thrillers / Espionage. | FICTION / Thrillers / Political. | FICTION / Thrillers / Terrorism.
Classification: LCC PS3623.I44 S8 2021 | DDC 813 W55--dc23
LC record available at https://lccn.loc.gov/2021913595

Epigraph

"The entire United States is
within range of our nuclear weapons;
a nuclear button is always on my desk.
This is reality, not a threat."

North Korean Supreme Leader Kim Jong-Un

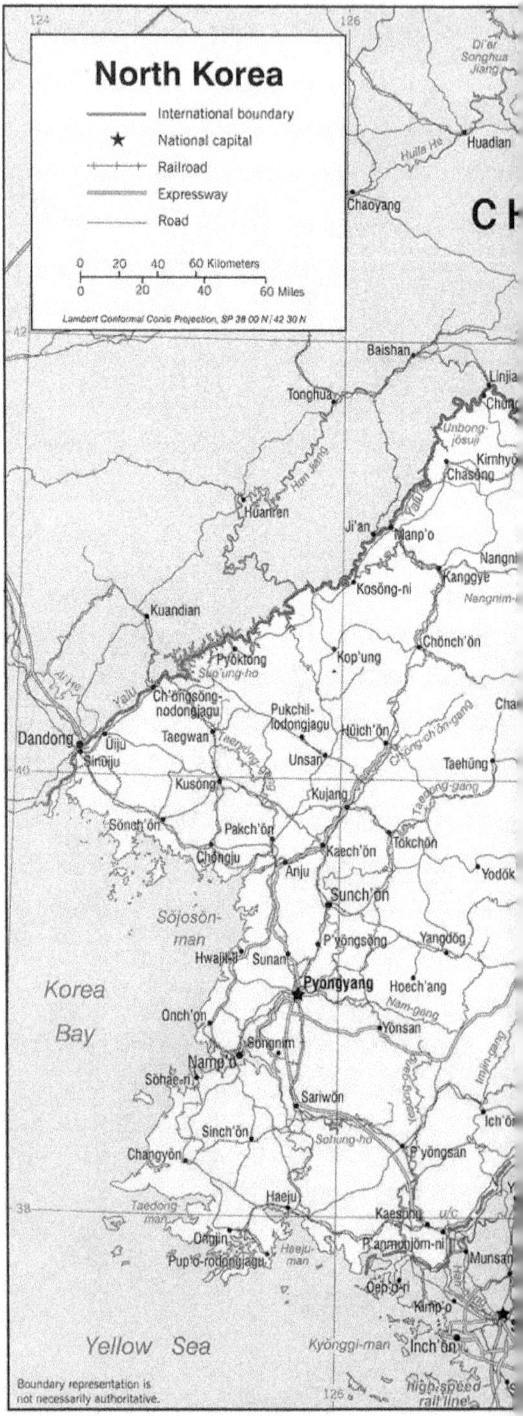

North Korea
International boundary
National capital
Railroad
Expressway
Road
0 20 40 60 Kilometers
0 20 40 60 Miles
Lambert Conformal Conic Projection, SP 38 00 N / 42 30 N
Boundary representation is not necessarily authoritative.
Korea Bay
Yellow Sea
Sŏjosŏn-man
Taedong-man
Haeju-man
Kyŏnggi-man
Pyongyang
Dandong
Sinŭiju
Ŭiju
Kuandian
Huanren
Tonghua
Baishan
Chaoyang
Huadian
Ji'an
Manp'o
Kanggye
Kosŏng-ni
Chŏnch'ŏn
Kop'ung
Pyŏktong
Ch'ŏngsŏng-nodongjagu
Taegwan
Pukchil-lodongjagu
Hŭich'ŏn
Unsan
Kusŏng
Kujang
Sŏnch'ŏn
Pakch'ŏn
Chŏngju
Anju
Kaech'ŏn
Tŏkchŏn
Sunch'ŏn
P'yŏngsŏng
Yangdŏk
Hwaju-ri
Sunan
Hoech'ang
Onch'ŏn
Yŏnsan
Songnim
Namp'o
Sŏhae-ri
Sariwŏn
Sinch'ŏn
Changyŏn
P'yŏngsan
Haeju
Kaesŏng
Ongjin
Pup'o-rodongjagu
P'anmunjŏm-ni
Munsan
Kimp'o
Inch'ŏn
Taehŭng
Yodŏk
Chasŏng
Yalu
Sup'ung-ho
Ch'ŏngch'ŏn-gang
Taedong-gang
Nam-gang
Sohung-ho
Imjin-gang
Han
High-speed rail line
124
126
42
40
38

Base 803021AI (C00700) 5-05

Chapter 1

Lee Chul-Moo stood before the U.S. immigration officer at Toronto's Pearson Airport, doing his best to appear relaxed. Canada was one of only six countries globally with U.S. pre-clearance operations at entry points outside the United States. Customs and Border Patrol (CBP) established these offices at strategic international gateways to prevent terrorists and others viewed as a security risk from reaching U.S. soil. Lee certainly didn't consider himself a terrorist, but only time would tell if he might be considered a security risk. He was on his way to New Mexico, where he was about to begin a new job at Los Alamos National Laboratory.

It was December, and a blizzard was dumping snow across the region. Despite the brisk temperature in the terminal, he could feel the sweat dripping from his armpits. Outwardly, there was no indication of the inner turmoil he felt as he stood before the immigration officer. Flight departures and arrivals blared from the loudspeaker with such regularity that he was having trouble concentrating. And concentration at this moment was vital to everything.

"Name?" Was it his imagination, or did the CBP official fill the small booth that served as his office? He was mammoth-sized, and his stern look made Lee wonder if he should turn back and try his luck in another line. But it was too late now. The man was motioning to him to come closer. He swallowed hard and found his voice.

"Jason Lee." He spoke the name with confidence. It rolled off his tongue, giving no clue to the CBP officer that it was not entirely true. On the surface, Jason's mouth, however, felt like sandpaper and his stomach like a monkey fist. Jason Lee was, in fact, his legal name, and his passport was

100 percent legitimate. But Lee Chul-Moo was what his father's family, living in Pyongyang, North Korea, called him. Chul-Moo didn't appear on any official Canadian documentation – birth certificate, passport, school records, driver's license. These all bore the name Jason Lee.

"What's the purpose of your trip?"

"I'm starting a new job in New Mexico."

"Whereabouts?" The officer covered a yawn with his large, hairy hand before flipping through the Canadian passport.

"Los Alamos," Jason said.

"Is this your first visit to the United States?"

"I've never been there before. I just completed a Ph.D. program at the University of Toronto. I've been too busy at school and work to travel."

"Where were you working?" The officer looked up from the passport and scrutinized the Asian man standing before him. Late twenties, thin, unusually tall for an Asian, possibly six feet. He wore his hair cropped short in a crew-cut and sported black-framed, tinted eyeglasses concealing what most certainly were dark brown eyes.

"I had a part-time job at the Munk School at the university. It's a center for the study of Korea at the Asia Institute."

"Was Korean studies your major?"

"No. My degree's in physics. Korean studies is just a hobby. They had me reviewing Korean language documents and scanning scientific journals published in Korea."

The immigration officer nodded as he continued to scrutinize the passport. "Just a moment, Mr. Lee. I need to make a call." He picked up the phone and spoke briefly to someone on the other end.

"Okay." He put the phone down and handed the passport back to Lee. "Go with Officer Starkey," he said, pointing to an approaching CBP official. "He has a few additional questions for you, and then you'll be on your way." The officer dismissed him with a wave before he could reply, calling the next person to come forward.

Jason turned to go, but then spun around. "Is there

anything wrong?" His voice remained steady, but the sour taste of bile rising to the back of his throat nearly gagged him. He passed it off with a slight cough. It never occurred to him that Immigration would question his story. Years of preparation had prepared him for this very moment. Yet he was about to be turned away because this sleep-deprived bureaucrat didn't like how he looked.

"No. We just need some additional information." The man was speaking to him. Lee stepped back as he sensed someone at his side. It was the other immigration officer. It looked like he was going into secondary for questioning. Officer Starkey took his passport and led him to a small interview room nearby.

"Have a seat." Starkey scanned the passport and did a name search on the computer. He printed a page, retrieved it from the printer, and then took his seat in front of Lee. After perusing the paper for a moment, eyes darting back and forth, he looked up.

"Your mother's name?" he asked.

"Lee Ha-Yoon."

"Father?"

"I don't know." It always pained him to admit he was technically a bastard. "My mother immigrated to Canada in the 1980s from South Korea. She was single, working as a medical doctor here in Toronto. From what she told me, I know she met someone in her thirties. It was a brief affair. She got pregnant, and he didn't hang around. She never saw him again. She pretty much raised me by herself."

The facts were more complicated. Lee's father, Roe Min-Woo, grew up in South Korea. He and Ha-Yoon dated in college, but after medical school, she wanted to practice in Canada, and he wanted to remain in Korea. They stayed in touch and then reunited briefly, a year later, after his father traveled to Canada as a trade delegate. That's when she became pregnant.

Unbeknownst to his mother, Lee's father had long harbored fantasies about returning to North Korea, hoping to reunite with his family. They couldn't leave their home in Yanggang when the Korean Armistice Agreement was adopted three years after the Korean War ended. This same agreement established the Korean Demilitarized Zone along the 38th parallel.

His parents and two brothers eventually relocated to Pyongyang, but they could not leave North Korea. On July 10,1995, a couple of years after his fateful trip to Canada, Roe defected to the North, where he had resided for the past twenty-five years. At some point, the North Korean Intelligence Service (NKIS) recruited him to work undercover as a trade official, and he now traveled the world in that capacity.

"That must have been hard for your mother, being a single parent working in a demanding profession like medicine." Starkey looked at Lee for affirmation.

"We lived in Seaton Village here in Toronto. There's a big Korean population, so she had tons of support. My mom felt strongly about maintaining Korean cultural traditions, so I had to attend Korean language classes and go to a Korean church. It was a good life." That last bit was a lie. Even though he lived in Koreatown, he could never overcome the feeling that he was a second-class citizen in Canada. From the time he was old enough to understand that he was different, it seemed that overt racism permeated every facet of his life, especially whenever he stepped out of Koreatown's bubble.

"Did you ever run into any North Koreans when you were growing up?"

"North Koreans?" Lee wondered where this was going. Surely, they didn't know about his trip to North Korea in 2011.

He and his father had connected for the first time in 2010 and agreed to meet in Europe just before he started college. They met in Paris, and although it was initially uncomfortable for him, they bonded in a way Lee had hoped for but never expected. Somehow, using his intelligence connections, his father orchestrated a trip to Pyongyang, where they remained for two weeks. That's when he met some of his father's friends working for the NKIS.

"No, I didn't even realize North Koreans were living in Canada. Are there many here?"

"About twenty-five thousand. Most are defectors. Our Canadian friends keep an eye on them for us, but they don't give us any trouble. Well, I think that's all I need, Mr. Lee. Have a nice trip." Starkey stamped Lee's passport and handed it back to him, then escorted him to a passageway that led out to the main concourse.

Lee pocketed the passport and walked through a door into the main departure area. He was still thinking about CBP's decision to pull him into secondary. He couldn't think of anything he'd said or done to raise suspicions. There was no record connecting him to North Korea, which was the one red flag the CPB officer had raised. Was it the same old thing, then? White racism against Asians? He hadn't felt that vibe from either of the men. They were professional in the interview. He shrugged his shoulders and dismissed it. Checking the departures display, he saw that his Air Canada flight was on time. He was on his way.

Chapter 2

Logan's cell phone rang as the Alexander clan was sitting down to an early Christmas Eve dinner. The lanky CIA Operations Officer excused himself from the table and moved into the living room to take the call. The chatter from the dining room faded to a murmur as he walked over to a window overlooking his parents' front yard. Forecasters predicted a white Christmas throughout Vermont, beginning Christmas Eve, and for once, they were right. Heavy snow was falling, blanketing Montpelier's main street in white. The grating sound of a snowplow at work broke the serenity of the moment.

Logan squinted at the display on his phone. It was a 703 area code, but the number was blocked. Probably Langley. They were supposed to call him this week about his upcoming assignment.

"Hello?"

"Hi, Mr. Alexander?"

"Yes."

"This is Lisa in the Directorate of Operations; I'm the special assistant for the Deputy Director for Operations. I'm calling to let you know your assignment was approved. The Chief signed off on it this morning. He wanted to tell you himself, but he got called downtown at the last minute. We can go over the particulars when you get back from your vacation, but he wanted you to know, especially since Los Alamos needs you out there in January. It doesn't give you much time to pack out."

"Thanks for the heads up, Lisa. We'll talk about it when I check in next week. Oh, and Merry Christmas."

Logan paused to collect his thoughts before rejoining

the others. Less than a month ago, John Murray, the Deputy Director for Operations (DDO) asked him if he would be interested in taking on a new assignment at Los Alamos National Laboratory. The Intel community's analysts and scientists traditionally have had good working relationships with the national labs, but the Directorate of Operations (DO) less so. Logan's assignment would remedy that. Murray also hinted there might be more to the job.

Logan knew the position was his if he wanted it. The DDO would make his wishes known to the selection committee, and they would rubber-stamp whatever he asked. Only then would the front office reveal the real reason they wanted one of their up-and-coming stars assigned to a domestic location where he would have little chance to use his formidable skills to recruit spies and produce intelligence. Logan was still puzzled over why the DDO tapped him for this assignment. Self-doubt crept in as he mulled it over, but ultimately, he dismissed his misgivings. The CIA wasn't marginalizing him. They valued his skill set, mostly when he was at the pointy end of the spear.

While the national laboratory at Los Alamos had many foreign scientists on its staff, they would be off-limits as recruitment targets because of special agreements and protocols between the lab and its foreign counterparts. Besides, the FBI was the lead law enforcement agency in the U.S. government responsible for intelligence and counterintelligence operations against foreign nationals on U.S. soil. They weren't about to let the CIA muck around in their backyard. The memorandum of agreement between the CIA and the FBI makes it pretty clear. Foreign operations outside of the United States belong to the CIA, but when it comes to operating on U.S. soil, the FBI's in charge.

Much of the bad blood between the bureau and the CIA dates back to WWII, right after Pearl Harbor, when President Roosevelt established the CIA's predecessor organization, the Office of Strategic Services (OSS). FBI Director J. Edgar Hoover lobbied Roosevelt to place the OSS under his command, but the president resisted because he recognized the value of having a genuinely independent intelligence organization. Roosevelt's rebuff ruffled Hoover's feathers, precipitating decades of sometimes collaborative, but more often than not, antagonistic relations between the CIA and the FBI. Fortunately, after 9/11, relations between the two organizations were much better.

Logan returned to the dining room and sat down next to his wife, Zahir. He reached under the table to squeeze her knee. She covered his hand with her own and leaned over to kiss him on the cheek. Along with the others, she laughed as their brother-in-law, Ryan, described his first-ever hunting trip with his father in hilarious detail. Ryan had asked his dad so many questions while they hunkered down in the deer blind that it scared all the deer away.

As Ryan regaled them with stories, Logan leaned over and whispered in Zahir's ear. "That was Murray's special assistant. Looks like we're going to New Mexico next month."

Zahir turned to look at him in surprise. After all, Logan was an intelligence officer with the CIA, not a scientist. He had a good track record recruiting foreign agents. Why would the CIA waste his talents by sending him to New Mexico? Before she had a chance to voice her concerns, Logan's mother, ever perceptive, tapped her wine glass with a knife. The room quieted down before she spoke.

"Something you'd like to share with the rest of us, Logan?" She folded her arms on the table, leaning forward with an expectant smile. There were few secrets in the Alexander household.

Logan paused before speaking up. Normally he didn't talk about work at home, but they would find out soon enough anyway. "We're being reassigned to Los Alamos in New Mexico. They want us there in January." There was a moment of silence, and then everybody began talking at once.

Logan held up his hands. "Look, I don't know much more than what I just told you. That was my boss's special assistant on the phone. Langley's looking for a better lash-up with the science and technology community. They don't want there to be any daylight between the Intel folks and the national labs. Many of the threats we're facing from China, North Korea, Russia, and Iran to name a few, are in the cyber and nuclear realms. We have to stay on top of our game and figure out what the bad guys are doing. Working with the labs is part of that effort."

"Son, I'm sure that if the CIA is sending you to Los Alamos, they have a good reason. They're sending the best. They're sending an Alexander." Harry Alexander spoke with pride in his voice. A native Vermonter, he understood independence and patriotism. He had lost one son, Cooper, to the war in Iraq, and Logan had almost been killed in an ambush while deployed as a Navy SEAL to Afghanistan.

The room went quiet. The log in the double-sided fireplace had burned low, and there was a slight chill in the air. Logan wanted to get up and toss more wood on the fire, but he waited until his dad was through talking.

"I'm sure I've told you and your brother how proud of you we all are. We're grateful to have been so blessed with you, your sister, and your families." Harry's voice cracked, and he wiped an eye. He rarely showed his emotions, but when he did, it all poured out.

Logan hugged his dad and then went over to throw in another log. He stirred the glowing embers, now crackling as the fire flickered, caught the draft, and burst into flame. He scanned the faces at the table. Logan's young son, Cooper, knelt beside him. "Why's Pops crying, Daddy? Is he sad?"

"No, son, he's not sad. Sometimes people cry when they're happy." He wrapped Cooper in a bear hug and then turned back towards the table. "Hey, it's snowing like crazy out there. What do you say first thing in the morning we build a fort?"

"Can we have a snowball fight?" Cooper asked.

"Oh yeah, buddy. We're going to have the best snowball fight ever."

Chapter 3

Martina Ramirez was a woman of steely determination. A veteran of the war in Afghanistan, she moved to Albuquerque after her honorable discharge from the Army to pursue a bachelor's degree in criminology at the University of New Mexico. She was an MP in the Army, so a career in law enforcement seemed like a logical choice, although she didn't know exactly where it would take her. Martina wasn't interested in graduate work or a career in law per se. So, when she found out that Centerra-Los Alamos was hiring veterans to beef up its security contract with the national lab, she applied in her senior year. Fifteen years later, she was still there.

"Hey, Ramirez. What's on the docket today?" Peter Hanlon, her deputy in the Security Police Officer's (SPO) unit, burst into the office without knocking. He handed her one of the cups of coffee he was carrying and plopped down in a chair by her desk. A strapping Marine with four combat tours in Iraq and Afghanistan under his belt, Hanlon also ran the Special Weapons and Tactical Operations unit for her.

The SPO unit was a busy office. With 280 employees, Martina was responsible for all aspects of security at Los Alamos. The lab's 13,000 employees worked in 1,000 buildings spread out over roughly thirty-five square miles of the property. It was a massive operation.

"Thanks for the coffee, Peter," Martina said.

"Black, no sugar."

"That's how I like it," she said. She took the lid off the cup and inhaled the aroma of freshly brewed coffee. It was one of her favorite times of the day before things got too crazy. She took a sip and then set the cup down.

"We have several new employees checking in today. Reach out to the badge office to see if everything's in order concerning their clearances and documentation. I also want to make sure all the new employees receive their security briefings before checking in for their assignments. You're speaking to the group in the general orientation session, right?"

"Yep. I'll kick things off at 0930. You saw my updated slides, right? They've got the new Department of Energy guidelines on reporting foreign contacts and the non-fraternization policy with people from criterion countries. Do you know if these are all new hires?"

Martina pulled up a list on her computer and ran through it. "Looks like there are three interns in the group. The rest are foreign scientists, and transfers from the other labs."

Her secure line rang. "It's CIA," she said, looking at the unknown caller ID.

"Hey, Lisa. What's up?"

"Hi, Martina. I'm calling to let you know the DDO has finalized his choice for the new liaison position. I'm secure-faxing his resume to you right now."

"What's his name?"

"Logan. Logan Alexander."

Martina grabbed a pen to take notes as she spoke. "He's from the operations side, right?"

"Yes. You'll love him. He was a Navy SEAL before joining the Agency and has experience working against hard targets abroad for CIA. You're lucky to be getting him."

"Any idea when he plans to arrive?"

"He was on leave last week, but I have him on my calendar for 1100 this morning. I spoke to him the other day and mentioned you were looking at a January arrival. He's married and has a son in elementary school. They'll be packing out in a couple of weeks."

"Do you know if he has any preferences regarding housing? There are rental properties in Los Alamos and White

Rock if he wants to be in close. If that doesn't work, tell him to check out Santa Fe and the Española Valley. The only downside with those is a thirty- to forty-five-minute commute.

"If he hasn't already, be sure to tell him to get on the Los Alamos website. Lots of resources for new hires. I look forward to meeting him." Martina hung up and turned her attention back to Peter.

"Sorry. That was about our new liaison officer. It looks like they've identified an Operations Officer to fill the billet. Name's Logan Alexander. It sounds like he's our kind of people. Former SEAL and field experience as an operator."

"Oorah." Peter bellowed the Marine call with enthusiasm. He eyed his boss with a mischievous grin. "Name sounds familiar. I know you've wanted to get someone over from the operational side of the Intelligence Community. What do you have in mind? Are we going to start running covert operations out of the lab?"

She gave him her "don't mess with me" stare. "I'm serious about this, Peter. I've felt the need to beef up our counterintelligence program for a long time. But I keep getting pushback from Washington. Congress won't authorize a new position, and DOE says we're already over budget with new contract hires. I figure if I can get the CIA to loan us a body for a couple of years, we'll get the resources we need without having to foot the bill out of our budget.

"The intelligence we get from the Agency is pretty clear. The Russians have been eating our lunch since the days of the Cold War. Don't forget the Rosenbergs, Klaus Fuchs, Theodore Hall, Oscar Seborer. And those are just the spies we know about."

Peter held up his hands as if to ward off a blow. "Hey, I'm with you, Martina. I remember you telling me about how you had to clean up that mess from the Wen Ho Lee case."

"That was a nightmare. It was all over the press. I'd only been here a couple of months, and this scandal broke. It made us look like amateurs. Morale was at an all-time low."

"I got a feeling for what you went through with that Venezuelan case we had a few years ago. Pedro something."

"Mascheroni. Pedro Mascheroni."

"Yeah. That's the guy."

"We need to do more," she continued. "We're a prime target. The Russians, Chinese, Iranians, Venezuelans, North Koreans. I want to get out in front of this threat now before we get hit again."

From the firm set of her jaw, Peter knew his boss meant business. It wasn't in her DNA to roll over when the going got tough. Martina came from rugged stock. She'd told him her story over beers one night after work shortly after he started working at the lab.

Martina's roots were in Mexico, going back several generations. Her paternal great-great-grandfather left home in Matamoros at the age of sixteen right after the American Civil War. He worked as a cowhand, driving cattle from Texas to the railheads in Kansas. He eventually settled down in New Mexico, where he married and had eight children. By the time Martina came along, there were aunts and uncles and cousins aplenty, spread across the Southwest, although most of them stayed in New Mexico.

After the military and graduating from college, Martina married, but it didn't work out. Her husband treated her with respect while dating, but it all changed after they said their vows. The first and only time he hit her was because dinner wasn't ready when he got home from work. He'd stopped off at his favorite watering hole with the guys and was more than a little wasted by the time they dropped him off, too drunk to drive his car. He was sober enough to take a whack at her, though. She left him passed out at the kitchen table, his slack face drooped over a bowl of black beans and rice. One of her favorite Nancy Sinatra songs, "These Boots Are Made for Walkin" was playing on the radio. She never looked back.

"I'm serious about this, Peter. Logan Alexander is going to be one busy guy."

Chapter 4

Jason Lee felt a tinge of exhilaration, mixed with relief, as his Air Canada flight raced down the runway, engines roaring. He loved that moment of transition when, straining against gravity, they became airborne. The pilot banked southeast in the direction of Chicago and climbed to thirty thousand feet. Jason had a two-hour layover at O'Hare, and from there, it would be non-stop to Albuquerque on American.

As he sat back in his seat, Jason replayed his run-in with CBP. He couldn't think of anything alerting he had said or done to make the immigration officer flag him for secondary. His documentation was authentic, and his story was rock solid. Maybe it was just a random check. He'd noticed a couple of other passengers being pulled in for questioning as he was leaving Immigration. Could be there had been a security threat.

The experience cemented one thing in his mind. The key to his survival and success would be his ability to stay under the radar once he got to Los Alamos. During his two-week visit to North Korea, his father's friends in the NKIS suggested that there might be ways he could help them out. They made it clear they weren't talking about spying. They just wanted him to find a way to get to the U.S. and land a job where he could tell them about American society. They hinted it would be even better if he could obtain a security clearance and get access to national security information.

Fresh out of high school, Jason hadn't overthought it. Sure, he wanted to make his father proud, but realistically, what would he be able to do? He never imagined he would earn a Ph.D. in physics and get a job at America's preeminent national lab.

Of course, there were early indicators he would do well in his studies. He attended the Fieldstone School, a private secondary school in Toronto offering A-level certificates and an Ontario high school diploma, where he excelled in math and science. Around the same time, publishing sensation Amy Chua popularized the concept of Tiger Moms, in her book *Battle Hymn of the Tiger Mother*, where a Chinese approach to strict discipline and tough love drove children to succeed. From his perspective, Chinese moms had nothing over their Korean counterparts. His mother had encouraged him to achieve for as long as he could remember. Neither failure nor mediocrity was an option.

What would his father's friends say now if they found out he would be working at Los Alamos, where he would learn as much as he could about the American nuclear program? He thought back to a ten-minute meeting with Supreme Leader Kim Jong-Un just before returning to Canada a decade ago. Kim explicitly pointed out that North Korea's nuclear program was of paramount importance to him. It was the only leverage North Korea had over the Americans. Without it, the U.S. would feel emboldened to accelerate its hostile policies against the North.

Jason kept up with developments between North Korea and the U.S. in the intervening years. Despite modest inroads made with the outgoing U.S. administration, including a summit between the supreme leader and the U.S. president inside the Demilitarized Zone (DMZ), the official North Korean line remained that U.S. policies towards the North were hostile.

The sound of a service trolley rolling down the aisle disrupted Jason's reverie. He hadn't heard the flight attendants distributing refreshments, so absorbed was he in his thoughts.

"Anything to drink, sir?" The flight attendant raised an eyebrow as her manicured fingers tapped the edge of the trolley.

"Just water, please. How long is it to Chicago?"

"An hour and thirty-five minutes," she said as she poured his water into a plastic cup and reached past the passenger sitting in the aisle seat to hand it to him. "Traveling on business?"

"Yes, thank you," he said, accepting the cup.

"Enjoy your flight." She had already turned away and was serving passengers in the row behind him.

Looking out the window, Lee could see a pale, milky cloud expanse beneath the plane. There were streaks of pink emanating from one edge. At thirty thousand feet, it was probably minus forty degrees outside, with only the thin envelope of the aircraft's fuselage protecting them from freezing.

As he sipped his water, his thoughts turned to a conversation with his mother the night before. He had never told her about his trip to North Korea ten years ago, nor had he revealed his meeting with his father's NKIS buddies. He was sure she would disapprove. They hardly ever discussed politics, especially relations between the two Koreas. His maternal grandfather had passed away in Seoul ten years ago at the age of eighty-seven, and his mother had not been back to the homeland since his funeral. In many ways, her thinking in the years since had become more Canadian than South Korean.

"It will be lonely here without you, Jason."

"I'll miss you too, Mom. You should come to visit once I get settled in." He sat down and hugged her.

She pulled away. "I don't know." She sighed and stared off into the distance.

His mother was lonely, he realized. She had been so busy with her medical career and raising him that there was never much time for friends. Some acquaintances from work occasionally got together, and she knew people from church, but in all these years, he had never known her to have a love interest. She rarely mentioned his father. Could it be that she was still in love with him? Is that why she had remained single, despite his defection to the North even after all these years? She was entering her sixth decade, and opportunities for love were growing less promising with each passing year.

As if reading his mind, she fixed her gaze on him. "I heard from your father last week."

"What? Did he write?" Jason was shocked by her announcement. It had been years since his father's name had come up in conversation. Jason was chary of talking about him, particularly because of his father's business with the NKIS and his own past visit to the hermit kingdom.

"No. Actually, I spoke with him. He's in Mexico."

"Mexico? What's he doing there?"

"Business. The Mexicans seem to be walking a tightrope with the North Koreans. Your father says they're trying to improve trade between the two countries, but the Mexicans do not support full diplomatic relations for now. He thinks the U.S. talks with the North may have given Mexico confidence to move forward with this."

When they said goodbye a decade ago, his father made it clear that they could have no outward contact, lest it negatively impact Jason's prospects in the West. In the unlikely event they were to meet, it would be in a neutral country, far away from the prying eyes of Western intelligence agencies. As a further precaution, his father advised him not to discuss his trip to the North with anyone. Nor was he to ever mention his father's intelligence affiliation.

In many ways, Jason was ambivalent about his tenuous ties to the North. He recognized the regime for what it was, a corrupt dictatorship ruled by a megalomaniac. While there, he was struck by the extreme poverty and suffering of the North Korean people. His father, on the other hand, had a rosy outlook and took solace in his close familial ties.

Jason realized he had been holding his breath as his mother relayed the details of the call. He exhaled slowly. "Did he say anything else?"

"Only that if things go well, he expects to travel to Mexico several times a year. He has a position in the Ministry of External Economic Relations. If Mexico reinstates the North Korean ambassador, they will consider establishing a permanent trade mission there. He thinks he could be appointed to head that office.

"He asked how you were doing. I told him about your job."

Jason's head was reeling. The NKIS now knew about his job at Los Alamos. His mother was an unwitting conduit of information that would be welcome news in Pyongyang. Was it possible he would get to see his father again? The next time in Mexico? As he explored the possibilities, he became aware that the plane had begun its descent to O'Hare. As they broke through the clouds, he caught sight of Lake Michigan sparkling far below. The shoreline and Lake Shore Drive ran parallel to the downtown area where skyscrapers reached for the sky.

He felt a sense of exhilaration as he took in the sights looming below. This was real. He was in the United States. Work begun a decade ago was about to come to fruition. Nothing could stop him now.

Chapter 5

Checking in and out of CIA Headquarters was a whirlwind of meetings and briefings. On the home front, Logan and Zahir toyed with the idea of his moving to Los Alamos first, with family following at the end of the school year. Ultimately, they decided they didn't want to be apart for that long. Logan had been TDY to the Middle East more than either of them cared for in his last assignment, and it put a decided strain on their marriage. Although Cooper would have to change schools midterm, and they would have to rush to pack out, it was worth it to remain together.

Logan's meetings at Headquarters and around the Intelligence Community were eye-openers. Aside from operational meetings with various geographical components in the Directorate of Operations Logan was briefed by specialists in the Counter Proliferation Center (CPC) and the National Counterintelligence Center (NCIC). He also had meetings at the FBI, DOD, DOE, and on Capitol Hill. CPC was setting up a briefing for his Q clearance, DOE's special security clearance to access their Top-Secret Restricted data.

One appointment stuck with him more than any of the others. It was a lunch he attended with Senate Foreign Relations Committee staffers featuring a recent North Korean defector's talk. The defector didn't speak English, so a Korean-speaking interpreter from the Agency's defector resettlement office was brought in to interpret his remarks.

The speaker had been a prisoner in North Korea's gulag, a system of internment camps scattered around the country. The United Nations Commission on Human Rights and independent organizations such as Amnesty International repeatedly speak out about the severe human rights abuses inflicted on a gulag prison population estimated to number nearly a quarter million. Pak Min-Kyu was lucky to have escaped from this living nightmare with his life, from what he told them. Torture and mass starvation are the norms in Kim Jong-Un's gulag, with tens of thousands of prisoners perishing every year.

"I entered the prison system when I was fifteen years of age," said Pak. "My father was executed, days before my incarceration, for stealing a pot of kimchi. My mother, younger brother, and I were rounded up and taken to this prison in the countryside. Life in North Korea is difficult for the average citizen, even if you live in Pyongyang and have food to eat. But in these camps, we were regarded as sub-human. We were treated worse than animals. We slept on the floor, even in the winter, and had only rags for clothing. The guards were sadistic, beating us for the smallest offense."

"What kinds of things would they do?" one of the staffers asked.

"I'll give you a few examples. They will shock you, but you should know that this behavior is considered normal in the camps. In one case, the guards found out that a girl there was pregnant. I think it was when she began showing. They made everyone stand in the courtyard and forced us to watch." Pak's voice faltered, and his lips began to quiver. He looked at the interpreter, who gave him an encouraging nod.

"They dragged her out of the barracks, stripped her clothes off, and then ..." He wrung his hands and continued. "Two of the guards held her down on the ground, and then the third guard jabbed his bayonet into her vagina. Not once but over and over again. She was screaming for help, and blood was gushing out of her. The guards were laughing, treating it as a sport. She was almost dead, and they left her there to bleed out. It took less than thirty minutes for her to die, but she was in excruciating pain." He took a deep breath and continued.

"Another time a prisoner was caught trying to escape

from the camp. Again, the soldiers made everyone stand outside and watch the spectacle. This time they turned two vicious guard dogs loose on him. He stood no chance. The dogs ripped into his flesh, and when they tasted his blood, they went mad. They tore into his body. At first, he tried to make himself as small as possible, curling up into a ball. But they nipped and tore at him until he couldn't withstand it. He began to flail around with his arms, trying to protect himself, but he was no match for them. Finally, one of them bit into his neck and would not let go. We watched him die right there in front of us.

"As bad as these atrocities were, the worst was yet to come for me. To understand this, you have to know something about the North Korean system. The only loyalty allowed is to the supreme leader. Forget about country, family, and friends. These have no value in North Korea. Our teachers brainwash us from an early age to report our parents, relatives, and friends who disrespect the supreme leader to the authorities. One day in the camp, I overheard my mother muttering to herself that she hated the supreme leader for what he had done to our family. I felt that it was my duty to inform on her, even though inside, I must have known it would not turn out well. I was seventeen years old.

"After I informed the guards of my mother's crime, they came for her. It was in the nighttime, and she was screaming as they took her away. 'What have you done? What have you done?' she cried as they dragged her out of bed by her hair.

"That is the last time I saw my mother." Pak looked down at the floor, too embarrassed to make eye contact with his audience.

The room went silent. Logan looked at the others seated at his table. There was no sound as they shared in Pak's anguish. Tears rolled down one staffer's cheeks as she struggled to grasp the horror of all he had shared with them. The revelations took their toll on Pak as well. He continued to stare mutely at his shoes. If the anguish on his face matched that in his heart, he was emotionally wounded, possibly beyond repair.

Telling these stories of life in the gulag to government officials and human-interest groups was Pak's admission price to the U.S. He had no family left in North Korea. His mother and most likely his brother, too, were victims of Kim's cruelty. As a defector, North Korea considered Pak a traitor, an outcast forever. There would be no going home for him. He might build a life for himself in the U.S. with the Agency's financial help, resettlement, and job training. But only he could tame the demons that surely gnawed at him day in and day out.

Pak somehow managed to recover his poise sufficiently to continue speaking for another fifteen minutes. There was a brief Q&A; however, the air seemed to have gone out of the room. After the audience gave Pak a polite round of applause, he left.

The congressional staffers sitting at Logan's table looked to be in their early twenties, just out of college. Pak's revelations must have hit them pretty hard, he thought. They looked shell shocked. With two combat tours as a Navy SEAL under his belt, Logan had witnessed first-hand the horrors that despots like Bashar al Assad and Saddam Hussein committed against civilians in Syria and Iraq. He experienced the depravity of the Taliban and Islamic State. Even so, Pak's recitation of life in the North Korean gulag had numbed him.

The human toll was enormous, but it was not the only thing weighing on his mind. As he walked out of the Capitol building, Logan was scrutinizing Pak's story from the perspective of his new responsibilities at Los Alamos. He was beginning to get a glimpse into the reasoning behind the DDO's desire for a better lash-up between the operational side of the CIA and the national lab. If someone as cruel and unstable as Kim Jung-Un were to acquire nuclear weapons, there was no telling what horrors he might unleash upon the world.

The only country, aside from the U.S., with the slightest

hope of reining in Kim, would be China. For decades following the Korean War, Beijing and Pyongyang had a fraught relationship often characterized by the Chinese as "closer than lips and teeth." In the 1980s, as China began to expand its trade relations with the West, North Korea distanced itself ideologically from its neighbor. But still, despite frequent tension between the two communist nations, North Korea remained very much dependent upon China.

Should it choose to do so, China could be a moderating force in the region, especially when Kim's saber-rattling causes tensions to rise on the peninsula and with the United States. Logan knew that, while it was unlikely the Chinese approved of Kim's nuclear ambitions and frequent ballistic missile tests, there was no doubt they took some measure of satisfaction in the foreign policy problem North Korea presented for the United States.

On the downside for China, as long as tensions on the Korean Peninsula prevail, it was unlikely the U.S. would abandon its military presence in South Korea. There were about 25,000 American soldiers garrisoned at Fort Humphreys, twenty miles south of Seoul. It's been a thorn in China's side to have the U.S. military camped out in their backyard, one that was unlikely to go away anytime soon.

Chapter 6

Martina Rodriguez finished strong, clocking a six-minute final mile in her daily run to the county golf course. She liked to start her day with a vigorous workout to clear the cobwebs from her brain. The extra dose of endorphins was addictive, and something the Army veteran looked forward to. She paused to take in the sunrise over the Jemez Mountains. It had frozen overnight, and from a distance, she could see what looked like a deep snowfield at the base, while higher up, the rocky outcrops wore a dusting of snow resembling white frosting on a cake. Streaks of golden sunlight penetrated fluffy white clouds, casting shadows over the rugged foothills.

Back home, Martina showered and dressed. She had an 8:30 a.m. meeting in her office with an analyst from the National Security Agency (NSA), regarding the results of a recent collection initiative targeting counterintelligence threats. She took Sherman, her eight-year-old German shepherd, for a quick walk around the block, fed him, and left the house for her meeting.

Harriet Wilson, the NSA briefer from Fort Meade, was already waiting for her when Martina reached the office. Wilson was active-duty Army. The twin silver bars on her shoulder board indicated she held the rank of captain. Wilson had a compact build. Her close-cropped afro framed a youthful face. She couldn't be much older than twenty-five, yet the Afghanistan Campaign ribbon embellished with two Bronze Stars on her chest indicated she was no rookie.

"Captain Wilson, welcome. I'm Martina Rodriguez. Head of security." Martina led Wilson over to a conference table. "What time did you get in?" she asked.

"About 6 p.m. last night," she said.

"Where are you staying?"

"I'm at the Holiday Inn on Entrada."

"Can I get you anything? Coffee? Water?"

"Some coffee would be great."

Martina put on a fresh pot of coffee. "This will just take a few minutes. Do you take anything with it?"

"Just a little cream," Captain Wilson said.

"I see you've spent a little time in the sandbox." Martina gestured in the direction of Wilson's ribbons. "Had the pleasure myself. October 7, 2001."

Wilson's eyes grew round. "Get out. You were part of the initial invasion force?" She asked, referring to the first troops deployed to Afghanistan by President George Bush, following Osama Bin Laden's attacks on the Pentagon and World Trade Center on 9/11.

"Yeah. I was supposed to get out in 2002, but I didn't want to miss that one. SOBs." Martina frowned. Her blood pressure went up every time she thought about the horror of 9/11 and al-Qaeda's assault against the U.S.

"Anyway, welcome to Los Alamos. I have to tell you, I'm so pleased about our lash-up with Fort Meade. When I reached out to you last month, I was struggling with the reality that I'm sitting on top of probably the biggest counterintelligence challenge in the Intelligence community, with precious few resources to combat it. Did you get a chance to look at the material I sent you?"

Martina had compiled a history of the lab's counterintelligence environment for Wilson, summarizing the security issues they had faced over the years. She had begun with the lab's inception in 1943 when they were known as "Site Y" of the Manhattan Project.

"Yes, thanks. It was useful background material." She bit her lip and looked squarely at Martinez. "You've certainly had your share of problems," she said. "And you've had to deal with a couple of big cases, especially Wen Ho Lee."

Martina grimaced. "Yeah. That one sucked. Mainly because it was all over the press, and there were Congressional investigations into whether the CIA was concealing information about technology transfer to China. No one knew what was going on."

"Right. I remember reading some reports our congressional liaison folks got from the Cox Committee. They were looking into whistleblower allegations about improprieties at CIA. It turns out, that wasn't the case. It was just bad blood between the whistleblower and the operations side of the house."

"We've always been stove-piped because we don't trust other agencies, or even components within the same agency, to handle our information properly," Martina said. They sat in silence for a moment.

"Well, here's to breaking down barriers," Harriet said, raising her coffee cup. "My boss specifically asked me to tell you NSA will do whatever we can to help you with your counterintelligence program." She set her coffee down and pulled a laptop out of her bag. As it was powering up, she resumed their conversation.

"You've heard about PRISM, right?" she asked.

"Everybody's heard about PRISM, thanks to Edward Snowden," Martina said, with a distasteful look on her face. Snowden was the former NSA and CIA contractor who, in 2013, blew the lid off the Intelligence community's global surveillance programs. He worked as a contractor at an NSA facility in Hawaii, when he walked off the job, taking thousands of classified documents. These reports detailed several of NSA's global surveillance programs in partnership with U.S. telecommunications companies and foreign allies.

Snowden went from Hawaii to Hong Kong, revealing the surveillance program's details to U.S. and Scottish journalists. Their reports in The Washington Post and The Guardian created a firestorm of controversy that shook the Intelligence Community's very foundations. Later, Wiki Leaks made additional disclosures. To avoid detention by U.S. authorities, Snowden fled to Moscow and remained there.

"Well, fortunately, people have short memories, or they just don't care who knows what they're doing," Harriet said. "And thankfully, our legal authorities under Section 702 of the FISA Amendments Act remain in place. We can access a wide range of data: voice, emails, voice over Internet protocols, files; you name it. If it's out there in a digital format, we have the legal authority to access it."

Martina was familiar with FISA, which stands for the U.S. Foreign Intelligence Surveillance Act, and also refers to the federal court that adjudicates warrants for electronic surveillance against foreign spies in the U.S.

"How do you even know where to begin?" Martina asked. "I mean, I think of all the data we store here at Los Alamos, and this is just this one place. You have worldwide responsibilities. How do you manage it?"

"Fortunately, we have some brilliant software engineers who give us the tools we need to cut through the clutter. One that I use daily is the Unified Targeting Tool—a web-based application that lets me enter search criteria, such as names, places, dates, and events, to build a query. The more information we have when we make our request, the better result we're likely to achieve. It allows me to drill down and discover salient details to make our case.

"What do you consider to be your primary counterintelligence threats?" Harriet asked.

"The Russians have to be at the top of anyone's list. We don't currently have any Russians working in the labs; DOE stopped exchanges between Russia and the U.S. in 2014. There may not be any Russians physically working here, but that doesn't mean they're not trying to penetrate our systems."

"As you know, cybersecurity has to be a big part of everyone's counterintelligence program," Harriet said. "The days when our enemies had to break in physically to steal our secrets are long gone."

"And that brings me to another big threat," Martina said. "The Chinese. You mentioned Wen Ho Lee. I don't know how much you know about that case. He did time in prison for spying for China, but the government mishandled his case. There were others with the same accesses Lee had who could have been spying for China. The government released him on appeal, and they paid out a lot in damages. There is no doubt he was guilty of mishandling classified information, but spying ..." Her voice trailed off. "It may not have been Lee, but I'm a hundred percent sure we're on China's target list."

"What about some of the other bad actors, Iran, North Korea?" Harriet asked.

"We worry about them. Given travel restrictions against Iranians and North Koreans, they don't pose a physical threat to our systems. Still, in the cyber realm, they've made persistent efforts to steal sensitive information."

Harriet turned her laptop so that Martina could see the screen. She pulled up the targeting application and opened up a new query. "There are different ways we can use this tool, but we can't just go on some kind of fishing expedition. Remember, we're building these queries under a FISA authorization. A judge has to rule on the merits of the warrant."

"Are the courts very supportive?" Martina asked.

"I think so. I mean, we have to make the case, but we have an outstanding record of getting our warrants approved. In the forty-some years the FISA court has existed, they've approved over 40,000 warrants. I think they've only rejected a tiny fraction of our requests. Sometimes they'll come back and ask us to modify a submission or provide additional justification."

"This is all very encouraging," Martina said. "I have a new employee beginning soon, who I expect will be in touch with your office quite a bit."

"Logan Alexander?"

Martina's jaw dropped. "How'd you know?"

"He was making the rounds in D.C. last week. Our office dealt with him on a China case a couple of years ago. Have you met him?"

"No. I've just seen his file."

"You're in for a treat. He's a real pro. Navy SEAL. He's

the real deal."

"That's good news, because right now, I could use a strong dose of the real deal."

Chapter 7

Jason Lee found the apartment on Rent Café, a helpful real estate app on the Los Alamos website. The property was located about thirty minutes north of Los Alamos off State Road 76 in Española, a city less known for its proximity to the national lab than its nearness to the Puye Cliff Dwellings. The Pueblo ruin is a designated National Historic Landmark attracting tourists from all over the world.

The apartment suited his needs perfectly. It was a furnished one-bedroom with a view of the Jemez Mountains. The Walmart in Santa Fe had most of the essentials he needed—towels, sheets, and kitchen items. It was the first time he'd rented on his own. He'd lived with his mother in Toronto all through graduate school, and although he loved her and appreciated the sacrifices she made for him growing up, he welcomed his newfound independence.

On Sunday morning, he was enjoying a second cup of coffee as he watched a popular weekly news program. The lead story had to do with the ongoing COVID-19 pandemic. The incoming administration had run on a campaign to pull out all stops to get the runaway virus under control. They were ramping up the production of vaccines and implementing improved distribution methods, but there was pushback in some quarters where misinformation and politics held sway over common sense.

What was happening in Pyongyang? Jason wondered. Was his father back home, or was he still in Mexico City? In the last year, South Korea had reported over one hundred thousand cases of COVID-19, making it unlikely the North had escaped its reach. There was less international travel to North Korea than to many of the other affected areas in Asia. Still, from what Jason remembered, sanitation in the North was substandard, particularly in rural areas. Fortunately, his father's family lived in Pyongyang, thanks in large part to his dad's intel connections. Conditions there were healthier, and citizens had ready access to medical care.

Jason turned off the TV and decided to go for a run. It was noon, and the temperature was just above freezing. Growing up in Toronto, he was used to extreme cold and frequent snowfall. Anything above freezing was considered mild in his book. On the running app Map My Run, he found a six-mile run posted in El Rancho, a fifteen-minute drive from his apartment.

Twenty minutes later, he parked his rental car at the trailhead just outside of El Rancho and stepped into the freezing cold. A biting wind blew into his face—good thing he'd layered up before leaving the apartment. A half-dozen cars filled the small parking area just off the roadside. A group of runners was stretching or running in place to keep warm. A faded bumper sticker on one of the pickup trucks read "Santa Fe Trail Runners." As he prepared to set off down the trail, one of the women in the group approached him.

"Care to join us? We're just getting ready to head out."

"Are you guys the Santa Fe Trail Runners?" he asked, gesturing towards the bumper sticker.

"Yep. That's us. I'm Laurie Kim." She was dancing back and forth from one foot to the other, trying to keep warm.

"I don't know. I just moved here from Toronto. I don't have a lot of experience running at elevation. I'm Jason, by the way."

"You get used to it. We're at about 5,600 feet here, and we'll probably climb 600 feet or so at the highest point. You're welcome to join us."

"Okay. I'll give it a shot. I found this route on Map My Run. It looks like it's about six miles, round trip."

"That's the one. You need to stretch?"

"Yeah, if you don't mind." While he was stretching,

Jason checked out the other runners. It was about fifty-fifty men and women. Most looked to be in their twenties or thirties. Young professionals. The group was pretty diverse—a couple of African Americans, a Latino, and some Europeans. Besides himself, Laurie was the only other Asian in the crowd. She looked Chinese, but with a name like Kim she was probably Korean.

After he'd finished warming up, Jason pulled a camelback out of the car and strapped it on. He caught Laurie's eye as he walked over to the group. "Hey, everybody. Say hi to Jason," she said. "Just in from Toronto. Let's go easy on him."

"Hey, guys."

They set off at a comfortable pace, and Laurie fell in next to him. She wasn't very tall, but she had a nice, smooth stride. "Do you run much?" she asked.

"I ran cross-country in high school and college. I'm not much of a gym rat. Usually, I try to get in three or four short runs before work—two or three miles. And then I'll do one longer run on the weekend. How about you?"

"I ran track in high school and college."

"What distance did you run?"

"Ten thousand meters."

"Where'd you go to school?"

"UCLA." Laurie had picked up the pace slightly and was still breathing smoothly.

Jason nodded. UCLA had a very competitive track and field program. If Laurie was on the track team there, she must be good. As they were talking, he began to feel the strain the altitude was putting on his lungs. His breathing was a little shallower, and the biting cold made his chest ache.

"We try to schedule a run every weekend," Laurie said. "In the summer, we might aim for some mid-week runs. It's cooler and stays light later. If you like it, look us up on Meetup. We post our runs on there. You going to be here long?"

"I'm just starting a job at Los Alamos."

Laurie almost stopped in her tracks. "I work at Los

Alamos. Been there two years. What department are you in?"

"I haven't started to work yet. I'm checking into LUMOS, the Laboratory for Ultrafast Materials and Optical Science, tomorrow."

"We might end up working together," Laurie said. "I'm at CINT, the Center for Integrated Nanotechnologies. We work with LUMOS all the time."

Jason nodded. It was hard for him to talk and run at this elevation. Running cross-country in and around Toronto, there was no elevation to speak of. He could feel the burn in his chest and cramping in his left calf. He had been so busy talking to Laurie that he hadn't paid much attention to his hydration. He took a long pull on the camelback. The water was icy cold, but it felt good going down.

Laurie gave him a little wave and pulled ahead to run with a skinny blond whose hair was pulled back into a long ponytail that bounced rhythmically with each stride she took. She glanced back at him to give him an appraising look. Jason watched with admiration as they picked up the pace, moving to the front of the pack. It would take time for him to adjust to the altitude change, but he was coming back.

Chapter 8

Logan and his five-year-old Labrador retriever, Trooper, left Washington on Friday morning and arrived in Los Alamos late Sunday afternoon. They made the two-thousand-mile road trip in three days, with stops in Nashville, Tennessee, and Norman, Oklahoma, to visit a couple of SEAL buddies from Iraq. Zahir and Cooper would fly out to join them in a week.

They had reached Los Alamos the night before and found a Hampton Inn that was pet friendly. He and Trooper had gone for an early run this morning. After a shower, he found someone on the housekeeping staff to take Trooper for a walk. The hotel was close to the Los Alamos campus. Logan had a general orientation at 9:30, but first, he had to check in with the badge office and find a coffee shop.

The primary vehicle access point onto the Los Alamos campus was on East Jemez Road. Logan pulled up at 8 a.m., and a security officer with a name tag that read Callahan came out of the building to greet him.

"Good morning. What can I do for you?"

"Good morning. I need directions to the Badge Office. Name's Logan Alexander." He pulled out his Virginia driver's license and handed it to Officer Callahan.

Callahan compared the picture on the license with the driver. Nice-looking guy, with a military bearing. He found Logan's name on the Los Alamos access list.

"The Badge Office is on the second floor of the Otowi Building." He pulled out a map of Los Alamos and marked the route. "We're here," he said, circling their location on the map. "The Otowi Building is just off of West Jemez Road. You'll pass a fire station on your right. Take the first left after that, Casa Grande Drive.

"How long are you going to be with us?" he asked as he handed the map to Logan.

"Depends on Ms. Ramirez, I guess."

"Are you going to be working security for her?"

"It's a new position; we're still working out the details."

"Welcome, call me Gary. I've worked for Martina for about ten years now. She's good people."

"Glad to be here. One more thing. Is there any place nearby to get a cup of coffee?"

"Yeah, the Otowi Cafeteria is just south of the Badge Office, but I like Hot Rocks Java Cafe, just past the fire station on the right."

Logan decided to stop by the Badge Office first just in case there was a line. Half a dozen people were ahead of him, but the personnel were efficient, and he was in and out of there in thirty minutes.

Gary's cafe recommendation turned out to be a good one. Not only did they have a nice dark roast on offer, but there was a selection of homemade pastries displayed on the counter.

"I'll have a large French roast and a blueberry muffin," he said.

"That'll be six-fifty," the cashier said as she rang it up. "Would you like it for here or to go?"

"For here, please."

Logan found a seat by the window. He had about twenty minutes before he had to be at the HR conference room. While eating his breakfast, he perused a local real estate magazine. He was pretty sure Zahir and Cooper would want to live in, or close to, Los Alamos, and given his druthers, he'd rather live close-in and forego a long commute.

"You looking to rent or buy?" The cashier had stopped by his table and was looking over his shoulder.

"Rent, probably," he said. "I think we're just going to be here a couple of years."

"My husband has a real estate company in town," she said, handing him a business card.

"McCann Realty," he said, reading the card. "Does he have many listings?

"Not a lot of rentals. Demand was pretty high throughout the fall, but he has some Southwestern-style properties close in that recently came on the market. Do you have a family?"

"Just three of us, and a dog."

"If you're free this afternoon, I'm sure he would love to show you around."

"That would be great. I've got to run right now, but if your husband's available around 4, that works for me."

"Perfect. I'll have Gene give you a call." She wrote down Logan's cell phone number and said goodbye.

The HR conference room held about thirty people. Twenty new employees and several Los Alamos staffers representing various departments filled the space. Logan found a seat and looked around.

The first speaker up looked like a jarhead out of central casting, Peter Hanlon. He introduced himself as Deputy Chief of the Security Police Officers (SPO) Unit, Martina Ramirez's shop. This was someone he was going to be working closely with over the next two years.

"Most people coming to the lab for the first time don't grasp just how big we are. We have over 1,000 individual buildings on our campus, including thirteen nuclear facilities. We patrol over 270 roads and have more than 13,000 employees, making us one of the state's largest employers."

Peter went on to describe the security challenges the lab faces. "We are a research facility that thrives on open communication to stimulate innovation and generate new ideas. At the same time, we play an essential role in our nation's national security. Every employee has a responsibility for protecting our classified information."

Peter discussed the role of the SPO office in the areas of physical security, background security, counterintelligence, and tactical response.

"The SPO office is managed by Centerra-LA. We have about three hundred employees on site. Our overarching approach, not only in the SPO office but across Los Alamos, is an integrated safety management process." He pulled up two slides, displaying the commitments and functions of their safety security process.

Security at the lab was first-class, Logan thought. He'd read up on Centerra-LA, which ranked as one of the top secure facilities management companies in the U.S. They were leaders, not just in nuclear security protection but also in other services such as federal and commercial security and fire and emergency support.

There were several other speakers throughout the morning. They broke for lunch at noon, and Logan was about to look for a place to grab a bite to eat when his phone rang. He didn't recognize the number. "Hello?"

"Hi, Logan. This is Peter Hanlon. We didn't get a chance to talk during orientation this morning. I know you have a 1400 hours meeting with Martina, and wanted to see if you were interested in getting lunch?"

"Sure. What'd you have in mind?"

"There's this little hole-in-the-wall taco place in town, La Mesa, that's hard to beat. You want me to pick you up?"

"No, that's okay. I need to run by the hotel to check on the dog after lunch."

"Okay." Peter gave him directions to the restaurant. "See you in a couple."

La Mesa was a typical taqueria, understated, but with smells coming out of the kitchen to make your mouth water. Logan recognized Peter from the morning briefing. He stood up as Logan approached, and the two men shook hands.

"Why don't we go ahead and order?" Peter said. "This place fills up fast for lunch."

"What do you recommend?" Logan asked.

"If you like beef, I'd go with the Southern rolled beef tacos. Three of those, and you'll have to add an extra thirty minutes to your workout."

Logan laughed. "Sounds good to me.

"I was pretty impressed by the security program,"

Logan said after the waitress took their order. "You guys have a lot on your plate."

"It's a big operation," Peter said. "But we've got good people. The one area where we've been weak, though, is CI." He leaned over and whispered the abbreviated term for counterintelligence.

Logan nodded his understanding. "I did some digging around before I left D.C. It seems like there were some high-profile espionage cases in the early days. Later on, there was the occasional high-profile case, but then things went quiet. Like anything, it's what you don't know that will come back and bite you."

"And that's why Martina reached out to the Agency for help. We asked Congress to authorize a new position to go after the CI threat. But they denied it twice. That's where you come in. She'll tell you all about it this afternoon.

"Changing the subject, I saw on your resume that you went to Navy a couple of years after I graduated. You wouldn't happen to be the Logan Alexander that played Navy football and was later scouted by the NFL?"

"There were a couple of players that year," he admitted. "But, yeah, that was me. I went to the combine in Indianapolis my senior year, just to see if I could compete. I held my own, and the Patriots wanted to draft me if I was interested." He was lost in thought for a moment as he thought how different his life might have been had he gone down that road, but he wouldn't trade the last ten years for anything.

"I didn't go to Navy so I could play professional football. I went because I wanted to be a SEAL."

"I hear you. I was with special operations forces in the Marine Corps."

"You talking about the Marine Raider Regiment?"

"When I first joined the Marines, we were known as the Marine Special Operations Regiment, but in 2014 they changed the name back to Marine Raiders, which is what we were called in World War II."

"Why'd you get out?"

"Too many deployments. Four assignments to war zones in seven years," Peter said. "My wife gave me an ultimatum—find a job stateside, or she was going to walk. I didn't want to lose her. How about you?"

"I got shot up while on patrol in Afghanistan. Uncle Sam gave me a one-way ticket to Walter Reed. I spent months in rehab, but the docs wouldn't certify me for active duty. It happens."

The two men were still for a moment as they thought about what might have been. Finally, Peter broke the silence.

"We ought to get rolling," he said. "That'll leave you time to check in on your dog."

Chapter 9

Logan and Martina had just settled into their chairs and were getting to know each other when there was a knock on the door. It was Peter. "Do you want me to sit in, Martina?"

"Yes, come on in. Have you met Logan?

"Yeah, we had lunch together."

"Let me guess," she said, looking at Logan. "La Mesa Taqueria."

"How'd you guess?" Logan asked.

"Oh, Peter has taken it upon himself single-handedly to keep that hole-in-the-wall afloat. What are we up to two now, three times a week?"

Peter had a pained look on his face. "What can I say? I must have been Mexican in a previous life." He gave her a mischievous grin.

Logan liked the easy banter between the two of them. A friendly workplace environment could make all the difference between enjoying your job or searching for the nearest exit.

"I met a fan of yours the other day," Martina said, looking at Logan.

He looked puzzled. "I don't know anyone here."

"Harriet Wilson."

"Harriet from NSA?"

"The same one."

"What was she doing out here?"

"We've got a new initiative going with the Fort. They're helping us with some collection on possible CI threats."

"Harriet's good people, and she's well-connected in the SIGINT world."

"As a captain? She can't be much more than twenty-five years old," Martina said.

"Family connections," Logan said. "Her father was a Brigadier General in the Air Force—Luther Wilson. He was a SIGINT specialist, and when he retired from active duty, he was offered the Deputy position at NSA. He worked there for ten years. Harriet was in high school and college at the time, so early on, she got to know her father's friends and colleagues on a social level. Many of those people are in senior positions in the Intelligence community now."

Martina was about to respond when her phone rang. "Sorry, let me take this."

She got up to take the call. "Hello?" As she listened to the voice, her brow creased, and her expression changed to one of worry. "When did this happen?" she asked. "How many are there? Order the tactical team to deploy. Have them get set up around the building, but I don't want anyone going in until we get there."

Peter jumped up and stood by her side, his face tense as he strained to hear what the caller was saying. Martina held up her hand to signal that she was almost done talking. "Also shut down all three vehicle access points, and I want everybody on lockdown until we have everything under control."

She hung up and faced the two men. "That was the watch office; we have a hostage situation in TA-3 Building 39."

"What do we know?" Peter asked.

"Not much. Building 39 is all technical shops. There usually are fifty people assigned to that area, but many are participating in an offsite team-building exercise today. We're not sure, but we think the perp is a guy by the name of George Taylor, who came through the Bikini Atoll Road vehicle access point at 2:15. He had an appointment at the Badge Office, but never showed up."

"Let's suit up," Peter said. "Logan, follow me. We've got tactical gear and an armory on the first floor." The two men raced for the stairs.

"I'll see you out front in five minutes," Martina said.

Moments later, the trio met outside the entrance to the Otowi Building. They were wearing flack vests and helmets and armed with Glock semi-automatic pistols. They climbed into Martina's car for the short ride to Building 39. Pulling into the visitors' parking area, they surveyed the scene, which looked like something out of a movie set.

The SPO Tactical Team had set up a perimeter around Building 39 and had beefed up security at the guard stations on Mercury, Pajarito, and Bikini Atoll Roads. There was no traffic moving within 100 yards of the facility.

A young SPO by the name of Garcia was running the tactical team's command post. He stepped up to brief Martina on the situation.

"Subject's name is George Taylor. He was supposed to stop off at the Badge Office, but instead, he drove over here, parked his car in the visitors' lot, and walked into Building 39. We pulled up video coverage of the entrance. He was carrying a rifle case and a handgun. No one spotted him coming, so he went right through those front doors. That's the last we've seen of him."

"Do we have any idea what he wants?" Peter asked.

"He had one of the hostages call over to the Admin Building. She said he was looking for a Rosemary Dietz."

"Rosemary used to manage the Technical Shops. She transferred to another DOE facility about a year ago," Martina said.

"Do you know what the connection was between Rosemary and Taylor?" Logan asked. "Maybe HR could make the connection for us."

Martina got HR on the line. "Jeannie, it's Martina. You know about the lockdown and the hostage situation at Building 39, right? We just found out the guy's name is George Taylor, and he's looking for Rosemary Dietz. Can you make any connection between the two?" Martina listened for thirty seconds and then hung up.

"Jeannie says that George Taylor was supposed to have a job interview with HR at 3 o'clock. She said there was a

Phil Taylor who worked at Building 39 for twenty years. He lost his job because of a sexual harassment charge Rosemary filed against him. She was not aware of a connection between the two men."

"Could be a relative," Logan said. He pulled out his cell phone and did a quick search. "Here's something."

"What is it?" Martina asked.

"An obituary," Logan said as his eyes browsed the screen. "Phil Taylor died six months ago of pancreatic cancer. His wife, Patricia, and son, George, survive him. There was a picture of George and Phil building a Habitat for Humanity-sponsored house in Albuquerque. The father-son team had helped construct over fifteen homes for the poor in recent years.

"Could be the son is trying to avenge his father if he thinks Dietz wrongfully accused him," Logan said.

"Best-case scenario is we resolve this situation in-house," Martina said." I don't want the bureau or the sheriff's office coming in here and taking over. It's too bad we don't have a hostage negotiator on staff. In my worst nightmare, I never dreamed we would need one at Los Alamos."

"I can do it," Logan said.

Martina and Peter turned to him in surprise. Peter spoke first.

"You're a hostage negotiator?" he asked, barely concealing his incredulity.

"Yep. I took a hostage negotiation course before my first deployment to Iraq. Believe it or not, it came in handy. I used it a couple of times out in the field."

"Tell me what you need," Martina said.

"First thing we need to do is establish a direct line to Taylor. I also need schematics of Building 39, intel on how many hostages there are, and where they are in the building. I'd like technical coverage of the room he's in, sound and video if we have the capability. I need someone to pull up any information we have on the Taylor case, see if we can contact the wife, and find out anything we can about George Taylor. That should be good for starters."

Martina stared at Logan in amazement, but she didn't miss a beat. "All right, you heard the man. Peter, you talk to the tech people and tell them we need video and audio for Building 39 pronto. Garcia, have someone speak to facilities management and get schematics of the building ASAP." She directed one of the other SPOs to follow up with HR to see what they had on the Taylor case. She sent another SPO out to Taylor's parents' house to reach out to his mother.

"I need to meet with the lab director and the senior management team so they can brief DOE. Hopefully, I'll be in and out of there in thirty minutes," Martina said. The meeting went slightly longer than that, forty-five minutes. She had a good working relationship with the senior management team, and they trusted her judgment.

"You're confident in this Logan Alexander fellow?" the director asked.

"Yes, sir. He's a trained hostage negotiator and has experience serving as a SEAL in Iraq and Afghanistan. He can handle it. I'm more concerned about keeping this under the radar. We're fortunate that we control our space and don't have to worry about a horde of reporters descending on us."

"You have my full support, Martina. Keep me updated. If you feel the need to call in extra help, be it the sheriff's office or the bureau, don't hesitate. We want to make certain our people get out of there safely."

"Yes, sir."

There was a whir of activity back at the command center. The tech shop had an off-the-shelf tactical video surveillance camera capable of providing live streaming coverage of the target room. One of the technical officers had identified a window he could approach by crawling on the ground out of sight of the people inside Building 39. He was in the process of installing it as Martina conferred with the others.

Peter was poring over a schematic of Building 39. "This is interesting," he said, jabbing his finger at a point on the diagram. "There is an underground tunnel that connects to the front office in Building 39. Many of the older buildings dating back to the days of the Manhattan Project had tunnels in them. They built them at the height of the Cold War when everyone was on high alert. We're not using them now, but they're still viable. What are you thinking?"

"If we aren't able to negotiate with Taylor, it may give us a better option than staging a frontal assault," Logan said. "Going in through the front door with guns blazing is never a great option with hostages' lives at risk."

The command center phone rang. Martina gestured to Logan to take the call.

"Hello," he said. There was a moment of silence, and then a raspy male voice spoke.

"Who's this?"

"This is the security office. Am I speaking with Mr. Taylor?" There was a pause. Logan could almost see the look of surprise on Taylor's face.

"What makes you say that?" he asked guardedly.

"We had a George Taylor who came in at 2:15 and never showed up for his appointment with HR. His car is in the visitors' lot next to Building 39. It's an educated guess."

"You have an advantage," Taylor said. "You know my name, but I don't know yours."

"Logan. Logan Alexander. You can call me Logan. What can we do for you, Mr. Taylor?"

"I want Rosemary Dietz here now."

"Ms. Dietz is no longer working at Los Alamos, Mr. Taylor. She transferred to another DOE facility about a year ago." There was a moment of silence as Taylor absorbed this information.

During this exchange, the video feed went live, and suddenly the tactical team had a live view into the room holding the hostages. There appeared to be a dozen frightened men and women sitting on the floor spaced out around the room.

Taylor was perched on a desk, waving a semi-automatic pistol in one hand and gripping a cellphone in the other, looking disheveled, with rumpled clothing, hair uncombed, and a week's growth of stubble on his face. An AR-15 semi-automatic rifle was propped up against the side of the desk.

Logan watched Taylor's face contort in rage as he absorbed the news that Dietz was not on the premises. Finally, he spoke.

"She has to pay," he shouted. "She ruined my father's life."

"Why don't you tell me what happened?" Logan asked.

"They charged my dad with sexual harassment," he said. "He worked here for twenty years and never had an issue like that. It was the other way around. It was her, Dietz, who was hitting on my father. He told my mother about it the first time it happened. Dietz's husband walked out on her three years ago, and she didn't have a man in her life. She'd walk by Dad's workbench and flirt with him. She would touch him. It made him uncomfortable."

"Do you mind if I call you George? I'm sorry about what happened to your family. It sounds as though it's been difficult for you. I can't promise we'll be able to get Ms. Dietz here to speak with you. But what about all those people that you're holding in there? They didn't have anything to do with this. Why don't you let them go, and everyone can go home?"

"He spent twenty years working here. These people were supposed to be his friends. No one came forward to support him because she was the boss, and they were just thinking about their own jobs. And then, he got sick with pancreatic cancer. No one called to see how he was doing, and no one bothered to pay their respects when he died. Twenty years, and because that lying bitch blackballed him, everyone treated him like scum. You get her here now," he screamed, and then hung up.

Chapter 10

Jason Lee smiled as he thought about his evening with Laurie. She had come over to his apartment after their run, and they cooked dinner together. She had a great sense of humor, and they laughed their way through the meal. Later, she wanted to watch one of her favorite TV programs. They settled on the couch together, and she cuddled up close to him.

Maybe it was the bottle of pinot noir, or perhaps it was just their chemistry, but pretty soon, they were kissing. Minutes later, she took his hand and led him into the bedroom. Before he knew it, they were pulling each other's clothes off and tumbling between the sheets.

Although their lovemaking was unexpected, it was as if they had known each other for some time. They took time exploring each other's bodies, new, but somehow familiar territory. Hours later, when they finally fell asleep in each other's arms, everything felt perfect.

In the morning, he was the first one up. He pulled on a pair of boxer shorts and tiptoed into the kitchen to make a pot of coffee. She came up behind him in the kitchen and hugged him.

"Can I make you some breakfast?" he asked.

"Just coffee; I need to get home so I can get ready for work."

They made small talk for fifteen minutes and drank their coffee. Laurie liked hers the same way he drank his, unsweetened dark roast topped with thick foamed milk. He wondered if she regretted staying the night and was just being nice to him. But those thoughts were dispelled when she stood up to go. She hugged him tightly and gave him a long, passionate kiss, her tongue exploring his lips and mouth.

She pulled back, out of breath, and laughed. "Any more of that and I may have to call in sick," she giggled. They said their goodbyes, and after Jason had cleaned up and dressed, he had a bowl of cereal topped with blueberries and left for Los Alamos.

Jason had parked his rental car just outside the apartment. Across the parking lot, an Española Valley High School bus was pulling away from the curb, a horde of high school students settling into their seats, staring intently at their electronic devices.

Traffic was light on the ride into Los Alamos. He checked into LUMOS at 8:30 and discovered that it shared space with the Center for Integrated Nanotechnologies, Laurie's workplace. He looked for her throughout the morning but didn't see her. His boss, Norman Chen, suggested he spend the morning meeting his colleagues and familiarizing himself with their research.

The lab supported a diverse range of research projects: diagnostics for materials at extreme temperatures; the study of plasmonic, metamaterials, and electromagnetic phenomena; X-ray imaging and spectroscopy. The latter was Jason's specialty; he would have access to the most advanced equipment on the planet for his research: ultrafast optical microscopes, optical amplifiers, optical pumps, and more.

At 12:30, he and two other researchers working in his field went into town for lunch. They had a lively discussion about their research as they ate. Before they knew it, it was 2 o'clock; they paid their bills and left the restaurant. The other two were driving straight to Albuquerque to catch a flight to Los Angeles, where they were presenting a paper on their research to colleagues at Sandia National Labs.

As he approached the gate to Los Alamos, Jason noticed that traffic had backed up a half-mile from the entrance. By the time he reached the guardhouse, it was almost 3 p.m.

"Sorry, but all the entrances are temporarily closed," the SPO said.

"What's going on?" he asked.

"There's an incident in TA-3," he said, eying Jason's badge. "It's a hostage situation. No telling how long it will take to resolve. You might want to call your boss and let him know you're stuck outside."

"Thanks," Jason said. He pulled to the side of the road and called Norman Chen.

"We're on lockdown. No one knows for how long," Norman said. "This could go on for hours. Why don't you take off the afternoon? Call Security in the morning."

"Are you all okay?" Jason asked.

"We're fine," Norman said. "Our area's not affected except for the fact that we're on lockdown and can't go anywhere. I heard it's Building 39 in TA-3, a hostage situation involving a dozen people."

"That's too bad. All right, maybe I'll return my rental car and shop for a car."

"You might try Lomas Boulevard in Albuquerque. There are several dealerships in that area".

"All right, thanks." Jason spent the next couple of hours shopping for used cars. He found a Jeep Wrangler he liked. It would be perfect for exploring off-road in the New Mexico backcountry. The car was two years old and only had twenty-six thousand miles on it. The dealership offered financing through a local credit union—$2,000 down and a good interest rate.

"If you have time, we'll detail it for you, and Gary, in customer service, will drive it to the airport so you can turn in your rental car. We should have it ready to go in about twenty minutes." The sales manager showed him to the lounge.

It was a slow afternoon, and Jason was the only person waiting. He pulled a bottle of complimentary water out of the fridge and settled down to check his email when his phone rang. He didn't recognize the number.

"Hello?" There was a moment's hesitation before the caller said anything.

"Jason?" He sat up, startled. He would recognize that

voice anywhere, even though it had been years since they last spoke.

"Dad?" he asked. "Where are you? Are you still in Mexico?"

"I see you spoke to your mother. Yes, I'm here through the end of the week, and then I have a couple of days before I fly home. I thought if you are free, that we could see each other, possibly Saturday?"

Jason's mind was reeling. For one thing, he couldn't believe he was talking to his father, and secondly, that they might get together so soon. "Yes. Where do you want to meet?"

"I'll be staying at the Hotel San Carlos on Bellamah Avenue in the Sawmill area, about ten minutes from the Albuquerque airport. Use the lobby telephone to check on the room number. The reservation is under the name Gardner. If you come early, I'll order breakfast."

"Eight o'clock early enough?" Jason asked.

"That's fine. And, Jason?"

"Yes?"

"I'm looking forward to seeing you, son."

"Me too, Dad. See you Saturday." Jason hung up and then exhaled, realizing that in his excitement, he had been holding his breath.

"Is everything all right, Mr. Lee?" It was the sales manager.

Jason got to his feet, a sheepish grin on his face. "I just had a call from an old friend I hadn't spoken to in years. Took me by surprise."

"Your car's ready." He handed Jason two sets of keys and led him outside, where his car sat gleaming in the afternoon sun. A sign on the windshield, "I'm going home with Jason," made him laugh. It was the first car he could call his own.

Chapter 11

The tactical team huddled around the video monitor, watching the feed from Building 39. George Taylor was strutting around the room, talking to himself, and then out of the blue, roaring in anger.

"This guy's about to lose it," Logan said. "We're not going to have a protracted negotiation with him." The team had just heard updated reports from HR and the SPO who had gone out to speak to Taylor's mother.

Mrs. Taylor was reluctant to reveal any details about her son, but when the SPO impressed upon her the severity of the situation, she had relented and began to talk.

"George was angry about the way Los Alamos treated his father," she said. "He couldn't let it go. That woman tried to seduce my husband, and when he wouldn't go along with it, she set him up. I knew my Phil, and he would never cheat on me, never." Her mouth tightened into a thin, severe line.

"Phil was going to fight it. We were going to get a lawyer and take her to court, but then he came down with pancreatic cancer, and all the fight went out of him." She sighed, the worry lines creased her face and made her look ten years older than her actual age. "He gave up, but George wanted to take up the fight for him. Phil didn't have anything left. Eight months ago, his cancer progressed, and by June, his body couldn't take any more.

"After my husband died, George wasn't himself. He was angry all the time and talked about how that woman, Dietz, was going to pay for what she did to our family. I never thought he would take it this far."

"Mrs. Taylor came across as very depressed," the SPO

told the tactical team. "Not only did she lose her husband, but in a way, she lost her son too."

HR spoke up next, referring to the official file of the investigation into Dietz's sexual harassment charge against Phil Taylor. It was true, the evidence against Taylor was thin. No one else had corroborated the woman's account of his alleged impropriety. Was there a rush to judgment? Dietz proved to be more convincing in her testimony than Taylor, and Los Alamos sent Taylor packing.

They were interrupted by a phone call. It was George Taylor.

"Logan?"

"Hey, George. It's me. How are you holding up?"

"How am I holding up?" he screeched into the phone. "How am I holding up? I'll tell you how I'm holding up," he said. "If Dietz isn't here within the hour, someone is going to die, and every hour after that, someone else is going to die, until you bring me that woman."

"Whoa, George. Even if we could locate her, it would take several hours for her to travel to New Mexico from Los Angeles. And don't forget, we can't force Dietz to come here. When she hears what's going on, I seriously doubt she'll want to come. I'll tell you what. How about we send you some food and water for now, and I'll let you know first thing we hear from her?" There was a moment's pause as Taylor considered Logan's offer.

"All right, you can send some food, but don't try anything."

One of the SPOs was dispatched to a sandwich shop in Los Alamos. He was back in forty-five minutes with the food and drinks. In the interim, Logan had been poring over the schematics of Building 39 and discussing an action plan with Martina and Peter.

"We need to move now," he said. "Taylor's under a lot of pressure, and he can't see a way out. At some point he'll figure out that we aren't going to give him Dietz, and he'll deliver on his threat. Our best chance is to use the food delivery as a little diversion, just enough activity to catch him off guard when we come up through the tunnel.

"I'll take the lead in the tunnel, and if possible, try to neutralize him, but if it looks like he's going to start shooting, I'll take him out."

"I'll back you up," Peter said.

"I'll deliver the food," Martina said. "Let me know when you're in place and want me to move."

Ten minutes later, Logan and Peter were in the tunnel moving at a brisk trot. They knew from the drawings that the tunnel was two hundred feet long. At the end there was a flight of stairs leading up to an office, which in turn opened to the room where Taylor and the hostages were located. When they reached the door, Logan signaled Martina—two clicks on the radio—to begin walking to the entrance of Building 39.

As Martina approached the door, it opened and one of the hostages stepped out. It was Renee Edwards, and she looked scared. In the background, Martina could see a shadowy figure—Taylor.

"Put the food down," he yelled. "Back up, with your hands in the air. Don't try anything or you'll be sorry."

Martina set the bags down, making a deliberate show of keeping her hands in the air. As she backed away, she whispered to Renee, "It'll be okay. Don't worry."

One of the SPOs signaled on the radio that Martina was in the clear. Logan turned the knob on the door and pushed it open a crack. There wasn't a sound; the room was empty. He stepped inside. It was eerily quiet, but then he heard Taylor yell at Martina. Good, the diversion was working. Timing was going to be critical in the next thirty seconds. He wanted to be certain that Martina was out of harm's way and at the same time none of the hostages were in the line of fire.

He crossed the room and cracked the door leading to the room where the hostages were being held. Where was Taylor? There in the shadows behind the main entrance. One of the hostages was just coming through the door with the bags of food. Damn, it was too risky. He needed more separation.

The food bearer went left to a small conference table. The other people in the room were stirring, but none of them moved, waiting for Taylor to tell them what to do. Taylor secured the door and stood inside the doorway surveying the room, arms at his side. He gripped a Glock automatic pistol in his right hand.

This might be his best shot. Suddenly, Taylor looked up. One of the women hostages had seen Logan and let out an involuntary gasp. Taylor followed her gaze and spotted Logan. He started to raise his gun.

"Drop the gun, Taylor."

"Logan? You bastard."

Logan didn't hesitate. He had to take the shot. The first shot hit Taylor in the chest. The force of the round spun him around, and he lost his grip on the pistol. It dropped to the ground with a clatter. Taylor grabbed his chest, but it was too late. The bullet had found a main artery and he was bleeding profusely. Soon he would be dead.

The hostages were screaming in terror. Peter came into room and his familiar face had a calming effect on everyone. Logan keyed his radio and spoke the words Martina was waiting for.

"One bad guy down. All the hostages are safe. All clear."

A moment later the front door burst open, and members of the tactical team poured into the room. They checked everyone for injuries or signs of trauma. No one was physically harmed, but it was clear they were still in shock. A psychologist was brought in to talk with them individually, and those who were able to remain were debriefed by the SPOs.

In the after-action brief, Martina praised her officers for their professionalism and courage. She saved most of her praise for Logan, who had stepped into unfamiliar territory and performed seamlessly. She now understood what the people at Langley meant when they said she was lucky to be getting him on loan. He had already proven his worth, although not quite in the way she had envisioned.

Chapter 12

The week raced by for Jason. As thrilled as he was about his new job and his burgeoning relationship with Laurie, he was distracted by thoughts of the upcoming reunion with his father. Saturday morning, he was on the road by 6:30. It took him a little over an hour and a half on I-25 to reach the Hotel San Carlos in the Sawmill area of Albuquerque.

He parked his car and walked through the hotel lobby, with its colorful display of indigenous art, and found the courtesy phone.

"Hotel San Carlos, Reception. This is Karen speaking. How may I assist you?"

"Yes, hello. Can you put me through to Mr. Gardner's room, please?"

"One moment." There was a brief pause, and then the phone was ringing.

"Hi, it's me," he said. He was careful not to use his name or reveal any details that might identify him to anyone listening. His father had cautioned him before to be circumspect in their dealings, particularly over the phone. You never knew who might be tuned in.

"Room 526," was all he said.

Jason took the stairs to the fifth floor. It was just a couple of minutes after 8 a.m. The corridor to his father's room was quiet except for a housekeeping cart parked near the service elevator. The door to his father's room was ajar, and a Hispanic room service waiter was leaving. He nodded to Jason as he wheeled the room service cart away. His father looked up, sensing Jason's presence.

"Dad." The word was barely out of his mouth when his father crossed the room and wrapped him in a bear hug.

After a moment, he released him, holding him at arm's length.

"Come in, come in," he said, clapping him on the back. He steered Jason through the door. Once inside the room, he switched from English to Korean. "They just delivered breakfast. I hope you're hungry."

Jason loved the sound of Korean. Since he'd left Canada, he hadn't spoken a word of it. Although she grew up in Los Angeles, with its sizable Korean population, Laurie didn't know any Korean language. Her dad was a software engineer, and her mom was a professor, but unlike his mother, they weren't that interested in passing on the language and customs of South Korea to their offspring.

Jason surveyed the table. It was like a buffet; there was so much food. There were breakfast pastries, bacon and eggs, hash browns, and more. His dad steered him to a seat with a view of the mountains.

"Oh, I forgot something," he said. He went into the bedroom and returned moments later with a small, gift-wrapped package that he placed next to Jason. "It's a graduation present. I'm sorry I couldn't be there for your big day."

Jason picked up the box and held it in his hands. His father's gesture touched him. He unwrapped the box to find an Apple smart watch. "Dad, you shouldn't have," he said. He knew the newest generation Apple watches were over $500; on a North Korean intel officer's salary, it was prohibitively expensive.

"It's nothing. I wish I could do more." He sat down across from Jason and began dishing out the food.

Both of them were hungry, and conversation lagged for a minute as they dug in. Jason's dad belched and patted his lips with his napkin. "Chul-Moo," he began, using his Korean name, "you've brought honor to our family with your achievement. Now, I suppose I should call you Dr. Lee," he said.

Jason laughed. "Not necessary, Dad."

His father grinned, but then his expression turned serious. "Tell me about your studies and your new job."

"My Ph.D. is in physics, and most of what I've worked on is theoretical. I'm working on the LUMOS team in the Center for Integrated Technologies.

"What does LUMOS stand for?"

"It's the Laboratory for Ultrafast Materials and Optical Science."

"It sounds impressive," he said. "What will you be doing?"

"I'll be using ultrafast laser systems to perform imaging and spectroscopic experiments to develop new materials. Everything we do has a national security element to it. Los Alamos is the oldest lab in the Department of Energy, with sixty percent of its budget going towards nuclear weapons research. Besides that, our science, technology, and engineering research impact many non-military fields.

"Do you remember when you visited North Korea, meeting the supreme leader?"

"Yes, of course. I only met with him for ten minutes, maybe less, but I remember the subject he was most interested in—nuclear weapons."

"He doesn't know you are working at Los Alamos yet, but he will consider it an intelligence coup if you agree to help us."

Jason had been starstruck when he first met Kim, but in the intervening years, he had come to see him for what he was, a ruthless tyrant. He couldn't share these feelings with his father, who no doubt was under Kim's spell. He needed to appease him.

"As a foreigner, I doubt I'll be working on anything that is weapons-related. You never know, though. I imagine I'll meet many people there, some who will be doing weapons research. Scientists love to talk about their work. Perhaps I'll pick up something useful from them."

"You're a good son, Chul-Moo." His father looked thoughtful. "We'll have to think about a new communication plan. I assume your mother told you about the new position in Mexico City?"

"Yes, she mentioned it."

"Based on the meetings we had with the Mexicans, I'm confident we'll be opening our new trade office there before the end of the year."

"Do you think they'll ask you to head up the office?"

"You never know. The supreme leader has the final say on foreign appointments. My reputation in the ministry is good, and I have the minister's support, so I stand a better than even chance of getting the job."

"Will we be able to see each other more often?" Jason asked.

"I was thinking the same thing," his dad said. "I doubt I would be able to make frequent trips to the U.S. if I'm in that job. The Americans keep track of North Korean officials' comings and goings, so there's no doubt I would be on their radar.

"You, on the other hand, might be able to move about more freely."

"In our security briefing, they told us to report any contact with people from criterion countries – China, Russia, Iran, North Korea, Belarus. Besides that, we must document any foreign travel, private and work-related.

"Foreign travel would be hard to hide because there's a record of it," Jason added.

The senior Lee stroked his chin and pondered the problem. "I think we should take it slow initially. Here's what I have in mind." He went over to the desk and unplugged a laptop and brought it back to the table, clearing away some of the dishes to make room. He sat down and motioned to Jason to move his chair closer.

"Do you know anything about the dark web?" He asked.

"Do you mean the deep web?" Jason asked.

"No, they're different. Most search engines can't access information on the deep web. It's not indexed and typically contains sensitive or private information. The dark web is a part of the deep web. The information there isn't indexed either, and it requires a virtual private network and a browser like the Onion Router to gain access. Many people engaged in illegal activity, and those who want an extra level of privacy, use the dark web. Let me show you."

His father clicked on the Onion Router icon on his screen and logged on. "When I send a message this way, it bundles the data into packets."

"Is this data encrypted?" Jason asked.

"Yes. It's encrypted when it enters the network. The router breaks up these individual packets and moves them around the dark web to relays or nodes. Each relay strips away a layer of encryption until the packet reaches the exit relay. From there, it sends the packet on to its final destination. No one can track this data."

"How does the VPN come into play?"

"There are two different ways to combine the router and a VPN, but my favorite is called Onion Router over VPN. This way, you connect to your VPN first to access the network. Using the VPN ensures your Internet service provider can't detect that you are using anything special, which adds another layer of protection. Here, let me show you."

His father backed out of the router and then logged on to his VPN. Then he repeated the procedure for accessing his router. "See, it's not that hard. Let me give you an address, and tonight you can send me a test message from your laptop," he said.

"It's important that no one but you has access to the computer with this software. The software itself is not illegal, but the dark web has a lot of illegal activity on it, and it could raise suspicions about why you are using it. You would never access this from your work computer."

"I think I've got it. Do you recommend a specific VPN?"

"There are many. NordVPN and Surfshark VPN are both good."

"Thanks." Jason committed his father's address to memory and made a mental note to send him a test message later that evening. He wanted to please him, and besides, it didn't seem like such a big deal to share information that was probably unclassified anyway. He would know where to draw the line if the time ever came.

Chapter 13

Zahir and Cooper arrived from D.C. Saturday afternoon. Logan met them at Albuquerque International Airport to drive to their new home in White Rock, about ten miles from Los Alamos. Logan had followed up with McCaan Realty earlier in the week and looked at several rental properties in the neighborhoods around the lab.

White Rock seemed the perfect location. Their house was a three-thousand-square-foot, pueblo-style dwelling not far from Chamisa Elementary School, where Cooper would be going. White Rock Canyon Trailhead was a short distance down the road.

The movers had delivered their household effects the day before, and Logan managed to unpack enough of their belongings that Zahir and Cooper didn't have to stay in a hotel on their first night.

"Why don't we take a little hike while it's still light out?" Logan said. "I stocked the fridge this morning; if you feel like cooking, or we can go out. You decide."

"The hike sounds like fun," Zahir said. "Let me change first. Have you seen my hiking boots?"

"Sneakers should be fine," Logan said. "We won't go too far into the canyon. I was out there a couple of times this week, and it's very walkable up near the rim."

The entrance to the trailhead was only a hundred yards from the house. From White Rock Overlook, the view into the canyon was dramatic. Steep, rocky cliffs dropped nine hundred feet to the canyon's bottom, where the Rio Grande River wound across the canyon floor like an unraveled ribbon.

"Wow," Cooper said. "Those rocks are purple."

Logan followed his gaze. The sheer cliffs below them formed a palette of brown, black, and purple hues. "A long time ago, this area was volcanically active. When the lava hardened, it turned into basalt. That's what all these colored rocks are on the cliffs.

"Look, there's a snake on that rock."

"Where?" Cooper asked.

Logan pointed to an ancient petroglyph depicting a menacing serpent. "The people that lived here thousands of years ago were storytellers. These drawings they left behind tell us about their lives. They didn't write books in those days, but they created this beautiful artwork to depict their world."

They explored the rim until Cooper was tired and then walked back home. "Let's go out," Zahir said. "I'm too beat to cook."

"Mexican or Southwestern is probably best in White Rock," Logan said. "There's a Mediterranean and a Vietnamese restaurant too, but I haven't checked them out yet."

"I want tacos," Cooper said.

"It looks like Mexican," Zahir said, tousling her son's hair.

Logan drove by Cooper's school on the way to the restaurant so he and Zahir could see it. Cooper would be finishing second grade at Chamisa.

Logan spotted Martina in line as they walked into the restaurant. "Would you like to join us?" he asked, as he made introductions.

"I'd love to," she said.

After scouring the menu and telling Zahir what they wanted, Logan and Cooper visited the men's room while the ladies ordered.

"Logan's already made a name for himself," Martina said, as the waitress collected their menus. "But I'm sure you've already heard about it."

Zahir looked confused. "What happened? He didn't say anything to me."

Martina told her all about Logan's heroics during the

recent hostage crisis. "It was a bad situation. We could have lost a lot of people, but he knew how to handle it."

Zahir studied Martina. How could Logan be so blasé about a life-and-death situation that he didn't even mention it? She shrugged her shoulders. "Logan's like that. All-in all the time."

"What's that mean?" Martina asked.

"It's one of those informal SEAL expressions that capture the SEAL ethos. Ready to take on any challenge. All Logan ever wanted was to be a SEAL, but Afghanistan squelched that dream. He nearly lost his leg in an ambush. After the medics patched him up, they sent him to Walter Reed for rehab. He worked hard to get back in shape, but it wasn't enough; the Navy released him on a medical discharge."

"How did you two meet?" Martina asked.

"It's a long story," Zahir said. "Logan's brother, Cooper, and I were dating. He was an Army Ranger in Iraq, and I was a DOD civilian translator assigned to his unit." Zahir heaved a sigh. The memory was still raw in her mind.

"Cooper died in an ambush on patrol one night; he stepped on an IED and was killed instantly. He always walked point. He cared so much about his men that he was always ready to put himself in harm's way to protect them."

Martina's hand covered her mouth. "I'm so sorry. I didn't know."

"It's all right. I was a wreck for months," Zahir said. "Logan's family helped me get through it. His sister, Millie, let me stay at her place in Boston until I could get on my feet."

They were interrupted by Logan and Cooper returning.

"Mom, you should have seen this guy coming out of the bathroom. Dad said he was Native American. He had long hair with a red headband." Cooper's eyes suddenly grew round with excitement. "It's him."

"Martina, it looks like you have some new friends."

"Nantan, long time no see." Martina jumped up and hugged the man. "This is the Alexander family—Logan, Cooper, and Zahir. They just moved here from Washington."

Nantan gave Cooper a mock salute. "Welcome to New Mexico. You'll have to visit our pueblo once you finish moving in. Martina can tell you the best time to come; festivals are the most interesting."

"How is your family, Nantan?" Martina asked.

"Thank you for asking. Everyone is fine. The twins are finishing their last year of high school."

"They grow up so fast."

"Indeed, they do. I'll leave you to your dinner," Nantan said.

"What tribe does Nantan belong to?" Zahir asked when he was out of earshot.

"Pueblo. Jémez Pueblo," Martina said.

"Are there many indigenous people left in New Mexico?" Zahir asked.

"Twenty-three tribes," Martina said. "There are nineteen Pueblo tribes, three Apaches, and the Navajo Nation. You wouldn't know it by talking to him, but Nantan is chief of the Jémez tribe. He's also a famous artisan. Some of his ceramics are on display at the Smithsonian. The king and queen of Spain even commissioned a piece of his when they visited the States."

"How did you get to know him?" Logan asked.

"It was one of those unexpected encounters. For the most part, the Pueblo tribes don't allow outsiders inside their communities except for certain feast days, so we probably never would have met. But one year, my father and I were driving back from delivering a horse to a buyer in Prescott, Arizona; I was in high school at the time. We were on I-40 near Laguna. The visibility was low because it was night, and we got caught in the middle of a blizzard. Suddenly out of nowhere, there was this truck in front of us spinning off the road into a ditch. We pulled over to help. It was Nantan and his pregnant wife on their way to deliver the twins.

"Dad got them out of the truck and gave them a ride to the hospital. Then we went back with Nantan to help him get his truck out of the ditch. We've been friends ever since."

Martina smiled at the memory.

"I'm surprised that they can keep people from going into their villages. Is that so they can maintain a level of autonomy?" Zahir asked.

"They are independent jurisdictions. They have sovereign governments," Martina said. "But I think the real reason they limit outside visitors is to minimize external influences. They have their language and traditions. When the Spanish first came to New Mexico almost five hundred years ago, there were over a hundred Pueblo communities throughout the Rio Grande Valley. Today there are only nineteen. They're good people."

After dinner, they said their goodbyes. Cooper was so tired he fell asleep in the car. Zahir poked Logan in the ribs. "Why didn't you tell me about the hostage situation?" she asked.

Logan squirmed in his seat. "I didn't want to worry you."

She snuggled up next to him. "I worry about you anyway, Logan Alexander."

Chapter 14

Jason frowned as he hunched over the laptop. Installing the Onion Router browser and virtual private network recommended by his father had been easy. Composing his first message was proving to be a more significant challenge. His father had cautioned him not to let his guard down when corresponding with Pyongyang. He was never to include his real name or any personal details in these communications.

"It pays to be careful," his father said. "Although the browser and VPN are reliable tools, it doesn't hurt to go the extra distance to protect your identity."

"But realistically, if the FBI or NSA figure out that a message to Pyongyang came from Los Alamos, my goose is cooked," Jason said.

"Not necessarily," his father replied. "How many people work at LUMOS?"

"I don't know the exact number. The Center for Integrated Nanotechnologies has about a hundred, and we're a part of the center."

"That's my point. It could be any one of a hundred people who are in touch with Pyongyang."

Jason nodded his understanding but decided not to dwell on his misgivings. Sure, there might be a hundred suspects if the FBI were to open an investigation, but he would probably be a prime suspect, if only because of his Korean heritage.

Apprehension about the security of his communications with Pyongyang wasn't the only thing on Jason's mind. He wanted to please his father, but at most, he was ambivalent about helping the North Korean regime with its nuclear program.

Sometimes he found it hard to believe that his father was an agent for the North Korean Intelligence Service. As a trade official, what role could he possibly play in intelligence operations? He'd read somewhere that because North Korea didn't have that many embassies abroad, it used its foreign trade missions to collect intelligence. Much of this collection came from open-source technical materials and a few covert assets. Also, it was true their cyber capabilities were sophisticated, but their SIGINT operations were almost nonexistent.

Jason returned to the task at hand. He decided to send his father a list of people working at the Center for Integrated Nanotechnologies, including their phone numbers and email addresses. This information could hardly be considered sensitive; it came straight out of the Los Alamos National Lab's public website. But it would show the NKIS that he was trying to be helpful.

As he hit the send button, Jason felt a tingle of excitement, or was it doubt? Before he was done, though, he had one more thing to do: review the open codes his father had suggested he use in his email communications. The day's date at the top right side of any message meant everything was all right. If, on the other hand, he put it at the top left side, it indicated he was under suspicion. And if he signed the email "Your Friend," it meant he had plans to travel internationally. In the latter case, he would call a designated phone number once he was abroad, and somebody would arrange to meet him.

Jason's cell phone rang. It was Laurie. "Hey, I was just thinking about you," he said. "What's up?"

"Not much. Checking to see if you want to go for a run Saturday."

"With your running group?" he asked.

"Yeah. We're doing a six-mile run in the Santa Fe National Forest, the Quemazon Trail."

"How hard is it?" he asked, thinking about the toll last week's run had taken on his body.

"It's not too bad, around 1,500 feet elevation gain. Let me check my trail guide."

While Jason waited, he could hear pages turning as she searched her book.

"Okay, I found it. Quemazon is described as a moderate out and back trail good for both hiking and running."

"Sounds like fun."

"I'll send you a link for directions. It's about twenty-five minutes from your place. We'll meet at the trailhead at 9 o'clock; there's a parking area off Trinity Drive between 47th and 49th Streets."

They chatted about work for five minutes before Laurie said she had to go. "I'm meeting a classmate from UCLA for dinner. We used to run track together."

"Have fun. Thanks for calling; I'll see you Saturday," he said. He felt a pang of jealousy as he hung up. He had to admit; he was emotionally drawn to Laurie, despite the short time they had known each other. They had a lot in common, their work, their Korean heritage, their love of running, and, not least of all, their compatibility in bed. They were also very different. She grew up in Los Angeles and didn't speak a word of Korean. Her parents were professional and, it seemed, well off. She didn't have any siblings or close relatives. He sighed and got up to work on dinner.

Laurie was idly toying with her phone as she ran through her conversation with Jason. Was it her imagination, or did she detect a trace of jealousy in his voice when she mentioned her dinner date?

He'd be envious if he knew who she was seeing, Billy Chu, former UCLA track star and love interest. Billy was South Korean. After graduating from college, he returned to Seoul, where his father, a bigwig in the Republic of Korea (ROK) government, got him a job in their Ministry of Foreign Affairs (MFA.) They'd stayed in touch over the years; in his last letter to her, Billy mentioned a possibility the MFA would assign him to their consulate in Los Angeles. He'd called her earlier in the week to say he was working in the Science and Technology Section there and was coming to

Los Alamos on an area familiarization trip.

The next day, Laurie contacted the Office of Security and spoke with a new security officer by the name of Logan Alexander, to report her upcoming contact with a foreign national. He thanked her for calling and took down Billy's particulars. He reminded her to file a follow-up contact re-port with him, especially if she anticipated close and con-tinuing contact.

She smiled. *We'll have to see about that,* she thought to herself.

Chapter 15

Logan submitted a trace request on Billy Chu to CIA headquarters, Seoul, and the FBI field offices in Los Angeles and Washington, D.C., based on the information Laurie Kim provided. She was a little fuzzy on Chu's actual birth date but knew the year and month, November 1994.

Headquarters and Seoul were the first to respond with classified messages. Chu's father, Chu Ho-Won, was a career diplomat at the Ministry of Foreign Affairs; his mother was a housewife. The family had postings in Washington, New Delhi, Canberra, and Kuala Lumpur during Chu's formative years. The senior Chu was currently serving as South Korea's ambassador to Mexico.

After graduating with honors from Seoul's Yongsan International School, Billy Chu enrolled in UCLA's undergraduate College of Letters and Science in 2012, graduating with a B.S. in 2016. He stayed on for an MBA Program at the Anderson School of Management, graduating cum laude in 2018.

All of this was interesting but what grabbed Logan's attention was the last paragraph. Chu did not work at the Ministry of Foreign Affairs. According to a compartmented source, he used it as a cover for his position as an intelligence officer with the National Intelligence Service (NIS), South Korea's preeminent spy agency.

Logan scratched his head and stared out the window. He wasn't used to having a room with a view. In his earlier foreign assignments for the CIA, Logan was under non-official cover and didn't have a corner office. At Headquarters, he worked out of a sensitive compartmented information facility where there were no windows.

The technical geniuses from the CIA's Office of Technical Services had devised a secure messaging system for him to use at Los Alamos. To protect the technology, he had to lock his door, even if he stepped out for five minutes to use the toilet. Also, there had to be twenty-four-hour security in the building.

Logan re-read the message to make sure he hadn't missed anything. The header read Top Secret/SCI; the originator classified it that way because of its sensitive sourcing. There was a tear line on the second page, a watered-down version of the original intelligence, without the sourcing information.

Logan secured his commo system and placed the tear line in an envelope. He walked down the hall to Martina's office and rapped on the door.

"Come in," she said. "Hey, what's up?"

"I just got this in from Langley," he said, waving the envelope. He dropped it on her desk. "I think you're going to find it interesting."

Martina opened the envelope and scanned the contents. Her brow furrowed as she got to the paragraph regarding Chu's intelligence affiliation. "Is this from a reliable source?" she asked.

"I can't go into that," he said. "But from the source description, I would give it a high level of confidence."

"What's your take?" she asked.

"I'm a little concerned that Chu's coming out here masquerading as a Science and Technology officer for the consulate in LA. I didn't think of it, but we should send a note to Sandia and find out if he's been nosing around there too."

"I wonder what he's up to?" Martina asked, drumming her pen on the desk.

"Probably hoping to pump his buddy, Laurie, for info. I read up on U.S./South Korea nuclear relations before I left Washington. Seoul didn't have a nuclear power program until the 1950s, and it wasn't until the 1970s that they began building their first reactor.

"The U.S. pressured the South Koreans into signing the

Nuclear Non-Proliferation Treaty (NPT) in 1975, and that pretty much put a stop to their nuclear weapons program," Logan added.

"If I remember correctly, there was an incident in the early 1980s when the South Koreans began experimenting with small-scale plutonium extraction. That got them into hot water with the International Atomic Energy Agency," Martina said.

"Yeah, but they worked with the IAEA to make amends and got a clean bill of health in the 1990s," Logan said.

"Flash forward thirty years, and they have at least twenty-four nuclear power reactors operating in-country, and over the next ten years, they're planning to export eighty more reactors worldwide, to the tune of $400 billion," he continued.

Martina nodded appreciatively. "You did your homework. So where does that leave us with Mr. Chu?"

"Good question. I'll bet Chu is sniffing around to see if he can pick up any intel on U.S. discussions with North Korea."

"What discussions?" Martina asked. "The Six Party Talks are dead in the water."

"Yeah, but maybe the South Koreans think we're having ongoing bilateral talks with the North Koreans, behind closed doors," Logan said.

"Changing the subject, how well do you know Laurie Kim?" he asked.

"Not well," Martina said. "She's been here a couple of years. Socially, I've gone on a couple of runs with a running club she belongs to, the Santa Fe Trail Runners. What are you thinking?"

"It's not just a coincidence that Chu is visiting Los Alamos. He and Laurie went to school together and were close. She didn't phrase it that way, but it seems like she was going out with him. And besides, her family background is South Korean.

"Do you think she's still active with that running group?" Logan asked.

"I think so. Why?"

"I think I need to go for a run this weekend," he said.

Martina nodded knowingly. "They post their runs on the Internet. Maybe you'll get lucky and bump into Mr. Chu," she smiled.

Chapter 16

Saturday morning Logan and Zahir were up early. They took their coffee into the family room, which had windows on all sides looking out to breathtaking views of the Jemez Mountains. Despite their 6,000-foot elevation and temperatures in the forties, it was sunny and mild, typical winter weather in northeast New Mexico.

"I talked to the dean of the School for Liberal Arts at Santa Fe Community College yesterday," Zahir said, as she stood gazing out at the vista. Zahir had a Ph.D. in Arabic and was a native Farsi speaker; her career had been pretty portable thus far. Academic positions were highly sought after, but somehow she always found something, even if it was only tutoring jobs.

"Were they looking for an Arabic teacher?' Logan asked.

"Yes, but not until next semester. One of their faculty is taking a sabbatical then to write an Arabic language textbook. I have an interview with the department head and a person from HR this afternoon. They're looking for someone who can teach beginning and advanced classes."

"How much of a time commitment is it?" he asked.

"Nine hours of classroom, office hours, and class prep. Probably about twenty-five hours a week total."

"When's your meeting?" Logan asked.

"Two o'clock. It's about a thirty-minute drive from here," Zahir said. "I think I'll leave at one to be on the safe side."

"That works out. I need to be in Los Alamos at 9 o'clock."

"What are you doing?" she asked.

"Going for a run. I'm trying to meet this guy who's visiting one of our employees."

Zahir looked at him knowingly. She knew enough not to ask him any questions about his work. Logan was a great believer in "need to know"—the Agency policy that stipulated if you didn't need to know something to do your job, you didn't need to know it.

"I'll be back at noon if that works for you," he said.

"Great, I'll have lunch ready. Do you want to do something with Cooper after lunch?"

"I was thinking about showing him around Los Alamos." He checked the time and saw that it was 8 o'clock. "I've got to get going."

"Aren't you going to eat something?" she asked.

"I'll grab an energy bar and a piece of fruit to eat on the way," he called back over his shoulder.

Logan checked the weather and saw that it was forty-five degrees and holding. He dressed in his running gear, making sure to layer up, and then stopped in the kitchen to grab his food and fill his camelback with water.

"You want any more coffee, sweetie?" he asked.

"No, you can finish it."

He poured the rest of the coffee into a travel mug and left the house.

Logan followed directions to the Quemazon Trailhead and spotted a half-dozen cars parked a few yards from the trail. Runners were warming up by the side of the road and hydrating. He spotted Laurie Kim talking to two Asian males. He unloaded and went over to see if he could join them on their run.

Laurie spotted Logan and beckoned to him. "Hey, Logan, are you running the Quemazon Trail?" she asked.

"Yeah. I was looking for a running group to join and spotted this run posted online, so I thought I'd give it a try." He began stretching. "Do you have room?"

Laurie gave him a curious sideways glance as though she knew the real reason he had picked this particular run. "We're a pretty friendly bunch," she said. "Try it out. We usually try to get together for a run once a week.

"Oh, I forgot my manners." Laurie turned to the man

standing closest to her. "This is Billy Chu, an old friend of mine from UCLA, and this is Jason Lee, a colleague from the lab. Logan works at the lab, too," she added.

She waved to the rest of the group and introduced Logan and Billy. The men nodded and continued their warmups.

"I didn't know you were a runner," she said to Logan as she knelt to tighten her shoestrings.

"I used to be in better shape," he said, "but I got this titanium knee, courtesy of the Taliban, and it doesn't work as well as the original model."

"What happened?" Laurie asked as the group set off at a warmup jog.

"I got into a firefight with the bad guys, and they won."

"Were you in the Army?" Billy asked.

"No, Navy."

"Isn't that unusual for the Navy to be in a firefight in the middle of the desert?" Billy asked.

"For Joe Navy, I'd say that's probably true, but for a Navy SEAL, it's what we do these days."

Laurie's lips parted as she looked at Logan with new-found respect. Chu shuffled his feet, seeming embarrassed by his glib remark.

"You were a SEAL?" Jason asked.

"Yep, right out of college," Logan said.

"Where'd you go to school?" Laurie asked.

"Navy."

She nodded her head in appreciation. After about a mile, the lead runners picked up the pace. It felt comfortable, and Logan breathed with ease as he took in the scenery. The ponderosa pines were majestic, but forest fires had charred large swaths of the mountain.

"Are fires a big problem in the park?" he asked Laurie.

"The word *quemazon* means 'burned' in the local dialect," she said. "Before the turn of the century, there were low-intensity fires throughout this area every ten or fifteen years; hot enough to burn the undergrowth, but not destroy the ponderosa pines." She pointed towards the mesa above Los Alamos.

"When the loggers and sheepherders came here around 1900, they cleared the low-lying brush, and the pine trees started filling in. There were no burns for over a hundred years. In May 2000, the Cerro Grande Fire came through here and burned the entire forest." She sped up to run with Billy.

They were climbing now, and Logan was beginning to feel the burn. He and Jason were running next to each other.

"Jason, where are you from?" Logan asked.

"Toronto."

"Been here long?"

"No, just a couple of weeks. I finished a Ph.D. at the University of Toronto last year."

"Where are you working?" Logan asked.

"LUMOS, how about you?"

"I'm in Security. Man, look at those guys go," Logan said.

Billy Chu and Laurie had kicked it into another gear and were pulling away from the rest of them. They seemed to be racing each other. The rest of the group, not to be outdone, picked up the pace too.

"Laurie said she and Billy ran track together at UCLA. They're at a different level," Jason said.

"How about you?" Logan asked. "You're not doing too bad."

"I ran cross-country in high school and college but stopped in graduate school."

Up ahead, Logan could see Pipeline Road. Half a mile further, there were views of the Los Alamos Valley and Chicoma Mountain, the highest peak in the Jemez Mountains at 11,561 feet. When they caught up with the others, Laurie organized a group photo, propping her cellphone against a rock outcrop, with Chicoma as a backdrop. When they finished, Logan pulled off his left sneaker to check a hotspot on his heel. He applied a piece of moleskin to keep it from flaring up further and laced up his shoe.

They set off at a moderate pace; forty-five minutes later, they were back at the trailhead. The sun was higher in the sky, and it had warmed up several degrees. A runner named Gillie hauled a cooler filled with beers out of his truck. Logan snagged a bottle of Sweetwater and made small talk with several other runners before rejoining Laurie, Billy, and Jason.

"This is chilly, but it's nothing like Toronto," Jason was saying. "In the spring, as soon as the temperature rises above freezing, people are outside drinking."

"What do Canadians like to drink?" Laurie asked. "Molson?"

"You're not going to believe this," Jason said. "Budweiser."

"No way," Logan said.

Laurie walked over to Jason and pulled him out of earshot, hugging him as she whispered something in his ear. Logan took the opportunity to approach Billy Chu, who was idly swirling the beer in his can.

"That was a pretty impressive running clinic you and Laurie put on," Logan said.

"You weren't exactly eating our dust," Billy chuckled. "Laurie and I trained together for four years at UCLA."

"Go Bruins," Logan said.

"Are you a fan?"

"Not really. I'm not a big PAC-12 guy. When I played football at Navy, we were independent, but then joined the ACC in 2015. I tend to follow ACC teams.

"So what did you do out of college?" Logan asked.

"I went back to Seoul and got a job with our Ministry of Foreign Affairs."

Logan did his best to look confused. "You're South Korean? I thought you were Asian American."

Chu laughed. "No, Korean. My dad's a diplomat; we lived all over the world when I was growing up. I went to UCLA for my undergraduate degree and stayed on for an MBA."

"Where are you working now?" Logan asked.

"At our consulate in Los Angeles, as the Science and Technology officer. I spend most of my time working on energy security issues. Our two countries have gone down separate paths when it comes to nuclear energy. The U.S., for the most part, is no longer exporting commercial nuclear reactors, but we're ramping up our commercial nuclear power exports."

"Okay, and South Korea is no longer pursuing the bomb. So, what's the nuclear connection between the U.S. and South Korea now that the Six Party Talks are dead in the water?" Logan asked.

"The biggest markets for commercial nuclear reactors are in the Mideast and Southeast Asia. That raises concerns about the proliferation of nuclear technology. The U.S. and the IAEA developed the norms for international nuclear nonproliferation. We're a strong proponent of the NPT. Keeping lines of communication between our two countries open is the best way to avoid any missteps."

"Maybe we can stay in touch," Logan said. "I just started an assignment at the lab, and I'll probably be here for the next couple of years anyway. Let me give you my phone number. If you're ever back in town, let's have lunch." The two men exchanged phone numbers and said goodbye.

As Logan drove home, he vowed to keep an eye on Billy Chu. Maybe he was just an aggressive NIS officer doing his job, or maybe he was sniffing around the lab and his old love interest Laurie Kim because he had something nefarious in mind.

Chapter 17

When Billy Chu returned to Los Angeles on Monday afternoon, the first thing he did was complete his NIS trip report. His meetings with Laurie's colleagues earlier in the day were useful, and he made several new contacts. He requested background traces on all of them on the off chance the service was already in touch with any of them.

But it wasn't the scientists in Monday's meeting that dominated his thoughts. It was the security officer he met on Saturday's run with Laurie, Logan Alexander. He did a Google search on Alexander; there was quite a bit out there. Starting with that the NFL wanted to draft him right out of Navy, that he was a war hero, got shot up in Afghanistan, and went on to found a marine maritime company in Boston.

There was also some intriguing history around that timeframe. The Boston Globe linked Alexander to a high-profile paramilitary operation against a terrorist training camp in Bander Deylam, Iran, near the Persian Gulf, and a retaliatory attack on his Boston office by an Iranian terrorist.

Alexander disappeared for a couple of years and then reemerged in Hong Kong, where he set up a branch office of Alexander Maritime to penetrate the China market. Billy searched Dun and Bradstreet's database to see how they rated Alexander's company, yielding scant information. D&B listed Alexander's Hong Kong office as closed in 2018.

"Who are you, Logan Alexander?" Billy asked out loud. Alexander was sharp, too sharp to be working on the lower rungs of the security office at Los Alamos. Could he be intel?

Billy turned his thoughts back to his conversations with Laurie. His primary motive for reaching out to her had been to leverage her access at the lab. He didn't know how useful her contacts would be to him, but at least he was making inroads in a place that was of critical importance to South Korea.

He had to admit there had been a moment when he first saw her that he felt a stirring in his loins. They were close at UCLA, initially as teammates on the track team and later as lovers. They had periodic communications over the years, but both of them had moved on. Seeing her with that Canadian guy, Jason Lee, left him feeling somewhat deflated, but he was over it.

Early Tuesday morning, Billy was having coffee in his Normandie Avenue apartment in Koreatown when he received a text message from his father.

"Please give me a call when you get to the office," it said.

I wonder what that's all about? he thought. If it were personal, his dad would call him at home. Asking him to phone from the office meant that he wanted to talk to him on a secure line. There was a NIS contingent in Mexico City, and, as the ambassador, his dad was responsible for their intelligence collection program. He would have useful insights into their reporting and activities that might overlap with Billy's operations.

In a rare alignment of his cover duties and NIS operational responsibilities, Billy's primary focus in Los Angeles was energy security and weapons of mass destruction. Although his dad was not read-in on his specific cases, as a senior MFA official in the region, he would have seen Billy's intelligence reporting. Billy finished his coffee, got dressed, and left for work at 7:30. It was a short fifteen-minute drive to the consulate general.

When Billy joined the NIS, he was proud to become a member of the elite service. But recent scandals had tarnished its reputation, the 2017 revelations of NIS interference in South Korea's 2012 presidential race, and 2018 allegations of bribery by three former NIS directors and the president's office. There was a lot of work to be done to restore the NIS to its former elite status.

Billy was the sole NIS operations officer in Los Angeles. He shared a secretary, Susan Oh, with the consul general. Susan was already at her desk when Billy arrived.

"Good morning, Susan. Could you get the crypto key for the secure line out of your safe for me? I need to call my father."

"At the office?" she asked.

"Yes. I'll wait until a little after 8 to call. He usually gets in early, but we'll give him a chance to settle in," Billy said. He logged onto his computer to read the overnight intelligence reports and summaries of relevant news stories. Billy skimmed the material until 8:15 and then placed the crypto key into his secure phone and dialed his father's number.

"Hello? Ambassador Chu's office. May I help you?"

"Good morning, Mrs. Chang. Billy Chu here. Could you put my father on, please?"

"Billy, how are you? I was talking to your mother yesterday, and she was wondering if you will be coming to Mexico for the Lunar New Year celebration."

"I'm trying to get away, but my boss is such a slave driver."

Mrs. Chang laughed. She knew the consul general personally, having served with her at a previous posting in Ottawa. If anything, she was the polar opposite of a slave driver. "I'll tell her you said that the next time I speak to her. Here's the ambassador."

"Billy?"

"Hi, Dad. How's everything?"

"We're busy. We do a big Lunar New Year party for the Mexicans and the other embassies. But that isn't why I reached out to you." He paused for a moment before continuing.

"The NIS chief here has an active program targeting North Korean activities. Recently his contacts at CNI (the principal intelligence agency in Mexico) told him that Mexico was in discussions with North Korea to establish a permanent trade office here." His father cleared his throat and continued.

"The CNI asked us for traces on the North Korean delegation. The group's head turned out to be a South Korean defector to the North by the name of Roe Min-Woo."

Chapter 18

Martina, Peter, and Logan were driving north from Two Mile Canyon to Technical Area 55 (TA-55) for a briefing from the Plutonium Facility director, Dr. Tom Nelson. Logan had suggested the meeting following their hotwash of the hostage incident involving George Taylor.

"Taylor just waltzed in here and held twelve people hostage for the better part of a day," Logan said. "We were lucky everyone walked out of it alive."

"Except for Taylor," Peter said, making light of the hostage-taker's demise during the stand-off.

Martina dug an elbow into her deputy's ribs. "That's not funny, Peter," she said. "I agree; it's hard to feel sorry for anyone who would do what he did, but still, the man died."

Peter pursed his lips and remained silent. Martina must be getting soft in her old age, he thought. There hadn't been a violent crime at the lab in all the years he'd been there. But Logan was right. They couldn't afford to be complacent. Sometimes it took a fresh set of eyes on an issue to expose its weaknesses.

And TA-55 was an excellent place to start. The facility began processing plutonium in 1978 and continued uninterrupted for almost thirty years. It was probably one of the most, if not the most sensitive piece of real estate at Los Alamos.

They were fast approaching the forty-acre site, located in a restricted area. Martina drove through a double security chain-link fence strung with concertina wire at the top and pulled up next to Building 1, the administration building. The first thing that struck Logan was the scale of the operation.

"There are five main interconnected buildings in TA-55," Peter said as they walked toward the building housing the director's office. He pointed out a couple of support buildings, the warehouse, plutonium building, and a nuclear materials storage facility.

"There's a tunnel that runs between the plutonium building and the storage facility for transferring plutonium," he said. "You'll see when we walk around that there are many other smaller structures throughout the site used for security and storage."

"What's over there?" Logan asked, pointing to a sprawling building.

"That's the Chemistry and Metallurgy Research Building," a gravelly voice behind them said. "Hi, I'm Tom Nelson, director of TA-55. And you are?"

"Logan Alexander."

"Hi, Dr. Nelson. Logan's on loan to us from the CIA. He's helping us beef up our counterintelligence program. Dr. Nelson's been at the lab since the early eighties," Martina said.

The lab director appeared to be in his early seventies. A thin patch of stubble on his head contrasted with a full white beard. Unflinching deep blue eyes took in the three security officers. His silver-tipped bolo tie and blue jeans were a nod to New Mexican informality.

Dr. Nelson proved to be as unassuming as his attire suggested. Rather than giving them a standard PowerPoint presentation, Nelson invited them to hop aboard his four-by-four Land Rover for a driving tour of TA-55.

"I began working at Los Alamos in 1980, two years after the lab started processing plutonium," he said.

"Since then, our capabilities and mission have grown considerably. We're not only the leading plutonium science and manufacturing facility in the United States but also the gold standard for a range of national security programs like stockpile stewardship and nuclear terrorism mitigation."

"Can you explain how the stockpile stewardship program works?" Logan asked.

"Let me give you a little background. The National Nuclear Security Administration maintains the stockpile. In the early days, we conducted underground nuclear tests to assess our stockpiled weapons' stability and reliability. But, because of concerns about nuclear fallout stemming from these tests, we stopped doing them."

"When was that?" Peter asked.

"I remember it like it was yesterday," Dr. Nelson said. "September 23, 1992. It was code-named, 'Divider,' a twenty-kiloton test performed at the Nevada Test Site in Mercury, Nevada.

"After we banned the underground nuclear testing program, NNSA had to find a way to assess and certify the stockpile. Along with the other labs and production facilities, we developed a new science-based approach to certification without the risk associated with underground tests.

"We also worked closely with the Nuclear Weapons Council and the Department of Defense to make sure we were addressing their concerns."

Dr. Nelson pulled over to allow a tractor-trailer room to pass by. He pointed to the truck as it swerved around them. "Has Martina briefed you on our shipping operation?" he asked. Logan gave Martina a questioning look.

"Not yet," she said. "The Office of Secure Transportation, OST, administers the shipping program now," she continued. "And OST federal agents based in Albuquerque staff it. Back in the day, we transported nuclear materials in commercial vehicles, but because of a rise in international terrorism and domestic unrest, the DOE decided we needed tighter shipping and handling protocols. They phased out the commercial shipping operation and upgraded their equipment; now, we have three OST regional offices—Oak Ridge, Albuquerque and Amarillo.

"Did you hear the one about the stolen car?" Peter asked with a straight face. "Inside there was a rattlesnake, a bottle of whiskey, a gun, and a canister of radioactive uranium."

Martina gave Peter her don't-go-there glare, but he continued talking.

"This is a true story," he said. "Happened last year in Guthrie, Oklahoma. Police stopped this couple because their car had an expired tag, and they found all that stuff inside. The point is you can have the best science and high-tech shipping containers in the world, and people will still find a way to get around it."

Chapter 19

Billy Chu was struggling to concentrate. His attention was on his father's call about the South Korean defector, Roe Min-Woo. But standing opposite him right now was the reigning Los Angeles tae kwon do black belt champion, Gunther Moore, who was preparing to beat him to a pulp.

He and Moore were in a tae kwon do dojang (training hall) in Koreatown, where they worked out and sometimes competed in local tournaments. Moore was a retired jarhead and *sahyun* (master) owner of the dojang.

In 2005, Moore was the gunny sergeant for the Marine Security Detachment at the American Embassy in Kuala Lumpur, where Billy was in middle school. Moore's son, Ethan, was a classmate of Billy's at the International School of Kuala Lumpur and invited him to join his father's tae kwon do class on Saturdays.

Over the years, Billy had worked on his tae kwon do, progressing through the ranks until he attained his black belt. He enjoyed competing, but rarely could he get the best of Gunther Moore. Before he could refocus on the match, Moore took him down with a surprise spinning jump kick, rotating his entire body and head 360 degrees in the air before releasing a back pivot kick.

"Sahyun," Billy said with respect, as he took a deep bow. He then left for the locker room to shower and dress.

Billy ran into his childhood friend coming out of the locker room. "Ethan," he said. "Your old man's still got it. He took me down with a spinning jump kick. I didn't know he had that move in his repertoire. How old is he now? Forty-five?"

"He turned fifty last month," Ethan said. "He works at

it, and he's in here six days a week, training." The two men talked briefly about mutual friends from their days in KL and made plans to get together for drinks.

Billy drove over to the consulate and parked in his assigned space. He wanted to read the overnight intelligence reporting and review the notes he'd made during his father's call.

Susan had put on a pot of coffee and left the overnight messages on his desk. A sealed manila envelope marked Top Secret with his name on it caught his attention. Curious, he opened it before starting his reading.

The report was from Seoul; the NIS had a file on Roe Min-Woo. He'd been a minor trade official at the South Korean Ministry of Trade, Industry, and Energy when he defected to the North in 1995. The South Korean newspapers had not widely publicized his defection, which was typical in these cases. On the other hand, North Korea made a propaganda video showing Roe reuniting with his family in Pyongyang.

The NIS had put Roe's name on a watch list after his defection and tracked his movements over the years. Meanwhile, the National Police Agency conducted an internal investigation. They began by interviewing Roe's friends and teachers in Seoul, where they learned of his relationship with Lee Ha-Yoon.

The investigating officer subsequently interviewed Lee's mother and learned that her daughter had immigrated to Canada, where she worked as a medical doctor in Toronto. The mother mentioned that her daughter had borne a child out of wedlock, and the father was none other than Roe Min-Woo.

South Korea is a paternalistic society, and children are expected to take their father's surname. Women, on the other hand, rarely, if ever, take their husband's name after marriage—those women who give birth to children out of wedlock pass on their family name to the child.

"What is your grandchild's name?" the National Police Agency officer asked.

"Jason. Jason Lee," she said with a smile. "He recently earned his Ph.D. in physics from the University of Toronto."

Billy exhaled and leaned back in his chair, twirling a pen in his fingers. He stared vacantly at the wall across the room. The world seemed to slow down as he tried to digest this new information. Jason Lee from the University of Toronto could be none other than the Jason Lee he had gone running with last weekend in Los Alamos. Laurie's new love interest's father was North Korean.

It didn't necessarily mean anything. South Korea had changed remarkably in the years since the armistice brought an end to hostilities between the North and the South. In the early days following the conflict, there was a great deal of suspicion surrounding anything having to do with the North. Seventy-five years later, it was not uncommon for a North Korean defector to marry into a South Korean family.

Billy wondered if Jason had revealed his North Korean parentage when he applied to work at Los Alamos. He doubted it. Lee's mother may not have disclosed the father's identity to him. In some ways, it would have been easier for him not to know.

Billy was working on a rough draft of his Los Alamos trip report for his bosses in Seoul. He set it aside for a moment to document his contact with Jason Lee. It would be a professional courtesy for his service to convey Lee's father's information to the CIA. He couldn't do it himself, given his Ministry of Foreign Affairs cover in Los Angeles.

Seoul could flag the intelligence for CIA Headquarters and the Department of Energy. That way, the NIS wouldn't have to identify him as the person who connected Roe and Lee as father and son.

It would be too bad for Lee if he lost his job over this. But these national security programs have to run a tight ship. If Lee could prove he didn't know about his father's defection to the North, he might be able to keep his job. If not, he could be on the next flight to Toronto.

In a separate Eyes-Only message to NIS, Billy asked his boss to read him in on the Roe file. If North Korea successfully established a trade office in Mexico City and Roe was affiliated with it in any way, he might attempt to establish contact with his son.

Billy knew from NIS briefings at headquarters that the North Korean Intelligence Service often used their trade missions as espionage platforms. Given Los Angeles' proximity to Mexico, it was not inconceivable that Roe would try to enter the country illegally.

Chapter 20

Logan called a meeting with Martina and Peter in Martina's office to review the reporting on Jason Lee. He brought sanitized copies of the Headquarters' message, keeping the sourcing to himself. Logan was responsible for protecting sources and methods; this information was from the South Koreans.

He had a hunch Billy Chu was behind the reporting, although his name wasn't in the source description. He also suspected Chu's father, the South Korean ambassador to Mexico, had picked up the recent information on Lee's father, Roe Min-Woo, from the Mexicans.

It made sense that the South Koreans had kept tabs on Roe all these years, given his defection to the North. Still, that was twenty-five years ago; in police work, the equivalent of a cold case.

"I can't believe that peckerhead snuck through security," Peter said, referring to Jason. "How's it possible this didn't come up in Lee's background investigation?"

"Lee may be telling the truth," Martina said. "I pulled his security file, and under 'father,' he wrote 'unknown.'"

"Let's haul his ass in here right now and find out," Peter said. "I'll bet you ten bucks he flat-out lied."

"Is a polygraph part of your security processing?" Logan asked.

"No," Martina said.

"We may have a hard time proving he knew about his father," Logan said. "If Lee did know, we have to find out why he lied."

"He probably figured it would jeopardize his chances of getting a security clearance and a job at Los Alamos," Peter said.

"We've come a long way in terms of diversity, but we haven't started hiring North Koreans," Martina said.

"Maybe the father put him up to it," Logan said.

Martina and Peter both started talking at once. Logan held up his hands.

"Hear me out. We know from the intelligence that Lee's father works for the North Korean government. No one in North Korea gets to travel abroad on official business unless the leadership trusts them. Roe could be working for the NKIS. You know Kim is looking for intelligence on U.S. nuclear capabilities. Lee would be his dream agent."

"We have to open up a case on Lee," Martina said. "The last thing we need is a North Korean penetration of the lab.

"I'll need to bring the Bureau in on this too," she said. "They have primacy on espionage cases in the U.S."

"We don't always play nice together," Logan said. "But I agree, it's their turf, and they may be able to expedite some things like warrants if it comes to that.

"We may also want to bring our cousins to the North in on this, too, since he's Canadian. We should reach out to the Mounties and the Canadian Security Intelligence Service, to see what they know about him.

"One more thing," Logan said. "If we think this meets the giggle test, we should also reach out to Harriet Wilson at NSA and ask her to get a FISA warrant for Lee's phone and computer. If he's in contact with his father or other North Koreans, we might pick up something."

Martina had been jotting down the main points from their discussion. She went over the list with them. "Did I leave anything out?" she asked.

"I forgot to mention something else," Logan said. "Saturday, I went for a run with the Santa Fe Trail Runners. That friend of Laurie Kim's, Billy Chu, showed up from Los Angeles, and so did Lee. By the way, Lee and Kim seemed pretty tight. He couldn't take his eyes off of her, and she kept flirting with him.

"I could make a point of running with these guys. Lee said he ran cross-country in high school and college, so he's probably going to be a regular on the weekend runs. It would give me a way to keep an eye on him. Maybe I'll find out something."

"Good idea," Martina said. "Logan, I'd like to keep this matter in your channels for now, if that's all right with you. It's sensitive, and I don't want it to get into HR channels unless it becomes an espionage case. We should brief the lab director this week, so he doesn't get blindsided from Washington."

"When do you want to do it?" Logan asked.

"Sooner than later," she said as she perused her daily planner. "How about tomorrow at 9:30?"

"Works for me."

"Peter?"

"Yeah, that's fine."

"All right. I'll reach out to the FBI Field Office in Santa Fe. If they're available, I'll invite the Assistant Special Agent in Charge to tomorrow's meeting.

Logan returned to his office and made a secure conference call to the DDO's office. The Assistant Deputy Director for Operations, Greg Samuelson, came on the line.

"Hi, Logan. How're things in sunny New Mexico?"

"Greg, how are you? Congratulations on the promotion." Greg had been in the trenches with him studying Chinese language years before. He'd been on the fast track even then, and now he was on the seventh floor.

"I wanted to give you a heads-up. I don't know if you've seen the reporting we got from the South Koreans on the Canadian scientist working here whose father is North Korean. Anyway, I briefed the intel to the Chief of Security and her deputy just now. They're all over it, primarily because he denied knowing who his father was during his background investigation."

"I saw the reporting," Greg said. "Jason Lee, the University of Toronto, Ph.D. in physics."

"That's the one. Anyway, Martina wants to bring in the Bureau, task NSA to get a FISA warrant on Lee's phone and computer, and do a full-blown CI investigation."

"Do you think she's getting out in front a little fast?" Greg asked.

"Maybe. Martina got burned a few years ago on the Wen Ho Lee case; I think she's determined that not happen again."

Logan gave Greg a gist of the earlier meeting and got the go-ahead to coordinate the case with the relevant internal and external participants. He spent the rest of the morning contacting the counterintelligence center and the Korea and Canada desks.

As Logan was leaving work that afternoon, he mused over the fact that he was beginning a full-fledged counterintelligence investigation, something he'd anticipated, just not in his first few weeks at the lab.

Chapter 21

Jason Lee yawned as he flipped through the last research paper his boss had given him to read. He felt intellectually invigorated and, at the same time, daunted by the breadth of research the lab was conducting. This paper, *Terahertz Metamaterials for Linear Polarization Conversion and Anomalous Refraction*, was as nerdy as it gets.

His boss had not assigned him to a specific team or project yet; he was still reading in and getting a feeling for the lab's mission.

Earlier in the day, he'd spent a couple of hours talking to one of the scientists involved in upgrading the U.S. stockpile's aging plutonium cores, used to trigger nuclear weapons. Their team was under a lot of pressure to begin production, she said, but safety problems and cost overruns had delayed progress.

"I thought safety here was paramount," Jason said. "What happened?"

"I'm personally only aware of one incident," she said. "But there are reports of others. In July, one of my colleagues was weighing plutonium oxide powder, and when he removed his hands from the glovebox used to handle it, some of the powder got onto his skin and protective gear. The air monitors detected the contamination. Altogether, a dozen or so people were exposed."

"Were you there?" Jason asked.

"Yes."

"I'm sorry to hear that. What are you doing for it?" he asked.

"There's not much I can do. I get tested once a week, and so far, everything looks normal. I'm just keeping my fingers crossed."

At 6 o'clock, Jason shut down his computer and headed for the exit. He and Laurie planned to meet for beers at Barrels and Bottles, a brewpub in Los Alamos, after work. Jason arrived first and grabbed a high-top near the window. Moments later, he spotted Laurie crossing the street. She was one of those women who didn't realize how beautiful she was. She walked with poise and confidence, unaffected by the male heads turning on swivel sticks as she passed by.

It was a new experience for him to be this close to a member of the opposite sex. It wasn't that he hadn't been interested in girls in high school and college. It was just that, between academics and sports, he never was able to make time for them.

"Hi." Laurie flashed a smile and hugged him.

"Hey," Jason said. "Is the high-top okay, or did you want to sit at a table?"

"We're just having beers, right?" she asked.

"Are you hungry? We could get some appetizers," he said.

They ordered beers and selected a couple of appetizers from the menu. "How was your day?" he asked.

"It was amazing," she said. "This guy, Patrick, I used to work for was the project lead for a technology called Kilo-Power. The idea was to create a new type of nuclear reactor technology suitable for outer space use. He briefed us on their program today."

"Wow, that's amazing."

"Yeah. Their team figured out how to scale the reactors to different missions. The smallest low-watt reactors would be capable of fueling missions beyond, say, the International Space Station."

"You're talking deep space?"

"Yes. Imagine setting up a permanent base in deep space. A forty-kilowatt reactor would be sufficient to power a suitable environment for humans on Mars.

"Anyway, one of the strategic goals at Los Alamos is to commercialize advanced technologies. Los Alamos, NASA, and the National Nuclear Security Administration collaborated early on developing space reactor technology. Now, they feel the private sector can take it to the next level. That's what Patrick and his partners are planning to do."

"It seems like it would be a win-win for everyone. I don't know how these things work," Jason said. "I assume the lab and their partners would license the technology to the private sector, which in turn would create new jobs."

"That's the beauty of it. If you ever get tired of doing pure research and want to capitalize on your education, there will be more and more opportunities for that.

"Changing the subject, how was your day?"

"Not as exciting as yours. I'm working on a couple of short-term projects for my boss. He thinks it's a good idea for me to have broad exposure to LUMOS's research areas. I'm hoping to nail down something longer-term this week."

"What are you interested in?" Laurie asked.

"You may have given me an idea," he said. "I've done some research into PU-238. You know it's the only safe and reliable radioisotope to be used on U.S. space missions for the last fifty years. In the late eighties, the U.S. stopped manufacturing PU-238; they had to rely on Russia until they started manufacturing it again in 2011.

"It's not unlike what happened with U.S. space launches. NASA shut down the Space Shuttle program in 2011 and had to rely on Russia to put U.S. astronauts into space for years."

"Yeah. At $90 million a pop, that was a real bargain."

"That's my point. Along comes SpaceX, a private company, and they launch the first American manned space mission in more than a decade, this year."

"The private sector is stepping up big time for these national security programs. So, getting back to your research interest, how does this tie in?" Laurie asked.

"I'm wondering if there's another PU-238 waiting to be discovered. Ultimately, will PU-238 be up to the space exploration challenges posed by these new missions?"

"You may be on to something," Laurie said. She reached

across the high-top and caressed his hand. "Are you doing anything for dinner?" she asked.

"I hadn't planned anything," he said. "What did you have in mind?"

"I have a bunch of veggies to use up. I was thinking about making a stir-fry."

"Do you need anything?" he asked.

"No, I think I have everything I need." Laurie continued to stroke his hand.

The waiter brought their bill. As they were heading out to the parking lot and their respective cars, Laurie stood on her tiptoes to kiss him.

"By the way, I forgot to mention my roommate is out of town tonight. If we finish dinner early enough, maybe you can stay for dessert." She laughed and jumped into her car.

Chapter 22

Roe Min-Woo was exhausted. The flight from Mexico City to Pyongyang via Dalian, China, typically took twenty-six hours; however, screening measures to combat COVID-19 and a blizzard in northeast China's Heilongjiang Province slowed air traffic to a crawl. He departed Mexico City on Tuesday and just missed his Wednesday morning Air Koryo flight to Pyongyang. The North Korean national airline had a fleet of Russian-made Tupolev Tu-204 aircraft, but their next flight wasn't until Saturday, putting him in late Saturday night.

He scratched his head, irritated by the delay. Wandering over to the arrivals area information desk, he inquired about land transportation to Pyongyang.

The attendant yawned in boredom and absently clicked on her computer. "You can take the high-speed train from Dalian North Station to Dandong, and then catch the Dandong Express to Pyongyang Thursday morning at ten o'clock. That will get you in by six p.m. the same day."

"How long is the train ride from Dalian to Dandong?" Roe asked.

"On the high-speed train, it's a little over two hours."

Roe withdrew a pack of Zhonghua cigarettes from his coat pocket, shook one out, and offered another to the woman. She declined, wagging her finger. He lit his smoke and took a long pull, exhaling loudly. He'd purchased several cartons in the duty-free shop for his bosses at the NKIS. At fifty *renminbi* a pack, they were much sought after by North Korean businessmen and government officials.

He thanked the woman for the information, gathered his things, and went outside into the biting wind to queue up for a taxi. Moments later, a shiny blue-and-white Volkswagen Santana pulled up.

"Dalian North Train Station," he said. "How far is it from here?" The driver turned down the radio; he spoke with a rasp as he clutched a cigarette between two nicotine-stained fingers.

"Nine miles, sir. We should be there in fifteen minutes."

Roe stared out the window; Xinghai Park's Ferris wheel stood in stark contrast to the backdrop of modern skyscrapers and classical buildings in the vicinity of Zhongshan Square, named after Sun Yat-Sen, the founder of modern China.

Roe had transited numerous Chinese cities over the years on official business, but Dalian was his favorite. Looking east, he could make out the Korea Bay, beyond which was North Korea. He would have preferred to overnight in Dalian. Still, given the vagaries of international travel, especially during this global pandemic, it was more prudent to get to Dandong today and not have to worry about making his mid-morning connection to Pyongyang tomorrow.

The two-hour trip to Dandong was uneventful. After checking into a budget hotel, he decided to do some sightseeing. From the Friendship Bridge, he gazed across the Yalu River to North Korea.

He had only been gone for a week, but he was already lonesome for home. He had not confided to Chul-Moo when they met in Albuquerque that he was married to a North Korean woman and had two high-school-aged children who attended Pyongyang Number 1 Senior-Middle School. After resigning himself to the fact that Ha-Yoon would never leave her practice in Toronto to join him in Pyongyang, he'd married Hanna, the only daughter of his parents' best friends.

Theirs was a simple ceremony by South Korean standards. As an official in the NKIS, he had some standing in North Korean society. Hanna's family rented a ballroom in Pyongyang's Koryo Hotel; he wore a dark suit, and Hanna wore the traditional silk Hanbok dress. For him, the oddest guests at their reception were the traditional live rooster and hen wrapped in colorful cloths, beaks stuffed with chilis and flowers, placed on a table just inside the entrance to the ballroom.

As was customary, there was no honeymoon. Roe returned to work the next day, as did Hanna, an administrator at the Ministry of Agriculture.

Roe stopped at a sidewalk restaurant and ordered barbecued seafood skewers and a bottle of Yalu River Beer. A plastic enclosure kept the wind out, and a heater near his table warded off the cold air. He wolfed down his food in a few minutes and hurried to pay his bill. It was two o'clock, and he wanted to visit the Korean War Memorial Hall, also known as the Museum of the War to Resist U.S. Aggression and Aid Korea. He flagged down a taxi.

"Jinjiang Street, please," he said.

The taxi driver appraised him through the rearview mirror. "Where on Jinjiang Street?"

"I think it's number 68."

"Ah, yes, the Dandong War Memorial. Are you North Korean?" he asked.

"Yes, I'm here on business and had some free time on my hands this afternoon."

"It's a short ride. I believe the museum closes at four-thirty today," the driver said.

"My father was in the army during the war. After U.S. troops began operating north of the 38th parallel, his unit deployed across the Yalu River to help North Korea. He said the worst time for him was the Battle of Chosin Reservoir when a hundred thousand of our soldiers surrounded the Americans. It was so cold the Americans couldn't dig foxholes, so they piled up frozen bodies in place of sandbags.

"In early December, the enemy tried to evacuate through a valley down to the sea. My dad's unit was waiting for them at the Funchilin Pass. It was the worst firefight my father ever experienced. Luckily he survived."

Roe nodded, a somber look on his face. His father had told him stories of the ferocious fighting that first year of the war. China's help had been crucial, but they paid a steep price with over fifty thousand casualties at the Battle of Chosin Reservoir alone.

Chapter 23

Logan and Martina filed into the Los Alamos director's office. The FBI Assistant Special Agent in Charge (ASAC) of the Santa Fe satellite office, Anthony Brown, was already seated at the director's conference table. He rose to greet them.

"Martina, good to see you again." Turning to Logan, he said, "I don't believe I've had the pleasure."

"Logan Alexander." Logan shook Anthony's outstretched hand. "Nice to meet you. I've only been here a couple of weeks."

"Where are you coming from?" Anthony asked.

"Washington. I'm on detail to the lab from the CIA."

Anthony didn't say anything, but the arched eyebrow gave away his misgivings about having a CIA officer on his turf.

Logan took note of Anthony's apprehension and spoke up to dispel any concerns the ASAC might have.

"To be clear, I'm not here in an operational role. The DDO and Secretary of Energy authorized this position to beef up the lab's counterintelligence capabilities."

"So you're a counterintelligence officer?" Brown asked.

"No, I'm an Operations Officer home-based in the DO," Logan said.

The national lab director and his deputy came into the room and took their seats. "Martina, this is your meeting. Tell us what you've got."

"I'm going to turn it over to Logan to brief the information since he first brought it to our attention," Martina said.

Logan took fifteen minutes to walk the group through the intelligence reporting on Billy Chu, Jason Lee, and Roe

Min-Woo. They listened attentively to his presentation as he ticked off the highlights.

"So what's your take on all of this, Logan?" Brown asked.

"Right now, I'm mostly concerned about Jason Lee. He's possibly lied his way into a sensitive national security position.

"I'm less worried about Billy Chu. He may have concealed his intelligence affiliation to preserve his ability to work undercover in future foreign field assignments. And I wouldn't be surprised if his intelligence responsibilities overlap or correspond to his energy security role for the Ministry of Foreign Affairs.

"Roe Min-Woo is a big unknown. Up until now, he hadn't come across our radar. We know North Korea likes to use its foreign trade offices for intelligence collection. But that can work to our advantage. If Roe gets the job in Mexico City, we might be able to put someone up against him and find out what he's up to." Logan paused for a moment to let what he'd said sink in. "That said, the most immediate potential threat is Jason Lee."

"And the only thing you've got on him is his non-disclosure of a relative from a criterion country. Is that right?" the FBI agent asked.

"Correct. We don't have any collateral to support our concern Jason Lee could be working against the U.S. for North Korea," Logan said.

"Anthony, I'm sure you've spent a lot of time petitioning courts for warrants," Martina said. "Do you have any experience with the FISA Court, and if so, do you think we could make the case for a warrant to them, given what we've got?"

"We tend to set the bar pretty high when we go in for a FISA warrant," Anthony said. "Just because someone is in touch with a foreign government is not evidence of wrongdoing. The contact could be entirely innocuous.

"If we have concerns, we'll typically open a case and gather evidence using the methods available to us under our authorizations. These could include, but not be limited to, direct contact with the subject, surveillance, public record searches, and interviews. After all that, if we feel we have sufficient evidence to make the case, we will submit a warrant application. If we've done our job, we should have no problem getting approval from the FISA Court."

"I take it from what you're saying, you don't think we have probable cause at this point," Martina said.

"I don't want to tell you how to run your investigation," Anthony said. "If it were the Bureau requesting a warrant, we would go through the steps I outlined. On the other hand, I believe you could make a case for an imminent threat to national security, given Lee's position at the lab and the North Korea angle."

"Do you have anyone in Canada who could reach out to the Mounties and CSIS to see if they have anything on Lee?" Logan asked.

"You said Lee was from Toronto?" Anthony asked.

"Yes. Lee's mother immigrated from South Korea, but Lee was born in Toronto. He seems to have lived there his whole life. The only travel we're aware of is a trip to South Korea for his grandfather's funeral ten years ago and a trip to Europe following his high school graduation."

"We have a legal attaché at the American Embassy in Ottawa. He would have contacts in all the right places. But I doubt they'll share anything with us."

Martina was making a list of action items. "Anthony, would you mind reaching out to them anyway?"

"Not at all. I'll contact the legal attaché as soon as I get back to the office."

"I can ask our people to talk to their contacts in CSIS and the RCMP, too," Logan said. "Sometimes they'll tell the Bureau something they haven't shared with the CIA, and vice versa."

"I think that's particularly true when it's a law enforcement matter as opposed to a strictly intelligence issue," Anthony said.

"Right," Logan said. "I just had an idea. Does it make

sense to have NSA approach the FISA Court for a warrant on Lee now while, at the same time, we go ahead and open up an investigation on him? That way, we're proactive, and if the court denies NSA's application, we'll still be collecting evidence to beef up our next application."

"I think it's a good idea," Anthony said.

"Sir," Martina said, turning to the lab director, "if it's all right with you, we'll leave it there for now, unless you have any questions. I'll get on your calendar later in the week with an update."

"Thank you," he said. "I don't have any questions at the moment. Anything else?"

"I think that covers it, for now," she said. "Anthony, do you have time to continue this over lunch in my office? We'll order some sandwiches and drinks."

"Let's do it."

Chapter 24

In the two weeks since the meeting with Anthony Brown, there had been modest progress on several fronts. The CIA's North Korea desk discovered that one of their field operatives had been in touch with Roe Min-Woo for three months in Cambodia nine years earlier. Roe was filling in for the recently deceased deputy trade counselor, who died in a car crash outside of the capital, Phnom Penh.

According to reports, the CIA officer bumped into Roe at a reception for foreign diplomats at the prime minister's residence. He knew Roe was North Korean immediately because he was sporting a lapel pin featuring the Hermit Kingdom's leader, Kim Jong-Un.

Roe and another North Korean were talking with the undercover CIA officer when they discovered he was an American diplomat. The two men immediately broke off contact, according to North Korean protocol, although, according to the report, Roe seemed interested in continuing their conversation.

Later, as the CIA officer left the reception, Roe was waiting for him in the garden. He indicated that he would like to pursue their discussion sometime.

Over the next three months, they met discreetly numerous times, never in the same location, in and around the Cambodian capital. Roe was reticent to talk about himself and never revealed any vulnerabilities. He seemed more worldly than the average North Korean and also demonstrated a superior knowledge of foreign affairs. The CIA officer concluded that Roe had all the attributes of an intelligence officer.

Separately, CSIS and the RCMP balked at providing the

Bureau reporting on Jason Lee. Their response was, essentially, show us the smoking gun first, and then we'll consider your request. Without definitive evidence of Lee's wrongdoing, it would be next to impossible to get anything out of them.

Logan was on his way to meet Anthony Brown for coffee at a coffee shop midway between Los Alamos and Santa Fe. He had suggested to the special agent that it would be more discreet for them to meet off-campus.

Brown was waiting for him at a small table towards the back of the coffee shop. It was midmorning, and there were only a few other patrons. After Logan sat down, Anthony got right to the point.

"Sorry the Canadians didn't come through for us on Jason Lee. I should have figured they'd resist reporting on a Canadian citizen."

"What did they say to your man?" Logan asked.

"That, absent any clear indication of wrongdoing, they are legally forbidden to share any details with a foreign entity."

"Does that mean you can't reach out to any of Jason's contacts in Canada? Teachers, teammates, relatives? You would need a good cover story for that because it could get back to Jason that people were asking about him."

"The Canadians would frown on that. Technically, if we're not working with them on an official basis, they don't want us mucking around in their backyard."

Logan frowned. He'd heard the Canadians had strict privacy laws regarding foreign law enforcement and intelligence agencies investigating Canadian citizens. Canada also had a broad interpretation of what it meant to be a Canadian person. It wasn't just Canadian citizens, but included anyone residing in Canada, regardless of their citizenship.

"We did find a report on Jason filed by U.S. Immigration. Customs and Border Patrol pulled him into secondary before he flew out of Toronto, and he claimed then not to know his father's identity," Logan said.

"It's hard to believe it never came up. Jason's maternal

grandparents knew who the dad was. It seems inconceivable that at some point, they or his mother wouldn't have talked about him," Anthony said.

"I agree," Logan said. "I think he's hiding something." He shook his head in frustration. "I met Jason a couple of weeks ago. When Laurie Kim reported her contact with Billy Chu, I decided to join them for a run with the Santa Fe Trail Runners. Jason was there too, and I had a chance to speak with him. He seemed like a nice enough guy. I'll start running with the group regularly and try to get closer to him."

"That sounds like a plan," Anthony said. "I've got a surveillance team that's underemployed. I'll put them out against him two or three evenings and weekends to start. If that's productive, we can ramp up the coverage. While the team's out there, they can also go through his trash at the apartment building. You never know what you'll find."

"Any way we can get into the apartment?" Logan asked.

"I'm going to need more than we've got to get a search warrant," Anthony said.

"That just leaves us with Billy Chu," Logan said. "I didn't stress this the other day, but Chu's father is the South Korean ambassador to Mexico and probably has his people keeping tabs on any North Koreans traveling to or living in Mexico.

"If Mexico and North Korea formalize a trade deal, and they assign Roe to Mexico City, he's going to be on Billy Chu's radar. Chu may suspect that Roe is NKIS, which would make him a high-priority target for the South Koreans. But even if he's only a trade official, Chu would have him on a watchlist because of Roe's relationship to Jason and Chu's energy security portfolio.

"I don't know how closely you follow North Korea, but there's a long history of North Korean illegals coming up from South America to establish themselves in the U.S. I'm not suggesting Roe would attempt to come to the U.S. as an illegal, only that the North Koreans have a history of working in that part of the world and may feel comfortable conducting intelligence operations from there," Logan said.

"I can't tell you the last time anything North Korean came across my desk," Anthony said. "Before 9/11, we mostly dealt with white-collar crime, bank robberies, and criminal threats. Nowadays, for the most part, it's counterterrorism, cybercrime, and counterintelligence. We've had some Chinese and Russian CI cases, but never North Korean."

"Let's stay in touch," Logan said, as they left the coffee shop. As he drove back to Los Alamos, his thoughts were on Jason Lee.

Chapter 25

Billy Chu deplaned the Airbus A320 at Benito Juarez International Airport; the three-and-a-half-hour flight to Mexico City had been uneventful. Once outside the terminal, he flagged down a taxi and gave the driver his parents' address. Despite congestion in the city of nine million, the drive only took thirty minutes.

This was his first trip to Mexico since his father's assignment a year ago. His mother had been coaxing him for months to join them for the Korean Lunar New Year. The Korean community in Mexico City numbered about nine thousand, many of whom would turn out for festivities at the ambassador's residence. They would wear native dress, the *hanbok*, dance, play games, and eat traditional foods like *tteokguk*, a traditional rice cake soup in beef broth. Since the holiday fell on a Friday, most Koreans would take Thursday off and make it a four-day weekend.

Billy missed his parents, but the clincher for him hadn't been the promise of home-cooked meals; instead, it was a cryptic comment from his father that the NIS station chief in Mexico City was running a covert source who might be able to shed some light on Jason Lee's father, Roe Min-Woo.

The ambassador's residence was a sprawling house in the heart of the Federal District. Billy passed through security and walked into an expansive entryway; he spotted his mother overseeing several workers stringing bright red paper lanterns in the archways and hanging colorful kites on the walls.

She spotted him from across the room; saying something to one of her helpers, she skirted a pile of decorations on the floor and walked over to greet him. She gave him a quick hug and then held him at arm's length, searching his face.

"I need to put some meat on those bones," she said with a twinkle in her eyes. Korean mothers are strict with their children when it comes to their schooling, but they tend to dote on their sons, even when they're grown men out in the world. "Are you getting enough to eat?" she asked as she caressed his arm.

"I'm fine, Mom," Billy said. "How are you?"

"We're almost finished decorating. I've been cooking for a week, but I've left the rest of it to the caterers. I think we're in pretty good shape."

"How's Dad?"

"He's busy, but he likes the job. He should be home in about an hour. Let me show you your room. We'll have drinks on the terrace at 6 and dinner at 7. It's just us for dinner, but I believe your father invited the NIS chief for drinks. He wanted to meet you." She nodded knowingly. His mother wasn't privy to the more sensitive aspects of Billy's job. She only knew that he worked for the NIS, and that was about it.

After she had shown him to his room, Billy showered and changed clothes. His father's voice, talking to someone he didn't recognize, wafted up the stairs. Must be the NIS chief, Billy guessed. He took the stairs two at a time and spotted his father and a man he didn't know standing in the foyer.

"Dad, how are you?" he asked.

His father clasped his outstretched hand, beaming with pride. "Billy, I'm glad you could get the time off." He turned to the man next to him. "I want to introduce you to Tan Chang-Woo. He's the NIS station chief here."

Billy took Tan's outstretched hand. "Pleased to meet you, sir. Billy Chu."

"Come, let's take drinks on the patio," his father said. He steered them towards a set of French doors that opened out onto a broad terrace overlooking a manicured lawn. He led them over to a well-stocked bar, tended by a silver-haired

Mexican servant.

"This is Juan, the best bartender in Mexico City. He can take care of your drink orders. I need to talk to your mother about some changes in the guest list for tomorrow. I'll be right back." He excused himself and disappeared into the house.

Billy and Tan took their drinks and walked away from the bar. "Let's talk over here," the NIS chief said, gesturing towards a thicket of trees. "The foreign ministry has had this residence for many years. One of our earliest ambassadors was fond of orchids and began cultivating several species that only grow in Mexico. Your father has kept up that tradition."

As they stood admiring the blooms, Tan lowered his voice. "We're fine talking out here." He removed a pack of cigarettes from inside his coat, and lit one, blowing smoke out the side of his mouth. He offered one to Billy, who declined.

"I saw your reporting on the scientist at Los Alamos," Tan said. "Quite a surprise."

"Jason Lee," Billy said.

"Yes. We've known about the father, Roe Min-Woo, for some time. I remember when he defected to the North. I was a young officer working in our counterintelligence section when it happened. It was an embarrassment at the time, but because he didn't have a sensitive position in the government, we didn't pay too much attention."

Tan paused for a moment, a pensive look on his face. "Strangely enough, Roe and I attended high school together in Seoul. We were both on the soccer team and knew each other; we weren't particularly close, but we were teammates. After graduation, we went our separate ways. I saw him once at a five-year reunion, and then the next thing I heard, he was in North Korea. It was quite a shock for our class. None of us knew anyone who had defected."

"Dad told me that you might have some insights into Roe," Billy said.

"I have a Mexican source in the National Intelligence

Center responsible for hard target operations—Russians, Chinese, North Koreans. When he learned about the trade talks with North Korea, he put one of his best covert officers under Ministry of Economy cover on the Mexican negotiating team.

"One night this officer invited Roe out and got him drunk. Roe didn't come out and say he was intel, but he admitted to having responsibilities other than foreign trade. When the Mexican dropped Roe off at his hotel, he arranged for a prostitute working for the service to accompany him.

"They had sex, and Roe passed out. She went through his things and found some photos stuffed into a concealed pocket in his briefcase, which she made copies of."

Tan reached into his breast pocket and pulled out several sheets of paper, which he handed to Billy. The lighting was dim, and the images were of uneven quality. They appeared to be head shots of Asian men and women. He flipped to the last one and held it closer to his face. His heart began to pound, and he stopped breathing. Staring back at him were two faces he knew intimately, Laurie Kim's parents.

Chapter 26

Logan re-read the Immediate — Eyes Only message from Headquarters. The cable originated on the Korea desk but included substantive comments from the Counterintelligence Center. The bombshell was the reporting from Billy Chu on his conversation with the NIS chief in Mexico City, who had shown him a photo of Laurie Kim's parents found in Roe Min-Woo's possession and the resulting investigation it triggered.

Logan's thoughts were reeling as he tried to grasp the implications of Chu's revelation. What could be the connection between the Kims and Roe Min-Woo?

The Counterintelligence Center took a stab at answering that question. Their reporting verified Dave and Ginny Kim currently lived in Los Angeles. Dave Kim was a successful software engineer who presided over a consulting firm named Digital Solutions. Ginny Kim was a mathematics professor at UCLA. Headquarters conducted extensive background checks on the Kims and found that neither of them was born in the U.S.; they had immigrated from Mexico in the early 1990's, settling in the San Gabriel Valley.

When Headquarters checked with Mexican officials, the latter advised that Dave Kim was born in Monterrey and his wife in Mexico City—both of South Korean women married to Mexican husbands. Both grew up and attended college in their respective hometowns. Dave later moved to Mexico City for graduate studies, where he met Ginny. They married and remained there for several years, working in their respective fields. They applied for their first Mexican passports in 1986, five years before immigrating to the U.S.

At Headquarters' request, Mexico's Institute of National

Investigation fast-tracked their investigation of the Kims and discovered glaring anomalies in Dave and Ginny Kim's backgrounds. Investigators could find no verifiable records or documentation of their early years in Mexico, practically from birth through undergraduate school.

There was no problem verifying their graduate school attendance and work history in Mexico City. But when they tried to locate family or friends predating their college years, they ran into a brick wall. Neither Kim claimed to have any living relatives on their graduate school applications.

Headquarters advised that their findings were preliminary. The investigation into the couple was ongoing, and this report would be updated as soon as additional information became available.

Logan toyed with a challenge coin on his desk. The Kim family revelations were like a stink bomb going off; they smelled to high heaven. Their ambiguous pasts and connection to Roe Min-Woo, no matter how tenuous, made no sense and spelled trouble without question.

Laurie Kim, on the other hand, came across as squeaky clean in comparison. Logan had asked HR to pull Laurie's folder. She was born in Los Angeles just a couple of years after her parents moved to the U.S. But it wouldn't hurt to double-check her information to be on the safe side. He picked up his secure line and placed a call to Anthony Brown, who answered on the third ring.

"Hello?"

"Anthony? Logan Alexander."

"Good morning. What can I do for you?"

"I just finished reading an alarming message from Headquarters. Did you get anything from FBI Headquarters on Laurie Kim's parents, Dave and Ginny Kim?"

"No, but that doesn't surprise me. Internal communication isn't the FBI's forte. Anything you can share?"

"I think I can pass you all of this. It's a pretty long message; I'll try to gist it for you."

Five minutes later, the silence on the other end of the line was deafening. "Anthony, are you still there?"

"Yes." The special agent's voice was tense. "I've heard of inept record-keeping, but this is over the top. How does someone not have a documented past for the first two decades of life? What I don't get is why the South Koreans haven't weighed in on Dave and Ginny Kim's mothers. They're allegedly South Korean, and you would think there would be a record of their immigration from South Korea to Mexico."

"I think we'll hear more from the South Koreans. They only found out about the connection between the Kims and Roe this week. They're probably scrambling to make sense of it too. I have some ideas," Logan said.

"Let's hear them." The special agent's voice had grown weary.

"Let's say the Kims came to the U.S. via Mexico as illegals; North Koreans masquerading as Mexicans. Their goal was never to remain in Mexico but to use it as a springboard for immigration to the U.S. They settled down, started a family, and built successful careers in business and academia."

"I don't think the basic scenario is that far-fetched," Anthony said, "though there are a lot of gaps. We have no idea how they managed it. Perhaps more interesting is how Roe Min-Woo fits into the picture."

"We don't know a lot about North Korean illegal operations," Logan said, "so take this with a grain of salt. The Kims have been here for thirty-some years and are living the dream. They've carved out a good life and, by all appearances, are model citizens. That's precisely what the NKIS would want them to do.

"They might be sleeper agents, waiting to be activated, or it could be they're already operational, and we don't know it."

"That's great, but it still doesn't answer the question about their connection to Roe Min-Woo and why he would be carrying a picture of them around in his wallet," Anthony said.

"Let's flesh this out a little bit," Logan said. "Suppose the Kims are, in fact, North Korean illegals. We don't know how they originally entered Mexico and were able to establish new identities there. But doing so enabled them to move forward with their ultimate goal—immigration to the U.S.

"Alternatively, the Kims could be precisely what they purport to be, Mexican immigrants who've made successful lives here in the U.S. Under that scenario, let's assume that Roe Min-Woo is a North Korean intelligence officer targeting sympathetic ethnic Koreans for recruitment.

"If the NKIS is running any other sources in the U.S., they would task them to spot potential recruits. As part of their recruitment process, they would provide assessment information and any identifying data they could obtain, including photos. The Kims might be targets in their own right, or maybe the NKIS knows about Laurie Kim's job at the lab and hopes to use the parents as access agents."

"That seems pretty far-fetched, Logan," Anthony said. "There are thousands of South Koreans in Los Angeles. Nothing we know about the Kims suggests that they would make good recruitment targets. Besides, under that scenario, how do you account for the paucity of information about their early years in Mexico?"

"I can't; it doesn't make sense. But you have to admit, they would make good targets for North Korea. How many Koreans in LA have a daughter working at a place like Los Alamos?" Logan asked. There was silence on the other end as Anthony pondered what he'd just said. Logan could almost envision the FBI agent nodding to himself.

"Logan, do you know if Los Angeles Division is in the loop on this new development?" Anthony asked.

"Headquarters did not info the LA Field Office," Logan said. "Maybe FBI Headquarters sent a message to them in their channels. I'll check with CIC and see if they can bring LA into the loop. You might want to check with Washington on your end to close the gap.

"One final thought just occurred to me," Logan said.

"What's that?"

"It's a tangent of the 'Kims as illegals' scenario. In this case, they have already recruited their daughter, and they've successfully penetrated Los Alamos."

"Wouldn't that be a bitch?" Anthony said.

Chapter 27

Jason Lee scrambled up Ravens Ridge, his breathing relaxed, as he left the Santa Fe Ski Basin's parking area behind him. It was early March, and temperatures were in the mid-fifties. The Santa Fe Trail Runners had scheduled this outing. Still, they canceled at the last minute when a sister club in Albuquerque announced they had extra tickets to elite runner Jim Ryun's talk at the University of New Mexico today. Everyone except Jason had accepted the club's invitation and opted out of today's run.

Jason had read about Ryun's exploits, most notably in 1964 when he became the first high school athlete to run a sub-four-minute mile. Jason respected Ryun's accomplishments, and he would have liked to hear what he had to say, but the urge to be outside in nature after a week in the lab was too strong.

The two months since he'd started his new job had flown by. He was content in almost every area of his life. Norman had green-lighted his assignment to a space reactor development project described optimistically as a MegaPower reactor. The project was an outgrowth of the KiloPower project Laurie had described earlier.

In his early meetings with the MegaPower team, Jason learned that the U.S. program was not abandoning radioisotope thermoelectric generator (RTG) technology. RTGs had powered dozens of U.S. space missions over the years and had been the mainstay in America's space reactor inventory. Three RTG reactors powered the Cassini spacecraft as it explored Saturn, spanning two decades from 1997 to 2017.

The U.S. invested in other space reactor technologies over the years in search of optimal reliability, safety, and durability. Nuclear electrical propulsion systems and heat-pipe power systems gained favor in the 1990s, but they alone lacked the capacity and reliability to power a crewed mission into deep space. In the next decade, the MegaPower team would incorporate the best of these technologies into a new MegaPower reactor capable of reaching Mars and beyond.

Jason emerged from the tree line and began to climb a jagged ridge to Lake Peak. He pulled out his cell phone to check his exact location. Looking east, he recognized from the contour lines on the map a treeless place called Penitente Peak. Notes from other runners advised that bighorn sheep sometimes frequented the area.

He pocketed his cell phone, took a swig of water from the camelback, and continued in the direction of Penitente Peak. He had taken no more than a few strides when he pulled up short, catching his breath. Not more than forty yards ahead, two bighorn sheep stared impassively at him from atop a steep ridge.

Jason guessed from their size that they were males. Both appeared to weigh over two hundred pounds and sported massive, curved horns that looked cracked in places, no doubt from frequent head-butting contests. They were feeding on rubber rabbitbrush, known locally as chamisa plants. They eyed him warily but did not seem too spooked by his presence.

Jason decided this was as good a place as any to eat lunch; he'd packed a sandwich and an apple. As he took in the scenery, his thoughts turned to Laurie. She had cooled towards him in recent weeks. When he asked her about it, she said their relationship was moving too fast and that she didn't want to make that kind of commitment at this point in her life.

It all started after a Valentine's Day dinner date. He'd reserved a table by the fireplace at a top-ranked contemporary restaurant listed on Tripadvisor in old Santa Fe. They enjoyed a sumptuous dinner, despite limited seating due to pandemic precautions. Later they ended up at his place.

They were in bed when she dropped the bombshell.

"Jason, you're a nice guy, and I enjoy being with you, but I think we need to slow things down," she said.

"I thought we were on the same page," he replied. "We share the same interests professionally and socially. I don't know what to say."

"I think we should see other people," she told him. "I'm not ready to be in an exclusive relationship."

He didn't have a lot of experience with women. To him, their relationship seemed ideal. Maybe he'd been naive about her true feelings towards him. He'd thrown himself into his work to ease the pain, but he couldn't stop thinking about her.

And then there was the deal with his father and the North Koreans. He was startled to learn that North Korea and Mexico were fast-tracking plans to open the trade office in Mexico City in the summer. His father was a shoo-in to head the office and would be moving with a small staff to temporary quarters in Mexico City in June. There they would busy themselves setting up their new office and finding permanent housing for the team. Since North Korea does not allow families to accompany its diplomats abroad (to better deter defections to the West), the officials assigned to Mexico City would likely share an apartment so they could keep an eye on one another.

Jason continued to feed his father borderline sensitive material from Los Alamos. The communication plan using the deep web, the Onion Browser, and a VPN bolstered his confidence about his contact with North Korea. He was able to justify his actions on one level, rationalizing that the material he was sharing was not that sensitive. But on another level, he knew that if U.S. authorities ever caught him in a clandestine relationship with North Korea, he was toast.

There had been one close call with Laurie in February. She had spent the night, and the next morning, because her phone had died, asked to use his computer to confirm a doctor's appointment. When she got on, she noticed the Onion Browser icon and asked him about it. He made up a bogus story about using the browser to research bitcoin investments he was considering. Fortunately, she bought his lie and let it go.

Jason finished his lunch and walked a few yards off the trail to relieve himself. It was 12:30, and he still had several more miles to cover. As he picked up the pace, he noticed that the two bighorn sheep had disappeared from the ridge. Spotting the animals had been the equivalent of a moose sighting back home in Canada.

The temperature had dipped, and he was chilly. He zipped up his fleece and pulled on a light pair of running gloves. Too bad the others had missed the run. They would be envious when he told them about the wildlife sighting.

Chapter 28

Logan, Zahir, and Cooper were en route to Laguna Pueblo, outside of Albuquerque. After meeting Martina's friend, Nantan, from the Jemez Pueblo, Cooper asked to visit one of the villages. Jemez did not have anything on the calendar in March, but Laguna Pueblo was honoring St. Joseph, husband of The Virgin Mary, today. They would be able to see indigenous people dancing and wearing traditional festive garb.

They were combining the visit with a trip to the airport. Logan was meeting Peter in Albuquerque at 3 p.m. to catch a flight to D.C. for Monday meetings at NSA and CIA. Zahir would drop him off at Albuquerque International on their way back to White Rock.

Meanwhile, they were driving west on I-40. Up ahead was a collection of small villages making up Laguna Pueblo. Rugged mesas with steep escarpments surround the pueblo, and in the distance, the snow-covered peaks of Mount Taylor rose to over 11,000 feet.

Logan parked on the street not far from San Jose de la Laguna Mission Church and Convent; it was 10:30. Native men, women, and children were moving to prearranged gathering spots, dressed in colorful costumes. Drums began to beat, and the performers started processing to the dance plaza.

"What are their clothes made from?" Cooper asked.

"The men are wearing kilts," Zahir said. "Deerskin or rabbit. The women's dresses look like cotton."

"Did you notice the difference in their shoes, Cooper?" Logan asked.

"The men are wearing leather sandals, but what do

those ladies have on?" Cooper asked.

"Those are moccasin boots made from rabbit fur, I think," Logan said.

A dozen drummers at one end of the plaza began pounding on their instruments as the dancers shuffled rhythmically in a circle to the beat. "This is called the Harvest Dance," Zahir whispered to Cooper.

"Do you see that building over there?" Logan asked, nodding towards a rectangular pit house. "That's called a kiva. It's a place for religious ceremonies. You can only go in there if you're a member of the Laguna tribe, and the only way to get in is by that ladder." He pointed to a weathered wooden ladder propped up against the wall of the kiva.

They walked around the plaza after the dance performance when Logan spotted a familiar face from work in the crowd, Laurie Kim. She was with an Asian couple old enough to be her parents. Logan had only seen the couple's blurry photo Billy Chu got from the NIS station chief in Mexico City, but he was pretty sure it was them.

He made his way over to where Laurie was standing. "Hi, Laurie. How've you been?" Logan asked.

"Logan!" Laurie seemed taken aback to see him there, or was she just surprised? "Is this your family?" she asked. "These are my parents, Dave and Ginny Kim. They're visiting from California. Mom and Dad, this is Logan Alexander; he works at Los Alamos too."

Logan introduced Zahir and Cooper. "What part of California are you from?" Logan asked.

"LA," Dave said. "We needed a breath of fresh air. The pandemic has hit California pretty hard."

"Over 50,000 people in the state have died from COVID-19," Ginny said.

"How many of those are in LA?" Zahir asked.

"LA County has about half of those," Ginny said.

There was a momentary pause in the conversation as everyone struggled to get their arms around such a large number. Finally, Logan broke the silence. "So how long are you here for?" he asked.

"Today's our last day," Dave said. "I had a client meeting in Albuquerque Friday. Ginny teaches at UCLA, but most of her classes are virtual right now, so she can work from anywhere, as long as there's an Internet connection." They chatted for a few more minutes and then said their goodbyes.

As the Alexander family walked through the open-air market near the plaza, Logan's thoughts remained on this unexpected encounter with the Kims. Nothing about their appearance or behavior suggested that they were North Korean secret agents. But then, he'd only spent five minutes with them, and they'd had thirty years to build a rock-solid cover legend if that's what they were.

Logan glanced back in their direction and could see Laurie having an intense conversation with her father. He wondered if she had told her dad that he was working security at the lab. Logan would have to document this brief encounter with the Asian couple, although he hadn't learned anything relevant to his CI investigation.

He caught up with Zahir, who was browsing for handicrafts in the street market. She found a pair of hand-coiled, hand-painted Laguna pots made by a well-known local artisan. The

shopkeeper was asking $500 for them, but she negotiated him down to $425.

It was a good thing Zahir was independently wealthy, Logan mused. Her mother was the niece of the former shah of Iran. The Pahlavis made a bundle, billions of dollars, in oil exports, from the time the shah ascended the Peacock Throne until the day Ayatollah Khomeini ended his reign. The Pahlavi Foundation had set up trust funds for the royals and sheltered the money in Swiss banks.

The crowd was beginning to disperse. Typically, Pueblo festivals offer an opportunity for tourists to mingle with locals in their homes, often to share a simple meal, but because of the pandemic, home visits were being discouraged. "You guys ready to go?" Logan asked Zahir and Cooper. "We can grab a bite to eat in Albuquerque before you drop me off at the airport."

"Are you sure there's time?" Zahir asked.

"Yes. We have about three hours until I have to meet Peter. If you're up for it, I heard about a popular burger joint on the way to the airport. Cooper, you good with that?"

Cooper was playing a game on Zahir's phone. He was intently focused, but at the mention of food, he looked up. "Burgers? Yay."

Chapter 29

Logan and Peter got into Dulles at 10 p.m. They had reservations at the Sheraton on Glebe Road in Arlington, Virginia, a short drive from Langley. Traffic was light on the Dulles Access Road, but it was after 11 by the time they checked into their rooms. Their first meeting in the morning was at 9 with the Counterintelligence Center.

"You up for some PT in the morning before work?" Logan asked.

"Oorah. What's a little sleep deprivation in the grand scheme of things?" Peter joked. "You want to go for a run or workout in the fitness center?"

"Let's go for a run," Logan said.

It was in the low thirties when they met in the lobby at 6 a.m. "Any good running routes around here?" Peter asked as they stepped out into the pre-dawn cold, stamping their feet to keep warm.

"The Washington and Old Dominion Trail (W&OD) is nice. It's about a half-mile from here off of Shirlington Rd. How far do you want to go?" Logan asked.

"Can we do four or five miles?" Peter asked.

"Depends on how slow you are," Logan said with a straight face. "You going to want breakfast?"

"Just coffee," Peter said. "And you'll have plenty of time to eat if you want to. It won't be the Marines holding things up."

"There's a Starbucks at Headquarters," Logan said, laughing over his shoulder.

"I used to run this route when I lived in D.C.," Logan said. "It's paved from Shirlington to Purcellville. Before the Civil War, it was the roadbed for the W&OD Railroad. They went belly up in the late 1960s; the Park Service converted it into a running and biking trail in 1974."

They clocked five miles in thirty-five minutes. Sunrise wasn't until seven o'clock, so it was still dark by the time they returned to the Sheraton.

"Maybe next time we can run it in daylight so we can see where we're going," Peter said.

At 8 o'clock, they pulled into the visitors' parking lot outside the main entrance to CIA Headquarters. A security officer retrieved Logan's staff badge from the automated filing system and issued a visitor's badge to Peter.

"Do you know who's going to be in the meeting with CIC?" Peter asked, as they went through the metal detectors and scanned their badges.

"Take a left. I'm not sure who all is going to be there," Logan said. "CIC will probably run the meeting. I expect East Asia, Latin America, Europe, and National Resources divisions will all have people there. Maybe the Counterproliferation Center too."

"How about the Bureau?" Peter asked.

"We'll see."

It was early, but there was still a line coming out of the coffee shop and winding down the hall. "It moves fast," Logan said. "We still have plenty of time."

"You spooks like your coffee," Peter said, marveling at the number of people waiting. They reached the front of the line in five minutes and placed their orders.

"It's true; we're a highly caffeinated group of people. Rumor has it that this is the busiest Starbucks in the country," Logan said.

"If there's time after our meeting, can we stop in the museum?" Peter asked.

"Anything in particular you wanted to see?"

"I heard the Agency has an original Enigma Machine; you know, the German crypto device from WWII."

"There are a lot of interesting pieces in their collection, going all the way back to the OSS days. We'll make time. Who knows when you'll get back here?" Logan said.

The cashier called their number and handed them their coffees to go. They went to the right out of the Starbucks towards a bank of elevators.

"We're meeting in the New Headquarters Building," Logan said as he headed towards an open lift.

There were a half-dozen people in CIC's conference room. Logan introduced Peter to Carol Hayes, CIC Deputy Chief, running the meeting, and the others.

"Okay, let's get started," Carol said. "I want to thank everyone for your work on this. To give you a sense of the high-level interest in this operation, I want to share an experience I had last week.

"Wednesday, I had a call from the DDO's office advising me that I was to accompany the DDO downtown Friday, where I would be briefing this operation to a senior U.S. government official.

"That official turned out to be the president of the United States. We went downtown with the president's daily briefer. When she finished her briefing, she left the room, and it was just the president, his national security advisor, the DDO, and me."

"How'd it go?" Logan asked.

"Well, from the feedback we got," Carol said. "You could tell the president was interested, and he asked good questions. We were in the Oval Office for fifteen minutes."

"Did the subject of a FISA request come up?" Peter asked.

"Funny you should ask," Carol said. "The president brought it up himself. He wants us to be proactive, using all the tools at our disposal to determine if the North Koreans have penetrated the lab."

"The president can't direct the FISA Court to issue a surveillance warrant," said Cal Healy from NR Division. "But knowing that he wants it will hold sway with the judge assigned to hear the brief."

"Even as we speak, NSA is putting together the application for warrants against the Kims, Jason Lee, and Roe Min-Woo," Carol said. "Lee and Roe fall under the FISA warrant request because they're foreigners; the Kims will be treated differently as Americans.

"You're meeting with NSA tomorrow, right?" Carol asked Logan.

"Yes. We're seeing Harriet Wilson," he said.

"You can tell her there's presidential interest in the case, so she might as well ask for everything she wants." Carol's eyes gleamed with excitement. "Let's go for broke. I want to nail these guys before it's too late."

Chapter 30

The house was on San Salvatore Place, backing onto Longden Avenue across from the San Gabriel Country Club's fifth hole in San Marino, a well-to-do Los Angeles suburb. The man had been observing the comings and goings of the couple living in the two-story pueblo-style home for two days.

He had visited a local library and logged onto several realtor websites until he found what he was looking for, an online listing. The house was not currently for sale, but a sales listing from 2019 showed an interior sketch and photos. The home was on the market for seventy-five days priced at $1.5 million, but was removed without selling in mid-March.

He lit a cigarette and inhaled. He was waiting for his contact to show up, a Filipino named Sammy from Long Beach. Sammy was a gangster in the Asian Hoods gang and had been active in and around LA for fifteen years. He was known for his ruthless wet work and for not getting caught. Despite almost two decades of busting heads and spilling blood, he had managed to stay below the radar.

The man in the car tensed as a dark figure approached the passenger door and rapped on the window. He lowered it a couple of inches. "Yeah?"

"I'm Sammy. I understand you wanted to talk to me." It was a statement, not a question. Sammy bent down to get a better look at the man inside the car. A plume of smoke obscured his features, but he could tell the guy was Asian. "You gonna open the door or fuck around?" he snarled.

The door latch clicked, and Sammy slid into the seat. He took stock of the man. He was either a fool or had ice water running through his veins. Not everyone coming out to meet one of the Hoods on a dark street corner would be as relaxed as this guy.

"How'd you get my name?" he asked. "It's not like we advertise."

"Russian mob. My organization maintains a professional relationship with them for those jobs requiring your special expertise."

"So who are you, and what's the gig?" Sammy asked.

"You don't need to know who I am. It's better for you if you don't."

The two men spent thirty minutes going over the plan. "It looks to me from photos that the easiest way in is off of the back patio. There's a wireless security system in the house, but we can defeat it," the man said.

"How's that?" Sammy asked.

"We'll use a jammer to put radio noise in the air, preventing the hardware on the wireless system from getting a signal to the control panel. The sensor and the control panel won't be able to talk to each other.

"We should wait until we know the husband and wife are inside and have gone to bed. No one will see us once we get to the back of the house and onto the patio. The driveway's not well-lighted, and there's good screening from the next-door neighbors. There's a gate off of the driveway that opens to the backyard. I didn't see any motion sensors or cameras out there."

He pulled out a blueprint of the house. "The master bedroom is on the first floor," he said, pointing to a spot on the sketch. There's no one else staying in the house, and there are no pets. Unless they've changed the furnishings in the last several months, this is what the downstairs looks like," he said, pointing to two of the pictures.

"Do you have a picture of the patio door?" Sammy asked.

"Yeah." The man shuffled through the photos and pulled one out, showing the patio with a double door leading into a family room.

"Where did you say the master bedroom is?" Sammy asked.

"First floor, the opposite end of the house from the garage."

"Any special requests once we get inside the bedroom?"

"I want it to look like a murder-suicide."

Sammy nodded his understanding. "You know if there are any weapons in the house?"

"I'm not sure. Our targets both received special military training in their twenties, but now they're close to sixty. I don't think they'll put up much of a fight, but to be safe, we need to take them by surprise."

"I'll take out the man first," Sammy said. "It will be easier to handle the woman than the other way around. I'll need you to keep her quiet." He stared off into space for a minute and then checked the time, midnight.

"You know about the overnight parking restrictions?" Sammy asked. "You need a permit from 2 to 5 a.m. to park your car on the street; otherwise, you get towed. We'll be done here in thirty minutes max. Let's talk money."

"The deal's half now half when you finish the job." The man pulled out his cell phone. "I'm ready to wire $25K to the account number the Russians gave me. Is this the correct number?" He showed Sammy the cell phone.

"Yeah, that's good. You ready to do this tonight, right?" Sammy asked.

The man nodded yes. They left the rental car on the street, a fifteen-minute walk from their destination. It was quiet outside, with only an occasional car cruising by. The men walked without talking. When they reached the house, the man gestured toward the drive. They hugged the shadows, crouched low, creeping to the rear of the house.

When they reached the patio gate, the man withdrew a radio jammer and turned it on. It began emitting a silent signal. He nodded to Sammy, and the two men took stock of their situation. There were no lights on in the house. Outside it was pitch black; the only sound coming from the backyard was the croaking of frogs.

They crept onto the patio and sidled over to the double doors. Sammy withdrew a glass-cutter and suction cup and went to work. It only took him five minutes to cut through the tempered glass on the door. Both men held their breath as Sammy reached in to unlock the door and cautiously pushed it open. The hinges barely squeaked as he gave it a nudge. To them, it sounded as though a firecracker had exploded.

There were area rugs on the floor, softening their footsteps as they glided through the house to the master bedroom door. As Sammy reached for the bedroom door handle, the man, who was several feet behind him, glimpsed, then heard a shadowy figure running towards the bedroom from across the hall, shouting out.

"Who are you?" The intruder closed the gap and launched himself at Sammy.

The man ducked behind an overstuffed chair and crawled along the wall towards the family room. He could hear Sammy and the stranger grappling, and then a woman's scream from inside the bedroom. He had to escape. He rushed out of the house and sprinted down the driveway. Two blocks away, he slowed to a walk. Although the streets were deserted, the last thing he needed was for someone to report a suspicious figure running away from a crime scene.

He reached his car without incident. Sitting inside, he cradled his head in his hands. What just happened back there? He had a lot of questions and no answers. The only thing he knew for sure was that his bosses were not going to be happy that Dave and Ginny Kim were still alive.

Ten minutes later, San Marino was in his rearview mirror. He navigated the car onto Interstate 110 towards Los Angeles International Airport. Although the transportation hub wasn't open to the public because of COVID 19 restrictions, passengers arrived and departed twenty-four hours a day. His flight to Mexico City was at 5:30 a.m.

"Your flight is delayed an hour, Mr. Gardner," the ticket agent for Aeromexico Airlines said when he checked in. We are currently planning for a 6:30 a.m. departure. Please watch for updates on the flight information display."

William Gardner, AKA Roe Min-Woo, accepted the ticket and alias passport from the agent. He needed to find something to eat and a place to hunker down. He wasn't worried that he'd blown his cover; that seemed implausible, given the care he had taken. But someone had foiled his plan. The question was, who?

Chapter 31

Billy Chu corralled the skinny Asian punk, who was putting up a better fight than he'd expected. Billy feinted to the right and then delivered a bone-jarring kick to the man's head. He heard a crunch as he connected with the guy's chin, and he went down, out for the count.

Billy could hear the Kims behind their bedroom door arguing. Ginny was hysterical, sobbing that they were going to die, as Dave searched for his cell phone.

"Ginny, Dave, it's Billy, Billy Chu. It's safe to come out now."

Dave Kim wrenched the bedroom door open, his eyes wide with shock as he took in the inert figure on the ground and his daughter's former love interest hovering over him. Ginny Kim, clutching her nightgown to her neck, cried out.

"Billy, what is this? What are you doing here? Who is that?" She pointed to the limp figure on the floor.

"I'll explain in a second," Billy said. "Let me restrain this guy. He's not going to be a happy camper when he wakes up. Do you have any rope?"

Dave went to the garage and came back moments later with a length of cord. Billy used it to tie the attacker's hands behind his back and then propped him up against a wall. He stripped off the man's belt and wound it around his ankles, cinching it tight so that he could not walk. Searching the man's bag, he found a knife, handgun, and glass cutter. A worn black canvas wallet in his hip pocket contained a few dollar bills and a driver's license issued to Sammy Perez of Long Beach.

"No one else out there?" Billy asked.

"Not that I could see," Dave said. "You think there were

more than one of them?"

"I thought I saw someone else when I came through the family room," he said. He'd been too busy dealing with Perez, who was probably a gangbanger, given the tattoos covering his arms. "Let me take a look around outside. Please don't call 911 until I explain what's going on."

Billy searched inside and out but didn't see anything out of the ordinary. There was no doubt in his mind who the furtive figure running out of the house was—Roe Min-Woo. Billy's father had called him only hours before to report that the NIS chief's penetration of the Mexican police had bugged the North Korean Embassy and learned that Roe was on his way to Los Angeles to kill the Kims.

Billy had been close to the Kims when he and Laurie were dating. One of the first calls he made after moving to L.A. was to Laurie's parents. Speculation about their possible involvement with the North Koreans left him feeling decidedly cool towards them. If they were North Korean illegals, they deserved whatever they got, although getting murdered in cold blood by this lowlife was probably a step too far.

His mind was racing as he thought through what he would say to Laurie's parents. They didn't need to know who his actual employer was, especially if they were North Korean agents. He went back through the family room towards the master bedroom.

Dave and Ginny huddled by the door to their bedroom. Ginny had stopped crying. She eyed Billy suspiciously as he entered the room. "Can you tell me how you just happened to be here when this criminal broke into our house?" she demanded.

Sammy was beginning to stir. He groaned and tried to stand up but slumped over on his side, banging his head on the floor. He moaned and then passed out again.

"I got a call from my father tonight. I think I told you he's the South Korean ambassador in Mexico City. One of the people working for him received information about a planned hit against a Korean American couple from Los

Angeles. The North Korean Intelligence Service ordered the hit. It named you specifically as the targets.

"Of course, Dad recognized your names right away from the times he and Mom visited Los Angeles while I was at UCLA. Laurie and I were dating then, and we went out to eat several times over the years. He decided to call me directly to alert you while the embassy figured out how to get the information to U.S. law enforcement.

"I decided to come over right away to warn you in person. I didn't want to contact the police directly because I didn't know what the embassy planned to say to them."

Ginny began to shake; she raised a hand to her mouth to stifle a whimper. Dave frowned, a perplexed expression on his face. "But why would the North Koreans want to kill us?" he asked.

Billy was surprised by their bewildered reaction; it seemed so genuine. They were either great actors or just as confused as he was. Why did the NKIS agent have a picture of the Kims in his wallet when he traveled to Mexico City? Where was Roe now? And how did Sammy Perez fit into the picture?

"I should wait for the police to come," Billy said. "If I leave now and it comes out that I was here, it will raise more questions. I would prefer not to get my dad and the Ministry of Foreign Affairs involved, especially if this comes out in the press."

Dave called 911 and reported an intruder had broken into their home. He provided the information from Perez's driver's license.

"We're at 1961 San Salvatore Place," he said.

"That's San Marino, sir?" the dispatcher asked.

"Yes."

"Was there only the one suspect?" she asked.

"We think there were two, but one of them got away," Dave said. "The other one is tied up here inside the house. He is going to need medical assistance, but his injuries aren't life-threatening."

The dispatcher was already on the radio, calling for

assistance.

"This is dispatch calling all cars in the vicinity of San Salvatore Place. We have a code 459 underway at 1961 San Salvatore Place. That's 1961 San Salvatore Place. Possible two suspects. One is detained in the home and, and the other is on the run. Search the area for a suspicious male."

"We'll be there in five minutes, sir. Is there anything else?"

"No, nothing. Thank you."

Within minutes two patrol cars, lights flashing, pulled up outside the Kim residence. Dave Kim met the police officers at the front door and escorted them to where Billy had propped Sammy Perez up against the wall.

Three of the police officers spread out to search the grounds and to process the crime scene. One of the officers checked on Perez, who was still groggy from the knockout kick. He frisked the culprit and then put him in handcuffs.

The lead officer suggested everyone sit down in the family room, where he could take their statements. It was two a.m., and Ginny put on a pot of coffee. Over the next two hours, they walked through the events of the evening.

Billy took the lead, describing his long relationship with the Kims and the late-night warning from his father that they were in danger. He avoided speculation about the other intruder's identity because he did not know for certain what information the Mexican and South Korean governments had shared with U.S. law enforcement. The Mexican source was a sensitive intelligence asset, and any unauthorized disclosures could jeopardize his security.

Billy described his encounter with Sammy Perez inside the Kim residence. While Billy detailed his fight with the intruder, the police officer ran a background check on Perez, discovering a lengthy rap sheet for violent crimes associated with the Asian Hoods, a notorious gang active in Los Angeles.

Perez was a suspect in three murder cases in the last decade but somehow always escaped conviction. Snitches told the police Sammy was behind much of the Hoods' sordid history over the last decade. Inspectors in LAPD's Criminal Gang and Homicide Division had given Sammy the moniker Slippery Sammy for his ability to avoid incarceration.

The gangster was sitting up now, staring sullenly at the people in the room.

"What do you have to say for yourself, Sammy?" the police officer asked.

"Go fuck yourself," he mumbled. "I want a lawyer."

The officer sighed and slipped his notebook into a pocket. He gave his name card to Billy and the Kims. "Give me a call if you think of anything else," he said.

He walked over to where Sammy was sitting and hauled him to his feet.

"Sammy Perez, you are under arrest for breaking and entering, assault, and attempted murder." He then read Perez his Miranda Rights before escorting him out to the cruiser.

As Sammy stumbled out of the house, he turned and caught Billy's eye. "You better watch your back, pretty boy. You made a big mistake messing with the Hoods."

Chapter 32

Harriet Wilson's surveillance request made its way through the FISA Court with only minor changes from the presiding judge. CIA, FBI, and NSA were unanimous in their support for this step in the counterintelligence investigation into irregularities at Los Alamos. Without the collateral information this coverage could provide, their hands were tied, and they might never find the spy at the lab.

Logan and Peter met with Harriet at NSA the day after their meetings at Langley. They helped her tweak the targeting, putting Jason Lee and the Kims at the top of the list for surveillance coverage. Roe Min-Woo was an obvious target as well. Because he resided outside of the United States, U.S. intelligence and law enforcement agencies would pursue him under their National Security authorities, which did not require a FISA warrant. The Kims would also be treated differently because they were U.S. citizens.

When Logan and Peter returned to Los Alamos Wednesday morning, they were shocked to learn of the break-in and attempted murder at Dave and Ginny Kim's home. The FBI obtained the San Marino Police Department's information, which concluded the Kims were only the victims of an attempted burglary. They didn't have the benefit of Billy Chu's classified intelligence, relayed by the NIS chief in Mexico City, that pointed to a hit by Roe Min-Woo and the NKIS. This report raised more questions than it answered. Why the hell were the North Koreans so intent on silencing the Kims?

One positive outcome from this turn of events was that collection against the Kims would be easier to implement than ever. The San Marino Police, working with the

Bureau's Los Angeles Division, offered to survey the Kim residence to advise them on security enhancements they should make to improve their safety. Unbeknownst to the Kims, a specialist from the FBI's Science and Technology Branch at Quantico would join the team to install electronic surveillance equipment in their home.

Meanwhile, Logan, Anthony Brown, and a technician from the Bureau's Albuquerque Field Office were en route to Jason Lee's apartment in Española. It was 8:30 a.m., and Jason was in an all-day meeting with scientists from the University of Texas about a joint space energy study with the lab.

"Have you been out here before?" Anthony asked Logan.

"Española? No, I don't know Jason that well," Logan said. "I didn't make it out here when we were looking for a place to rent either."

"Where are you living?" Anthony asked.

"White Rock. We love it there. It only takes me fifteen minutes to get to work, and the family's happy with the neighborhood and school."

It was 9 a.m. when they reached Española. Logan found Jason's neighborhood and parked the car two blocks from his apartment building. Anthony knew the local demographic was mostly single people and young families. Everyone was either at work or school. A couple of runners ran by them outside of Jason's building, but they were busy talking and took no notice of the three men.

Logan was concerned they would draw attention to themselves as they tried to get into the apartment, but the FBI tech, Paul, was a pro; he defeated the lock in less than a minute, and they let themselves inside.

The apartment was a small one-bedroom with a nice view of the mountains. It was tidier than you would expect a bachelor pad to be. Paul headed straight for the kitchen table, where an Apple MacBook Pro laptop was sitting. He opened up a backpack and rummaged around, looking for something.

"Ah, here we go," he said, pulling a mouse cord and USB cable from a pocket. He compared them to the equipment on the table. Satisfied, he selected the mouse cord and began to replace the one installed on the computer.

"What's that going to buy you?" Logan asked.

"Remember a few years ago whenever you went to a conference, people were always giving out USB drives?"

Logan nodded. "Yeah, half the time they had malware on them, and if you plugged one into your computer, you were hosed."

"Well," Paul said, "the hackers are always trying to stay one step ahead of everyone else, and they knew it wouldn't be long before their targets figured out the USB drives had malware on them. Pretty soon, most people just tossed them in the trash when they got their goody bags.

"Then the hackers came up with the bright idea of using cables to inject malware into the computer. It's not as easy as giving your target a USB drive as a freebie at a conference. No one hands out power cords, but lucky for us, we have direct access to the computer."

Paul swapped out the virtually identical mouse cords and put Jason's original mouse cord into his bag. He rummaged around in a couple of drawers and found a spare mouse cord, which he swapped out too.

"Doesn't hurt to have a backup," he said.

"So, you're able to inject malware into his computer now?" Logan asked.

"Yes. What I did back at the lab was make a firmware modification to the microcontroller on the USB cord. Right now, it's loading the malware onto Jason's computer through keyboard strokes," Paul said.

"What kind of malware are you installing?" Anthony asked.

"Something I came up with. The rootkit will allow us to take over his computer, infect it with keyloggers and password grabbers. We'll be able to see everything he's doing," Paul said.

"Assuming he has antivirus software installed, won't

that detect the malware?" Logan asked.

"Nope. We'll use the malware to disable the antivirus software."

"You going to do any other technical enhancements while we're here?" Logan asked.

"You talked about the possibility of installing audio/video in here. The thing is, we don't have a good sense of how security-conscious this guy is. We don't want to do anything to alert him. Between the computer installation and NSA's coverage of his cell phone, we're going to learn a lot about Mr. Lee.

"Before we leave, I want to test our malware attack. It'll save us a trip back here if things aren't working right."

Paul pulled a laptop out of this bag and powered it up. He logged on and, within five minutes, was sending live commands to Jason's computer. Anthony and Logan looked over his shoulder.

"Is that Jason's file directory?" Logan asked, staring at Paul's computer screen.

"Yep. Right now, we own Mr. Lee's computer." Paul allowed the program to download the directory while they searched Jason's apartment for any clues he might be working for the NKIS. After an hour of scrutinizing every corner of the apartment, they came up with nothing.

Paul gathered up his equipment, and they took one last look around to make certain they had everything. As they let themselves out into the empty hallway, Logan felt mixed emotions. On the one hand, he was elated that they were one step closer to discovering if Jason Lee was spying for North Korea; on the other hand, it could be weeks or months until they had enough evidence to charge him with espionage.

Logan pulled the zipper up on his fleece. There was a biting wind blowing as they struck out across the parking lot to where they'd left the car. It was 11:30, and his stomach growled.

"Anybody up for lunch?" he asked.

Chapter 33

Jason Lee wrapped up his meetings with the two scientists from the Texas Innovation Center at the University of Texas, Austin, by 4:30 p.m. They identified several areas of possible collaboration in the fields of Artificial Intelligence and Space and Aeronautics. The researchers planned to meet monthly, alternating between the Los Alamos and Austin. Jason was straightening up their meeting room when he received a text on his cellphone from Laurie.

"Hi, it's me. Are you still at work? I need to see you."

He was surprised to hear from her. Since she'd told him that she wanted to dial down the temperature on their relationship, the two of them had barely spoken to each other.

He texted her back. "Just wrapping up meetings with a couple of guys from the University of Texas. About ready to head out."

"Want to meet me for a beer at Barrels and Bottles?"

Barrels and Bottles had become their favorite brewpub in Los Alamos. It was low-key, so much so that there were usually a couple of dogs belonging to patrons lounging around on the sawdust floor.

"Okay, see you in ten," he wrote. He wondered what was on her mind. Maybe she was rethinking their relationship.

It was just after 5 when Jason pulled into Barrels and Bottles. He spotted Laurie's car in the otherwise empty parking lot. On the weekend, you could barely find a parking spot, but this early on a weeknight, they had the place to themselves.

Laurie was sitting by herself in a booth away from the bar. She didn't see him right away when he walked in. Something about her was off, Jason thought, as he walked towards her table. Her normal personality was bubbly, effusing over everything. Now she was staring at her phone, frowning over something. Sensing his presence, she looked up, and her features softened.

"Hi, he said. He bent down to kiss the top of her head and then slid into the booth opposite her.

"What are you drinking?" he asked.

"It's a Hefeweizen. Do you want to try it?"

"Sure," he said. She passed the cloudy glass of beer across the table. He took a sip and made a face. "Tastes like bananas and bubblegum," he said. He handed the drink back to her.

"What makes it so cloudy?" he asked.

"It's the yeast. *Hefe* means yeast in German."

"It's too sweet for me. I think I'll have an IPA," he said to the waitress.

"Do you want to try Barrels and Bottles' IPA? We have a new batch from yesterday."

"That sounds good," Jason said.

The waitress was back with his drink in five minutes. Jason raised a glass to toast Laurie, but her head was bent down, eyes fixed on the swirling beverage as she absently sloshed her beer around.

"So, what's up?" he asked.

Laurie's brow creased. "It's my parents," she said. I'm worried about them."

"Did something happen while they were here?" Jason asked.

"No. We had a good visit. My dad had some client meetings in Albuquerque, but other than that, we spent tons of time together. It was after they got home. Someone broke into their house while they were sleeping."

"Are they all right?" Jason asked. "Did anyone get hurt?"

"The cops arrested a suspect who belongs to one of the Los Angeles gangs, the Asian Hoods. He was in my parents' house when the police got there. He had a knife and a gun on him, but no one got hurt.

"But this is where it gets bizarre. A second intruder ran away during the break-in because Billy Chu showed up."

"Billy Chu?" Jason couldn't mask his disbelief. "Your old boyfriend? What was he doing at your parents' house?"

Laurie leaned forward, her eyes intense. "My mother didn't go into any details, but she said the South Korean Embassy in Mexico got a threat report late in the day that someone was targeting my parents. Remember Billy's father's the ambassador there. The embassy was trying to figure out how to pass it to U.S. law enforcement, and Billy's father decided to call Billy to warn my parents. He knew them from when Billy and I were dating in college."

"What time did this happen?" Jason asked.

"My dad is usually in bed by 11, so it was after that."

"And Billy just showed up in the middle of the night? That seems strange. Why didn't he just call your parents?"

"I don't know. It was late. He probably figured it would freak them out. When he got there, the intruders were already in the house, about to go into my parents' bedroom." Laurie shuddered; she finished her beer and signaled the waitress for a refill.

"That seems reckless to me," Jason said. "He had no way of knowing who was in there or if they were armed. He could have been hurt."

"Billy has a black belt in martial arts; he's very confident of himself," Laurie said. "He was able to subdue one guy, the Asian Hoods person. But while Billy was fighting him, the other one got away. Billy told my mother that he looked Asian, but it was dark, and he didn't get a good description."

"What are they going to do?" Jason asked.

"The police are holding the gang member. His name's Sammy Perez. But Perez isn't talking other than to say the other Asian guy hired him to do this. The police found a pretty sizable wire transfer when they went through Perez's cellphone, and they're looking into that.

"But there's something more. Something bizarre. Mom was cleaning the house yesterday, and she was vacuuming in the spot where Billy said he spotted the guy hiding when he came into the house. And she found something he must have dropped."

"What was it?" Jason asked.

"A picture of my parents that I took when Billy and I graduated from UCLA. I remember it well because I took it on campus in front of the Bruin Bear."

Chapter 34

Logan set up a war room of sorts in his office. On one wall were photos of Dave and Ginny Kim, Laurie Kim, Billy Chu, Jason Lee, and Roe Min-Woo. He'd fed all the digital information he had on them into an Agency computer program that performed transactional analysis.

The CIA's Crime and Narcotics Center originally developed transactional software to analyze illegal drug and monetary transactions between the Colombian drug cartel, shipping companies, financial institutions, and individuals. It also linked phone records, travel data, and physical addresses to establish patterns of activity between individuals.

Logan had pinned three-by-five note cards containing key facts next to the corresponding pictures on the wall. It was still early in their investigation, and there was a lot they didn't know. Red arrows between individuals showed the type and frequency of connections between them. Billy Chu was included as a suspect only because he didn't fit neatly into any other category. The one true thing about Billy that Logan knew was how he misrepresented himself when he first visited Los Alamos.

One of Harriet Wilson's tasks, besides collecting current phone traffic associated with the six named individuals, was to use keyword search technology to conduct a historical review of phone calls and Internet communications going back five years. The Tailored Access Office at NSA had hundreds if not thousands of computers dedicated to collecting, storing, and sorting targeted communications.

The Prism and Upstream surveillance programs used by NSA to conduct these searches ran into trouble with privacy advocates during the Obama years, resulting in stricter controls on NSA's ability to collect and retain warrantless communications. Congress had recently reinstated these programs despite the clamoring of the American Civil Liberties Union. With any luck, Harriet would begin flooding his office with information in the coming days.

There was a knock on the door, and Martina poked her head inside. "Got a minute?" she asked.

"Sure," he said. "Come on in."

Martina pushed the door open. She noticed the wall display and walked closer to it to get a better view. "This is new, isn't it?" she asked.

"Yes, it's a work in progress. I find it helps me get a handle on a complex case if I can visualize it. I don't know how much experience you have working with NSA, but they are about to inundate us with information. If we don't get out in front of it, they'll blow us away."

"Peter said you had good meetings in Washington," Martina said as she sat down by his desk.

"Did he tell you Chief CIC's story about the president?" he asked.

"He did. I think it's a good thing for us, although the stakes are higher with the White House looking over our shoulder," Martina said.

"That's true," Logan said. "But on the other hand, if they don't have a clear understanding of the risks here and the limited resources you have to do your job, they will by the time this is over. You might want to resubmit your request for a full-time CI person."

"I'll think about it. I don't want to jump the gun until we have something to show for our work. If we're able to find the spy using the methods you're putting in place, I'm confident we'll be able to make a case for a full-time CI slot.

"If we had to pick the most likely suspect today, who would be at the top of your list?" Martina asked.

"That's a tough one," Logan said. "The smart money would point to Jason Lee because his old man's a North Korean intelligence officer."

"Yes, and ...?" Martina asked.

"Let me tell you a story. Do you remember Aldrich Ames?" Logan asked.

"The CIA spy who worked for the Russians?" Martina asked.

"Yes, one of the worst espionage cases in U.S. history. Ames compromised more sensitive assets than anyone except maybe Robert Hanssen.

"But here's the thing. Did you ever hear of Edward Lee Howard?"

"Sounds familiar, but I'm not sure," Martina said.

"Howard was a CIA officer, spying at the same time as Ames. But here's where it gets interesting. Ames worked at the CIA for over thirty years and spied for the Russians for almost ten of those. Howard had a three-year career at CIA and worked for the Russians for five years." Logan said.

"I don't get the connection," Martina said.

"Bear with me," Logan said, coming across the room.

"In 1985, a Russian KGB officer by the name of Vitaly Yurchenko defected to the U.S. In his debriefings, he identified Howard as a Russian spy. The Agency started an investigation against Howard and was spinning its wheels, trying to figure out if he was the mole.

"Some people think the Russians gave us Howard as a way of deflecting attention away from Ames, essentially allowing him to continue spying."

"So, you're saying Jason Lee may look like the obvious culprit, but that there could be someone else spying for the North Koreans?"

"I'm just putting it out there," Logan said. "It's a house of mirrors."

"What are you suggesting?" Martina asked.

"That we keep an open mind and not fall in love with the first lead we develop.

"In the intelligence world, there's no such thing as a coincidence. So, what do you think of this? A known NKIS intelligence officer has a son working here, and a suspect NKIS illegal couple has a daughter working here. I have a hard time believing that's a coincidence," he said.

"What's more, the two of them found each other within a week of Jason's arrival and almost immediately hooked up."

Martina frowned as the weight of Logan's words sunk in. "We can't afford to lose this fight. There's too much at stake," she said, clenching her fists.

"I promise you, Martina, we're going to find him or her, whoever it is. At some point, they'll have to show their hand, and we'll be there to nail their sorry asses."

Chapter 35

Roe Min-Woo was exhausted. He hadn't slept in three days, continually looking over his shoulder as he traveled back to North Korea from the United States. When Roe ran out of the San Marino home, his only thought was to put as much distance between himself and the crime scene as quickly as possible.

He'd been tense for the entire time he spent waiting for his flight at Los Angeles Airport, half expecting to be detained by police. Once he was in Mexico, he breathed more easily. That had been a close call. He didn't know who burst into the house just as he and Sammy Perez were about to kill Dave and Ginny Kim. It wasn't the police. No, they would have come in with lights blazing and guns drawn. This was a lone wolf. Maybe he was tipped off. But by whom?

This morning he was nervously waiting outside the office of the chief of the Reconnaissance General Bureau's Fifth Department, also known as Bureau 35. There was going to be an accounting, and he couldn't put aside the feeling that things would not go well for him.

"Comrade Roe, he's ready for you. You may go in."

Roe felt his heart flutter and his throat constrict. Breathe, he admonished himself as he rose and strode towards the inner sanctum. Outward confidence was paramount at a time like this. If he displayed even the slightest bit of fear he was feeling inside, the chief would cut him off at the knees.

"Comrade Roe, welcome home. I trust you have good news regarding your mission. I am anxious to hear all the details." The chief guided Roe to a chair and offered him a cigarette.

"Comrade, thank you for seeing me," Roe said as he

accepted the tobacco and a light. He inhaled deeply before beginning.

"I'm sorry to report that our mission was a failure," Roe said. "It was not because of poor planning or lack of intelligence. It was because we were betrayed."

"How so, Comrade Roe?" the chief asked. He held the cigarette away from his face, looking intently into Roe's eyes.

Roe swallowed hard and continued. He had decided to embellish his story somewhat to strengthen the argument he was about to put forward. Leaving the house in San Marino before completing his mission was not only the right decision but the only one he could have made to salvage North Korea's reputation in the face of an exposed double homicide.

"Despite excellent intelligence and vigilant surveillance, our enemies fooled us into believing that the conditions for our operation were ideal. We were no sooner inside the targets' house when an intruder and police arrived on the scene. It was as though they were forewarned."

"How did you manage to escape?" the chief asked, barely concealing his skepticism.

"Fortunately, they did not see me when they came into the house. The intruder came inside seconds after we breached the security system. We bypassed the alarm system as planned and moved towards the master bedroom when this man came rushing through the door.

"He threw himself at the hitman we hired through our Russian contacts, and the noise awakened the targets inside their bedroom. A moment later, I heard police sirens in the distance and knew there was no time to complete our mission and escape.

"I went out the patio door and over a neighbor's wall next door, trying to put distance between myself and the crime scene. I almost changed my travel plans because I assumed they would be searching for me at the airport, but they had no way of knowing my identity."

"Who saw you?" the chief asked.

"Only the hitman who sat with me in the rental car going over the plan. The intruder would not have seen me well enough to identify me, but he would have a general description. The husband and wife never saw me."

"You were so close," the chief said. "It's a shame you couldn't have done something."

Roe could sense an accusatory tone coming from his boss. He needed to defend himself without becoming defensive. "You know I would have done anything to complete the mission. It was never part of the plan that I would kill the targets. That's why we brought in the gangster from the Asian Hoods. He had the weapons on his person. I was not armed.

"In the dark, it was difficult to tell if the intruder had a weapon. He was a master fighter; I didn't see any way to take him down, liquidate the targets and escape without being caught."

"Who would betray you?" the chief asked as he ground his cigarette butt into the ashtray with more force than necessary. A drop of spittle escaped from his pursed lips, which he angrily brushed aside.

"The only people outside of Bureau 35 who knew about the plan were our Russian contacts and the hitman, Sammy Perez. All Perez had was contact instructions to meet me at a pre-determined location in Los Angeles. The Russians told him it was a break-in and a hit, so he had the tools he needed with him, but he didn't have any specifics about the target."

"Did he know who you were?" the chief asked.

"He asked, but I didn't tell him anything. I don't think he saw the license plate on the rental car, but if he did and cooperated with the police, they might be able to figure out my alias information."

The chief's features relaxed. "From what you've said, it seems unlikely the hitman would have said anything to anybody. We have a good relationship with the Russians, so I find it hard to believe they would leave you high and dry like that.

"I think I can save your ass when I brief this to the director. He hates to bring bad news to the supreme leader, so he can spin this along the lines that we may not have achieved our goal of eliminating Dave and Ginny Kim, but we got away without tarnishing our reputation.

"Meanwhile, comrade, we need to find out the identity of the man who came into the house after you. He knew something. The question is, how did he know it?"

Chapter 36

Based on Logan's recommendation, Martina decided not to adjust Laurie Kim's or Jason Lee's assignments or access to sensitive information. As repugnant as it was to think of them siphoning off classified information to pass to the North Koreans, it was essential to maintain the facade that all was well.

She, Logan, and Peter were going for a run on their lunch break. Spring was in the air as they climbed the rugged trail to Guaje Mountain's summit, where they would see spectacular views of the Jemez Mountains to the west and the Sangre de Cristo Mountains to the east. They stopped for a water break halfway there to take in the vista.

"Are you getting hammered with info from the tech ops yet?" Martina asked Logan as she drained half a bottle of water.

"Paul, the Bureau tech from Albuquerque, has been looking at the directories and files on Jason's computer," Logan said. "Jason hasn't been online much since we put the malware on his computer, but one thing jumped out at me when I looked at the programs he's running."

"What was that?" Peter asked as he stretched his arms over his head and rolled his shoulders back and forth.

"He's running The Onion Router and a voice privacy network on his laptop."

"What's the Onion Router?" Martina asked as they stowed their water bottles and resumed running.

"It's a software program that uses a series of network nodes to transmit messages between parties. Every time a message leaves a node, that node peels away a layer of encryption, making it almost impossible to decipher the original message.

"Normally, when you visit a website or send an email, your computer makes a direct connection with that website using TCP. If that connection isn't secure, a sophisticated hacker would be able to read the contents of your message.

"With TOR, your computer never talks directly to the website's server. Instead, it anonymizes your message by routing it through several nodes before it reaches its destination."

"Is it illegal?" Martina asked.

"It's not illegal to use it," Peter said, "although a lot of illegal activity on the dark web happens because people use it to conceal what they are doing."

"In all fairness, some people use it just because they like their privacy and don't want anyone looking at their browsing habits or their contacts," Logan said.

"Jason's also running voice privacy network software, which would give him another layer of protection," he added.

"None of this is illegal; it's perfectly legit. But it makes me ask the question, 'What are you so worried about?' Once Paul finishes mapping the directories, we can dig deeper into any suspicious-looking content."

They had reached the summit and sprawled out on the ground to take in the view. There wasn't a cloud in the sky, and the temperature was in the low fifties.

"We are beginning to get data dumps out of Harriet's shop," Logan said. "When NSA turns on the faucet, they can overwhelm you pretty fast. We're fortunate that Jason doesn't spend a lot of time on his phone.

"We've identified most of his contacts from the cell phone logs NSA gave us. The bulk of the calls were to and from Laurie Kim. There was a number in Toronto that turns out to belong to Jason's mother and quite a few work-related calls with colleagues here at the lab."

"Any unusual phone activity?" Martina asked.

"There's one number that I would say is suspicious. Surprisingly, that call occurred the same day as the hostage incident. I've looked at access logs to the lab that day, and Jason couldn't get back on campus because of the lockdown.

"I did a little digging and found that he went car shopping and returned his rental to the airport. While he was out, Jason received a call from this suspicious number that lasted for less than a minute."

"What makes that suspicious?" Peter asked.

"I'm pretty sure the person calling used a burner phone with a disposable SIM card. Using metadata from the telephone, NSA pinpointed the call's location as Mexico City in the vicinity of the Zona Rosa. The caller purchased a mobile prepaid SIM card at a 7-Eleven in Mexico City in early January. That same phone and SIM card was used to place a call to the reservations desk at the Hotel San Carols in Albuquerque earlier in the day. Mind you at this point we still don't have a voice recording, just linkage between these phone numbers.

"The Bureau requested records of the transaction from the Mexicans and discovered that a William Gardner used a credit card to purchase the SIM card. On a hunch, Anthony's man visited the Hotel San Carlos and asked if they had a record of a William Gardner staying there."

Martina got to her feet. "Let's keep moving. I've got a 1:30 meeting with the Director." She fixed her eyes on Logan. "So, what did they find out?"

"William Gardner was a guest at the Hotel San Carlos for several nights."

"Is there anything we can do with that information?" Martina asked as they set off running.

"Yes, I've asked NSA to see if they can get access to the voice recording of that phone call. I've run name traces on William Gardner, but we need more information to narrow it down and determine the connection, if any, with Jason Lee. So far, I've got everything from William Gardner, the actor, to William Gardner, the zoologist.

"I've got one more connection for you," Logan said. "I've been playing with this program that I told you about, the one that does transactional analysis. I decided to put all of Jason Lee's known contacts into this program and then ran the software to determine any connections between the various phone numbers.

"As expected, many of the Los Alamos employees knew each other and had multiple connections. But one number jumped off the page for me."

"William Gardner?" Peter asked.

"Why do you say that?" Logan asked.

"He's the outlier," Peter said. "It had to be him."

"But not for the reason you think," Logan said. "William Gardner is connected to two people on our list. One is Jason Lee, and the other is Dr. Ha-Yoon Lee, Jason Lee's mother. I think William Gardner is Jason Lee's father, Roe Min-Woo."

Chapter 37

Billy Chu was preoccupied with cover work in the days following the attack at Dave and Ginny Kim's house. He was initially concerned there would be blowback from the San Marino Police Department over his role in thwarting the murder attempt against the Kims. He figured that it would lower his profile if he kept busy with official duties for a week or two.

In keeping with his energy security portfolio, Billy traveled to Sandia National Laboratories, located at Kirtland Air Force Base, home to the 377th Air Base Wing and the Nuclear Weapons Center near Albuquerque. The Sandia lab arranged accommodations for visiting diplomats such as Billy on base at the Kirtland Inn.

Billy wanted to visit Sandia because one of their research studies had to do with testing nuclear waste storage canisters. South Korea was interested in improving its spent fuel storage. The U.S. stores spent fuel in storage pools or dry storage containers, but South Korea was running out of storage capacity.

South Korea's spent fuel storage problem was looming large. As the world's fifth-largest nuclear power consumer, there was insufficient storage capacity at South Korean nuclear power plants. Scientific advisors recommended constructing a temporary facility for near-term demands but felt that a deep underground facility was a better long-term solution. One problem they needed to solve was the container's long-term viability for holding spent fuel.

The researchers at Sandia showed Billy a controlled experiment they were conducting using stainless steel storage canisters. Each canister weighed twenty-two and a half tons and was sixteen and a half feet long. The scientists installed heaters and various instruments in each of the canisters to simulate nuclear waste conditions.

The goal of the experiment was to determine how much corrosion takes place over time and if it causes stresses or cracks that would render the canisters unsafe. If the experiment was successful, stainless-steel canisters might be a solution to South Korea's storage dilemma.

Billy had a break between meetings at Sandia and decided to check in with Laurie. It was too soon to schedule another trip to Los Alamos, given his recent visit to the lab, but maybe he could take Laurie out to dinner. Billy wanted to talk to her about the events at her parents' house. He walked outside and gave her a call.

"Hi, Laurie. It's me," he said.

Laurie was quiet for a moment and then spoke, "Billy. Where are you?"

"Albuquerque. I had a last-minute meeting at Sandia, and I thought I'd get in touch to see if you're free for dinner."

"How long are you in town?" she asked.

"I'm leaving tonight. I have an 8:30 flight on American."

"How about if I meet you near the airport, so you don't have to rush? I can leave work a little early and meet you at, say, 5:30."

"Why don't we meet in Santa Fe? That's about halfway, and you won't have to drive so far," he said.

"Okay, there's a popular steakhouse on Don Gaspar Avenue in Santa Fe that gets rave reviews."

"What's the name? I'll call ahead and make a reservation."

"Saltgrass Steak House," she said.

Billy called the restaurant, wrapped up his meetings, and then returned to the Kirtland Inn to check out. He had a couple of hours until his dinner date with Laurie and decided to leave early for Santa Fe. He'd never been to the state capital but had heard the city square in the historic downtown was worth exploring.

Billy poked around the galleries and antique stores

lining the plaza and then headed over to Saltgrass at 5:15. It was early, and there were few customers in the restaurant. He ordered a beer while he was waiting for Laurie. He was looking forward to seeing her again, but more than anything, he was hoping she could shed some light on the events at her parents' house.

"Hey."

It was Laurie. He was so immersed in his thoughts that he didn't see her arrive. He slid out of his chair and kissed her on the cheek.

"What were you thinking about?" she asked. "You looked like you were miles away."

He steered her to the seat across from him and signaled to their waitress. "We only have about an hour, so I thought we'd go ahead and order. Do you want a beer or wine?" he asked.

"How's the beer?" she asked.

"It's a pale ale from one of the local craft breweries," he said. "They just started selling it outside of their taprooms."

"So far, it's been popular," their waitress said. "My brother's one of their brewers, and if they can produce enough, they plan to ship it all over the state by the end of the year."

After the waitress took their orders and brought Laurie's beer, there was a moment of quiet. Laurie sipped her beer appreciatively, then leaned back in her chair with a thoughtful look on her face.

"What happened that night, Billy? I can't get out of my head what would have happened to my parents if you hadn't shown up when you did."

Billy looked deep into Laurie's eyes. They had known each other for years. He was a good judge of character, and Laurie was one of the sincerest people he had ever met. He could not fathom her being party to something as nefarious as a North Korean illegals operation. He wondered how much she knew about her parents' immigration history.

"You never told me your parents immigrated to the U.S. from Mexico," he said.

She looked confused for a moment. "It never came up. I was born in Los Angeles, and they never talked much about their life in Mexico. I know their mothers immigrated from South Korea and married Mexican men. I never knew my grandparents, and we never went to Mexico.

"But what's this have to do with someone breaking into their house to kill them?" she asked, a confused look crossing her face.

Billy took a deep breath. "Did your parents ever say anything to you about North Korea?"

Laurie's lips parted, and she stared at him as if he had gone mad. "North Korea?" She asked, "What does that have to do with anything?"

Billy was skating on thin ice. Laurie wouldn't be able to fake the look of disbelief on her face. She appeared to be genuinely confused. He needed to get to the bottom of this, but he was hesitant to reveal too much.

"Our embassy in Mexico City found out that there is some connection between your parents and the North Koreans."

"How do they know?" she asked.

Billy reached into his pocket and pulled out the copy of the photograph taken from Roe Min-Woo's wallet by the Mexican hooker. He slid it across the table. "This picture was in a North Korean intelligence officer's wallet and was shared with officials at our embassy."

Laurie picked up the photo of her parents, and her hands began to shake. "Don't you remember this picture? It was at graduation, and we were taking family photos on campus. This is one I took of my parents near the Bruin Bear."

Billy smacked his head. "No wonder it seemed so familiar," he said. "I thought I'd seen it before, but I couldn't remember where. How did a North Korean agent get this picture of your parents?"

"I don't know, Billy, but when I talked to my mother the other night, she told me she found this picture on the floor when she was cleaning up. He must have dropped it when he broke into the house," she said.

"Whoever it was must not have known your parents. He had the picture so that he could use it to identify them. He wanted to be sure he was killing the right people."

"But why?" she cried.

"Not because they were afraid of killing the wrong people," Billy said. "He wanted to be sure your parents were dead."

Chapter 38

Logan was studying the San Marino Police Department's interrogation report on Sammy Perez. There wasn't much there, mainly because Billy Chu had broken the gangster's jaw, making it impossible for him to talk. Perez had emergency surgery the day after the break-in, and the surgeons had wired his jaw together, holding it in place with plates and screws.

To make matters worse, Perez had the IQ of a half-wit and was illiterate to boot. It was virtually impossible to get anything useful out of him. The Los Angeles district attorney charged Perez with breaking and entering and attempted murder. At his arraignment, the judge set bail so high that the Asian Hoods would have to raid Fort Knox to spring him from the county jail.

It would be six to eight weeks before Perez's jaw healed. With any luck, he would have a change of heart during that time and decide to cooperate with the DA. It was a long shot, and besides, there was always the possibility that he didn't know anything; Roe Min-Woo hired him to do his wet work, nothing more.

The FBI Field Office in Albuquerque had better luck investigating William Gardner. As luck would have it, the head of security at the Hotel San Carlos in Albuquerque was a retired FBI agent who had a thing for technology. All public areas in the hotel were covered with high-resolution video systems, backed up daily, and stored digitally for five years.

Agent Brown invited Logan to accompany him to the hotel to meet with the security chief and review the relevant footage. They were gathered in his office on the main floor, just off the lobby.

"After we received your request, we narrowed down Gardner's check-in time and then pulled the files from our archives. We isolated the lobby feed as the most obvious place to start so you can visually identify the subject. We'll begin the clock with the hotel lobby feed five minutes before check-in. Let me see," he said as he searched through a file on his desk. "Here it is. Check-in was at 6:20 p.m."

The video began playing on the computer. The date-time stamp on the screen was the Friday after George Taylor attacked Building 39 at the lab and took the employees hostage. At 6:18 on the time stamp, an Asian male entered the hotel lobby and approached the reception desk. There was no audio, but they could view the scene from several angles due to the strategic placement of the hotel's recording devices.

"It's him," Logan said. He'd seen several headshots of Roe in recent weeks. The South Koreans had given them pictures of Roe as a young man before he defected to North Korea, and the Mexicans provided official photos from the North Korean trade talks in Mexico City. And now, here Roe was, captured on video checking into this hotel as William Gardner.

"William Gardner is Roe Min-Woo. There's no doubt about it. The question is, what was he doing in Albuquerque?"

"We pulled up a record of charges he made during his stay. He was here for three nights, and during that time, racked up mostly room service charges. The only one that stands out is this Saturday breakfast charge. He ordered enough food for two or three people. We dug around a bit and discovered he had a visitor that day," the security chief said.

"That might help narrow it down," Logan said. "Do you keep a record of room service tickets?"

"Yes, as a matter of fact, I asked the accounting department to pull up that charge. The kitchen uses a punch clock to track orders as a quality check." He pulled the ticket out of his file. "It looks like Mr. Gardner, or whoever he is, called in the order at 7:45. Room service delivered it to room 526 at 8:05.

"On the off chance the room service waiter, Manuel, would remember anything about this delivery, I called him in yesterday for questioning. It turns out Manuel had a pretty vivid recollection of Mr. Gardner. Gardner stood out to him because we don't get many Asian clients at the San Carlos. Also, he thought it unusual that Gardner didn't have an Asian name. But the thing he most remembered was that Gardner was a poor tipper."

"You said Gardner had a visitor that day. Did Manuel see him in Gardner's room?" Anthony asked.

"Briefly. He was mostly alone, except for Saturday when Gardner ordered the big breakfast. Manuel delivered the food and was just leaving Gardner's room when a young Asian male walked up to the room. He nodded to the man, and as he was wheeling his cart away, he saw the visitor enter the room and heard him address Gardner as 'Dad.'"

Logan and Anthony looked at each other; this could be the break they needed. "Does your video coverage of the lobby capture the courtesy phone?" Logan asked. He was thinking back to tradecraft 101. If you were going to have a clandestine meeting in a hotel and didn't want to advertise what room you were in beforehand, you would have your contact use the courtesy phone to have the hotel operator connect you to the room. You would speak only the room number over the phone, leaving no record of the visitor's name.

There was another reason for using the courtesy phone this way if there was uncertainty about your visitor's true intentions. Providing the meeting site's exact location at the very last minute made it virtually impossible to mount technical surveillance against the room.

"I have video coverage of the main lobby entrance and a separate camera that captures the courtesy phone. I also have coverage of all the hallways on every floor. Do you know who you're looking for?"

Logan and Anthony both nodded at the same time. "We have a pretty good idea," Logan said. "Let's see if it's who we think it is."

Moments later, they watched as Jason Lee entered the hotel lobby.

"Son of a bitch," Logan said through gritted teeth.

Jason walked over to the courtesy phone, placed a call, and then entered an elevator. The security chief held up his hand, and with a couple of mouse clicks, changed the feed to the fifth-floor hallway outside of Gardner's room. A Latino employee emerged from room 526, pushing a cart.

"That must be Manuel," Logan said.

"Yes, that's him."

A moment later, Jason Lee's figure filled the frame. He turned to scan the hallway and then crossed the threshold.

Chapter 39

The homeless bum dumpster-diving behind Jason Lee's apartment building gawked at the young scientist as he hefted a garbage bag and tossed it into the trash.

"What are you doing in there?" Jason asked the scruffy forager.

"Looking for something to eat," the man growled.

Jason shook his head and walked away. "You should try getting a job," he muttered.

"That's easy for you to say," the man retorted.

The bum grabbed Jason's bag and tore through it. There was no food inside, but he stuffed a bundle of personal papers he discovered into a knapsack he was carrying. He hopped out of the dumpster with greater agility than seemed possible and shuffled out of the parking lot. He walked two blocks and turned down a side street to where he had parked his Bureau car.

Special Agent Tim McGinty wasn't fond of dumpster duty. It was right up there with a two-week, midnight-to-7 a.m. surveillance detail he pulled last month against a suspected pedophile dealing in child pornography. It was worth it when they nailed that piece of shit trying to smuggle a twelve-year-old girl into a seedy motel on the outskirts of Albuquerque, where he was set up for a photoshoot.

McGinty was only six months out of the FBI Academy. Newly minted Special Agents couldn't expect plum assignments right out of Quantico. "Consider it character building," his boss, Assistant Special Agent in Charge Anthony Brown, told him.

This case could be his big break, though. Jason Lee was an up-and-coming star at Los Alamos, Ph.D. in physics from the University of Toronto. But he left one thing off his application when he applied for the job; his dad was a North Korean intelligence officer.

Hell, they were even working with the CIA on the Lee case. He'd met the Agency officer detailed to the lab, Logan Alexander. He seemed like a regular guy. He had to be if he was a Navy SEAL with combat tours in Iraq and Afghanistan under his belt.

McGinty picked up speed as he merged onto State Road 76. He couldn't wait to get back to the office, where he would painstakingly sift through each piece of trash in the bag, identifying, logging, and analyzing every scrap of Jason Lee's life.

Meanwhile, back at the apartment, Jason was powering up his computer. He hadn't heard from his father in two weeks. He wondered what the political environment was like in North Korea, given the recent leadership change in Washington. Things had been quiet for a couple of months, and then, out of nowhere, North Korea sent two ballistic missiles careening into the Sea of Japan.

North Korea was rolling out its equivalent of a diplomatic welcome mat for the new American administration. The newly-installed U.S. president's foreign policy team met with its Asian allies and frequent adversary, China, in mid-March to set out its strategic policy goals and expectations. But North Korea was probably feeling isolated. The former president wooed the supreme leader with summits and joint declarations, but this administration mostly ignored him. Jason thought back to his brief encounter with the supreme leader in Pyongyang shortly after coming into power. He wasn't particularly tall, maybe five-foot-seven, and probably weighed 300 pounds. Despite his stern, anti-American rhetoric, he was charming and outgoing during their ten-minute meeting. It was hard to reconcile that person with the ruthless dictator who demanded adulation and strict submission from his countrymen. Jason opened his TOR browser and signed on to the VPN. There was a message from his father.

"I have been traveling on State business and have barely had time to sit down at my computer. I hope you are well and that you continue to make inroads in your mission. I see from your recent emails that you are working on power equipment for long-distance space missions. While this is a fascinating area of science, our scientists are more interested in information concerning nuclear weapons at Los Alamos." There followed a short list of requirements: "What is the present nuclear weapons mission at Los Alamos? What can you tell us about Technical Area-55? Does Los Alamos have a bioweapons program? Is your access badge restricted? If so, what areas are off-limits?"

Fortunately for him, the answers to these questions weren't classified. However, he knew the security people at Los Alamos would take a dim view of this secret correspondence with his father. The last paragraph in his father's message contained both exciting and disappointing news.

"We are moving forward with our plans to set up the trade office in Mexico City, now that our Embassy is open there. The Ministry of External Economic Affairs has decided to fast-track my assignment, and I will be relocating permanently to Mexico City next month.

"Initially, our office will be operating out of the Embassy. Fortunately, I know the new ambassador and am confident he will help us get established. At some point I will be looking for separate office space outside of the embassy. One other colleague will be joining me there. I am hopeful that we will be up and running by May.

"When I first learned of the job in Mexico, I thought it would be possible for us to see each other more often. Now, I realize that this is unrealistic. I am concerned that I will come under greater scrutiny there than I am used to with my high profile at the embassy.

"We know that the Mexicans and Americans share intelligence. The Americans would like nothing more than to catch a North Korean Intelligence officer illegally in their country. That would be an embarrassment for North Korea, but I am more concerned about what it would mean for you and your career.

"We will have to find another way. I thought you might occasionally travel to Mexico, but we don't know yet if the Mexicans will have us under surveillance. If so, you could come to their attention. It will take months, perhaps years, to determine their level of interest in our activities. Maybe we can meet in a third country again."

Jason was beginning to feel that he was in over his head. There were so many things he didn't understand about his father's world; he wasn't a trained operative. He would have to depend upon his father's advice. He shook off his misgivings and set to work answering his father's questions.

Chapter 40

Tony Perez stood out like lipstick on a pig. A straggly ponytail hung limply to his shoulders, and two gold-capped front teeth flashed whenever he smiled. A menacing blue-and-gray *prajna* tattoo covered his muscular left shoulder and chest. *Prajna* was the Asian Hoods' misappropriation of the revered Buddhist symbol, which stands for wisdom. In gang culture, *prajna* is considered the incarnation of evil, the devil.

Unlike his brother, Sammy, Tony was the brains of the Asian Hoods. Cambodians had dominated the Hoods in Los Angeles for decades, but after he was court-martialed and booted out of the Army in 2010, Tony developed a following amongst LA's Filipino gang sub-culture. He rose to the top, mainly by securing a segment of LA's drug trade, but the Russian mob had tried squeezing the Hoods out in recent years.

Last year the two groups declared a truce; recently, the Russians came to the Hoods with a money offer too good to pass up. It involved taking out a South Korean businessman named Dave Kim in San Marino. Tony gave Sammy the lead on the hit, but something went wrong when he went out to do the job. From what Tony was able to piece together, Sammy and a Korean affiliated with the Russians went to Dave Kim's house in San Marino but got busted when the cops showed up.

One other person showed up, too, the one who kicked the shit out of his brother. No one knew who he was, and the Korean who accompanied Sammy disappeared before the cops got there, leaving Sammy to take the hit.

It was too early to tell, but it looked like Sammy might

do time for this job. Tony visited him in jail, and he didn't look too good. Tony talked to him in Tagalog, their native language, but Sammy couldn't say anything because his jaw was wired shut.

Tony wanted to make good on their deal with the Russians. They had wired $25,000 when Sammy went out to do the job and were being patient despite the setback; they wanted results. There was more money to be made with the Russian mob, but only if the Hoods could deliver.

Tony was on his way to finish what his brother hadn't done. He knew Kim's home address, but he wasn't about to go back to the house in San Marino; it was too risky. He also found out the Russians didn't really care about Kim's wife, Ginny; the one they most wanted dead was her husband.

Dave Kim ran a software company in downtown Los Angeles with offices located in Pershing Square. There was an underground parking garage in the office building, which usually emptied out by 6 p.m. Tony reconnoitered the garage earlier in the week and found there were no visible security cameras in the structure; the entrance was an unmanned, RF-activated gate.

Kim drove a late-model white Mercedes four-door SUV. His parking spot was along the garage's south wall, one level down from the first floor. During Tony's scouting visit, he noticed an unlocked storage room with cleaning supplies. Afterwards, he picked up a gray long-sleeved work shirt matching those worn by the cleaning crew at a secondhand clothing store. He was already wearing the fake facial hair disguise he picked up to go along with the clothing. He planned to change shirts in the storage room and make as though he was a member of the janitorial staff.

Tony reached the office complex at 6:15. The underground parking lot had a half-dozen cars parked in it. There was no overnight parking, so those people would be leaving sometime before midnight. Tony entered the storage room at 6:25 and changed into his disguise. He donned a ball cap to tuck in his long hair and used a hand mirror to check out his beard. After grabbing a trash cart on wheels, a broom, and a dustpan, he exited the storage room. He wasn't sure how long he would have to wait in the garage, but it would be best to blend in.

He heard the elevator door slide open, tensing as he waited for the person to emerge. It was a Caucasian broad, a beauty. Her high heels made a staccato clicking sound against the cement floor as she sashayed over to a loaded gray Porsche 911 Carrera parked near the Mercedes. She barely nodded to him as she unlocked the car and started the engine. The throaty roar filled the garage as the Porsche glided towards the exit.

Bitch, he thought to himself. Why was she cruising around in wheels that probably cost $150,000 while he was driving a 1971 Pontiac GTO that he and Sammy bought for $1,000 and painstakingly restored? Sure, his ride had a 400-horsepower fuel-injected V8 and a 426 Hemi transmission, but it just wasn't right.

Over the next hour and a half, three other cars left, leaving only Dave Kim and someone else's car. What if they came down together? At least they weren't parked near each other. Tony shuffled around the garage, pushing the trash cart. He wanted to be close to Kim's car when he came down. The silenced Titan 9mm pistol was tucked into the waistband beneath his work shirt, rubbing against his belly. He was using subsonic rounds to reduce the noise further. He planned to kill Kim before he got into his car and then conceal the body in the back seat or trunk.

Tony wasn't concerned about disposing of the body. It was too risky for him to be driving around in Kim's car with his corpse in the back seat. He just needed to make sure the man was dead and then get out of Dodge before any alarms went off. He was so immersed in his thinking that he almost missed the movement from the elevator. It was Kim. He was alone, but he was talking on his cellphone as he walked towards the Mercedes.

Tony angled himself to walk past the Mercedes as he walked towards the storage room. He would intercept Kim near his car. Kim was shouting at someone on the phone and barely glanced up as Tony approached. Kim finished his call and was fishing in his coat pocket for his key when he suddenly spun around.

He must have sensed that the cart noise had stopped when Tony reached into his waistband to pull out his pistol. Kim's mouth opened as if to say something, and his arms flailed trying to ward off the gun. But it was too late. Tony fired two rounds into Kim's chest from five feet away. He jerked and then went slack, sliding to the ground.

Tony crouched down next to the body and felt for a pulse; Kim was dead. He grasped the corpse under the arms and dragged it to the rear of the car. He found Kim's keys and opened the rear hatch, wrestling the body inside; he closed and locked the door.

Tony returned the cleaning gear to the storage room and walked casually towards the exit. As he passed the elevator, a woman stepped out and looked around, looking intently at the white Mercedes.

"Excuse me. Has anyone come down in the last fifteen minutes?" she asked.

"No, ma'am," he said. "It's probably been a half-hour since I saw anyone."

"That's strange," she said with a frown. "I could have sworn Dave said he was leaving." Suddenly her eyes grew round, and her hand went to her mouth. She was staring at Tony in horror.

Tony looked down and noticed for the first time that his shirt was covered in blood. "Shit," he cussed. This was not going well.

"You should have stayed in your office, lady," he said.

"Please," she said, backing up. She tripped on the curb and sprawled onto the sidewalk.

Tony pulled the pistol from his waistband, aimed, and fired two rounds into the woman's head. He ripped off the shirt and wadded it into a ball; he took off at a jog, pulling on the tee shirt he had been wearing earlier as he forced himself to look straight ahead. When he reached the street, he slowed to a walk. Turning a corner, he pulled off the beard, and removed the baseball cap.

Tony walked for another fifteen minutes towards a makeshift homeless shelter, a mini-tent city he had spotted earlier in the week. As he sauntered by, the cold-blooded killer casually tossed his wadded-up disguise through the open flap of one of the tents and kept on moving. Relief washed over him, and he finally allowed himself to breathe.

Chapter 41

Logan got off the phone and jogged down to Martina's office. "Someone murdered Dave Kim last night," he said. "I can't believe it. I just met him a week ago when he and his wife were here visiting Laurie."

"What?" Martina asked in disbelief. "The North Koreans?"

"We don't know. I just got off the phone with Anthony. The Bureau doesn't have any leads. Whoever did it was waiting for Kim in the underground parking garage at his office. The killer shot him twice in the chest at close range and then stashed the body in his car.

"The shooter also killed a woman from Kim's office. Security for the parking garage came by at midnight to lock things down and found the bodies. Hers was right by the elevators. Shot twice in the head. The police think she just happened to be in the wrong place at the wrong time. Might have seen the killer shoot Kim or somehow had contact with him."

"They don't have any suspects?" Martina asked.

"Nothing so far," Logan said. "Security in the garage was nonexistent. With COVID, most employees in the building are still working from home. The building management company cut back on security early in the pandemic as a cost-cutting measure. They also delayed a planned installation of security cameras in the garage until next year. No one saw anything.

"Anthony said the police are interviewing Ginny Kim at her home this morning. He wants to bring the detectives into the loop on the North Korea angle," Logan added.

"That could be a problem," Martina said, frowning. "It could compromise our CI investigation. We still don't have a handle on Dave Kim's relationship with the North

Koreans, if any; if law enforcement starts mucking around in our case, they could expose information we don't necessarily want out there.

"Has anyone talked to Laurie Kim?" Martina asked.

"I don't know," Logan said. "I imagine Laurie's mother contacted her as soon as she found out."

"This has to be the North Koreans," Martina said. "It's too much of a coincidence."

"Yeah, but how?" Logan asked. "We went back and tracked William Gardner's movements following the break-in at the Kim residence. Gardner caught an Aeromexico flight to Mexico City at 6:30, a few hours after the break-in. After that, he drops off the grid. He probably got rid of the Gardner alias and left Mexico in his true name.

"I'll send a message to Mexico City to ask the Mexicans for the most recent travel information they have on Roe Min-Woo."

"Let me get Peter in here," Martina said. After a quick conversation with her deputy, she called HR.

"Hi, Jeannie. It's Martina. One of our police contacts just advised us that Laurie Kim's father was murdered last night."

"Thank you for the heads-up, Martina; I got a call from Laurie's supervisor first thing this morning. Laurie's mother called her in the middle of the night with the news; they live in Los Angeles. Laurie is taking emergency leave; she's on her way to LA even as we speak."

"Thanks, Jeannie."

Peter came into the office and plunked down in a chair opposite Logan. He wore a perplexed look. "What the fuck is going on?" he asked.

Logan filled him in on what he knew from his conversation with the Bureau. "If I were the Bureau, I'd focus on that Asian gangbanger, Sammy Perez, and his associates."

"But Perez is in jail, and the bond is five hundred thousand. My bet is no one gives a shit about him because he's still cooling his heels in lockup," Peter said.

"According to the Bureau, the visitor log at the jail

shows only one entry, Tony Perez, Sammy's brother. He's a big shot in the Asian Hoods; has a reputation for being the brains of the gang. Allegedly Tony got the Hoods into the drug trade a few years back, but neither the Feds nor local law enforcement has been able to nail his ass on narcotics trafficking."

"I've got an idea," Logan said, "getting back to your concerns about briefing law enforcement on the North Korea angle. What if I go out to Los Angeles and interview Ginny Kim? We'd have to separate her and Laurie and drum up a reason for why the lab is even interested in this."

"We need to get buy-in from the Bureau and local law enforcement. My gut feeling is they wouldn't be supportive. Why should they be?" Martina said.

"For one thing, I'm a trained interrogator, not just military-style field interrogations, but ones like the police do. I took a course in techniques of investigative interviewing and advanced interrogation. A lot of it uses psychology and body language to determine if the subject is telling the truth. I've also met Ginny Kim. Granted, it was a short conversation, but for her, it would be a familiar face."

"I like it. Peter?" Martina asked.

"Laurie Kim is a smart cookie, and she's a person of interest in this investigation. We'll be tipping her off if we start asking her mom about North Korea, not to mention the mom, who, for all we know, is a North Korean illegal."

"How about this?" Logan said. "What if I backbench an FBI interrogator conducting the interview? The Bureau can set it up at the LA field office, and I'll observe the session remotely. I can feed the special agent questions and provide my take on Mrs. Kim's reaction to being questioned."

"I like that scenario better," Peter said. "It keeps you out of the picture but takes advantage of your expertise, so we get the most out of the time we have with her."

"All right. I'll work it out with Anthony, and I'll make sure Headquarters is on board with my travel to Los Angeles. I think it's best to do this sooner than later. It'll be tough on Mrs. Kim, given what she's going through right now."

"When are you thinking about going?" Martina asked.
"If I get approval and Mrs. Kim is available, I'll fly to LA tomorrow.

Chapter 42

Logan breathed a sigh of relief as he boarded his flight to Los Angeles. If he didn't have such a good relationship with Assistant Special Agent in Charge Anthony Brown, he'd be spinning his wheels at Los Alamos at the moment.

The senior agent in the Los Angeles Field Office was an Assistant Director of the FBI and thus outranked Brown. She was initially cool to the idea of having a CIA officer participate in Ginny Kim's interview, even remotely, but Anthony pleaded his case. When Anthony mentioned that Logan was a graduate of the U.S. Naval Academy, she relented because, as a fellow Navy graduate, she had a soft spot for those who served at sea.

The Bureau had scheduled Ginny Kim's interview for 10 a.m. tomorrow. That would give Logan ample time to meet with the FBI interviewer to review the case and get the lay of the land.

He checked into the Residence Inn in Beverly Hills and took a taxi to the FBI offices located in the Federal Building on Wilshire Boulevard. The receptionist had his information and asked him to wait in the lobby for a moment. She placed a call, and five minutes later, a young woman arrived to escort him upstairs.

They made small talk on the way up. She was originally from Minneapolis and had come on board with the FBI three years ago. After training at Quantico, the FBI dispatched her to the Los Angeles Division, where she expected to spend several years.

"This is Special Agent Conroy's office," she said, knocking on a door. "He'll be your primary contact during your stay."

"Come in," a voice boomed from inside.

Logan opened the door and found himself looking at two hundred pounds of solid muscle. Conroy was built like an All-Pro linebacker. Beneath an unruly thatch of blond hair, two inquisitive blue eyes assessed the CIA officer.

"Agent Conroy?" Logan asked. The two men did an elbow bump in deference to the social distancing guidelines posted all over the building.

"You can call me Ben," he said. "You must be Mr. Alexander?"

"Call me Logan," he replied.

"How was your flight?"

"Can't complain. It was on time and still had all its gear when we landed," Logan laughed.

Ben chuckled. "Are you staying nearby?" he asked.

"Yeah, the Beverly Hills Residence Inn. A ten-minute taxi ride from here."

"We better get down to business. We're set to interview Mrs. Kim tomorrow morning at 10," Ben said.

"I have to tell you; we were a little surprised when Anthony told us he wanted you to sit in on her interview. I haven't had anyone backbench me since I was a rookie agent."

Logan detected a slight edge to the special agent's tone. "Look, I'm not here to tell you how to do your job. There are aspects of this case that are especially sensitive because of the sourcing. How much do you know about it?" Logan asked.

"Not a lot," Ben admitted. "I didn't get involved until after the break-in at the Kims' house last week."

Logan spent the next two hours bringing Ben up to speed on the North Korea angle of the operation. "There's a lot we don't know," he admitted. "And the things we do know raise more questions."

"For instance ...?" Ben asked.

"Why did the Kims have such a shady immigration history from Mexico? How did Dave and Ginny Kim go from being penniless immigrants to successful professionals?

Why did a North Korean Intelligence officer have a photo of them in his possession? Why did the North Koreans want the Kims dead?

"One of our early theories was that the NKIS sent the Kims to the U.S. via Mexico as illegals with some general instructions to establish themselves and wait to be contacted. There are some holes in their background story—missing records and no known relatives to substantiate their claims. That's a red flag, but it's not conclusive," Logan added.

"The North Koreans are patient with these illegal operations. They may wait years before activating their people. Part of the reason for that is that it takes illegals a while to establish access to intelligence.

"The NKIS uses them for other things besides intelligence though. They may want them to work their way into a critical supply chain, like government information technology or shipping. Or they may just need them to sabotage a vital infrastructure asset, like the electrical grid or the water supply."

"How about the daughter, Laurie Kim?" Ben asked. "She's got a Q clearance and access to sensitive nuclear technology in her job at Los Alamos."

"We're looking into it," Logan said. "Her parents visited her in New Mexico the week before the break-in. I ran into them with my family at a Pueblo celebration. They seemed friendly enough, but Laurie and her dad got into a heated argument at one point. I have no idea what the issue was."

"Why don't we take a look at the interview room and where you'll be monitoring the meeting?" Ben said.

The two men walked down a short corridor to an inner office, a sparsely furnished space with a table and chairs, and what Logan presumed was a one-way mirror.

"Am I going to be on the other side of that mirror?" he asked.

"Yes. We'll swing by there in a minute. Oh, and while I'm thinking of it, you should plan to get here early tomorrow, so you don't accidentally bump into Mrs. Kim at reception."

"Is 9 early enough?" Logan asked.

"That should be fine, Ben said. "When she comes in, Shelly, the agent that escorted you earlier, will bring Mrs. Kim here. I'm going to have Shelly seat her closer to the door than this arrangement. I find people psychologically are more comfortable the closer they are to the door.

"After she's here and settled in, I'll come in, introduce myself, and begin the interview."

"Will there be a way for me to get a question to you, real-time?" Logan asked.

"I'll be wearing an earpiece. We have some high-tech ones that don't look too obvious. Worse case, if that fails, you could write out your question and have Shelly bring it to me."

"That works," Logan said.

"Let me show you where you'll be." Ben guided Logan back out to the hallway. They walked thirty feet and then turned right down a narrow corridor. Midway there was a windowless metal door. Ben opened it and ushered Logan into a small room equipped with a comfortable chair, table, notetaking materials, and audio controls for the interview room.

Ben went back into the interview room to test the earpiece and the sound feeding into the observation room. "The sound quality is great," Ben said.

"Ditto in here," Logan said. "I can hear you loud and clear."

They shut off the audio equipment and turned out the lights. "You feel like grabbing a beer?" Ben asked.

Logan looked at his watch; it was already 6 p.m. "Sure, I have a feeling we're going to be busy tomorrow."

Chapter 43

Laurie and Ginny Kim were huddled next to each other on a sofa in the family room. Neither felt like eating breakfast, but Laurie made a pot of coffee because both were exhausted from lack of sleep and dealing with the tragedy of Dave Kim's murder. Laurie held her mother's hand as Ginny repeated the chronology of events from the night of the murder.

"Your father was preoccupied. He had been for months. You probably sensed it when we visited you."

"I did. I thought maybe it had something to do with the business. Everyone's stressed out because of the pandemic; it just goes on and on. Businesses are failing, people are losing their jobs, and so many people are dying." Laurie sighed in despair. Her father was her rock; he was always there for her.

"I can't forgive myself for the fight we had when you guys visited. Dad wasn't himself, and I made some sarcastic remark that caused him to blow up. I didn't get a chance to apologize. I never thought when we said goodbye that it would be the last time I would see him alive." She started to cry.

Laurie's mother wrapped her arms around her and squeezed her tight as she rocked back and forth. They remained that way for several minutes until Laurie was cried out. She got up to get a tissue and wiped her eyes. Returning to her seat, she faced her mom.

"I need to ask you a question," she said.

"What is it?" her mother asked, a quizzical look on her face.

Laurie hesitated as though considering her words. "Did

you and Dad have a connection to North Korea?"

"What?" The look of shock on Ginny Kim's face was genuine. "I don't know what you're talking about. Where did you ever get such an idea?"

"Billy Chu. Billy was in Albuquerque on business, and we got together in Santa Fe for dinner. He said the old picture I took of you and Dad that you found after the break-in was discovered in a North Korean intelligence officer's wallet in Mexico City."

Ginny Kim shuddered, covering her mouth with her hand to stifle a cry. "You're sure it's the same picture?" she asked.

"Billy had a copy of it. I remembered it immediately."

Her mother rose and tottered over to a table. She picked up a picture and squinted as she stared at it. She walked back over to where Laurie was seated and handed her the photo. "Is this the same one?" she asked.

Laurie knew even before she looked at it that it was the same picture. She took it from her mother's outstretched hand and scrutinized it for a full minute.

"Yes. It's the one. Do you remember if you made any copies of this picture?" Laurie asked.

"No. There was just one. It was in a family photo album. I think it's on that shelf," she said, pointing to a floor-to-ceiling built-in bookshelf. "It's that red leather album on the top shelf."

Laurie retrieved the album and returned to the sofa. She began thumbing through it, pausing to reminisce as the photos brought back old memories. Toward the back of the album, there were several graduation pictures. Turning the page, she noticed a blank spot in the middle.

"It looks like it might have been in here," she said.

Her mother handed her the picture, and Laurie slid it into place. It was a perfect fit.

"If there was only this one picture, Dad must have given it to the North Koreans," Laurie said.

"Or someone else gave it to them," Laurie added.

"Do you remember the last time you saw the picture in

the album?" Laurie asked.

"Not really. You know how it is. You put pictures in albums and then forget about them. I'll bet I haven't seen that picture in years."

The two women sat there in silence as they pondered the mystery. The abrupt ringing of the house phone broke the silence. Ginny got up to take the call. She listened for a moment before responding.

"That won't be a problem. I have an appointment at the FBI Field Office on Wilshire at 10. Would it be all right if I come by to pick it up at, say, 9:30?"

She and the caller spoke for another minute before hanging up. Ginny sat still, wearing a puzzled expression.

"Who was that?" Laurie asked.

"No one you know," her mother said. "He was a business partner of your father's, Eric Wong. Eric was a silent partner. He invested in your dad's company over the years but never got involved with the nuts and bolts of running the business.

"Anyway, he just said something strange. He said he has been holding a package your father gave him two weeks ago in a safe deposit box. He claims not to know what's in it, but his instructions from Dad were to hand it to me if something happened to him personally."

"That is weird," Laurie said.

"I'll pick it up on the way to my interview with the FBI," Ginny said.

Ginny glanced at her watch and jumped up. "I need to get moving. It's already 9 a.m.

"When I get back, let's sit down and figure out what arrangements we want to make for your father. I know he wanted to be cremated; perhaps we can plan a memorial service later after it's safe to get a larger group together."

Thirty minutes later, Ginny pulled up in front of Eric Wong's office building. She texted him when she was five minutes away, and he was waiting there for her so she wouldn't have to park her car and risk being late for her interview.

Eric handed her a sealed, two-inch-thick manila envelope and expressed his condolences for her loss.

"Dave was a good man," he said. "I will miss him very much."

They said their goodbyes, and Ginny pulled out into traffic. She was itching to find out what was in the envelope, but she didn't want to be late for her interview.

Ginny caught all the green lights up Wilshire Boulevard and reached the Federal Building in fifteen minutes. After she parked the car, she decided to see what was in the envelope, before going up.

She tore the flap at the top of the envelope and pulled out a thick, typed document. As she began to read, her heart began to race. She re-read the first line and lowered the manuscript to her lap, gripping the edges so tightly her knuckles turned white.

"If you are reading this, it means that I am no longer alive. This document is my attempt to set the record straight about how I came to spy for North Korea and why I decided to end my relationship with the NKIS."

Chapter 44

Logan had a dull hangover; he couldn't keep up with the younger guys the way he used to. He discovered he and Ben had their wartime service in common. Ben was a jarhead who served in Afghanistan when Logan was deployed to Forward Operating Base Spin Boldak outside Kandahar. That gave them much to reminisce over and a lot more time to drink beer.

Ben took him to a favorite Bureau haunt not far from the Federal Building; two hours and two pitchers of beer later, and they were still going strong. Ben was ready for round three, but Logan suggested they call it a night, given their morning schedule.

It was 10:15 the next day, and Ginny Kim had yet to make an appearance. Logan was restless: the observation room was not well ventilated and was getting stuffy.

There was a knock on the door, and Ben stuck his head in. "They're on the way up," he said. "Shelly went down to the parking lot to see if Mrs. Kim had trouble finding a parking spot and found her sitting in the car in a kind of daze. She was reading a document that seemed to upset her. She's in the ladies' room freshening up and will be here in a minute."

"Okay, thanks for the heads-up," Logan said. It was hard to know what was going on with Ginny Kim. Was it her husband's murder or something else causing her to react so emotionally?

A moment later, the door to the interview room opened, and Ginny walked in. She looked stressed out, not unexpected, given the double shock of the break-in at their home and her husband's untimely death. She was clutching an envelope in her hand; she paced back and forth, unsure where to sit.

There was a knock on the door, and Ben stepped in. Ben was dressed in the conservative style of FBI special agents, a dark two-piece suit, white shirt, and muted tie. He was carrying a couple of bottles of water and notetaking materials.

"Mrs. Kim? I'm Special Agent Ben Conroy. Please have a seat." He motioned to a chair about five feet away from the table, near the door.

"Would you like some water? Sorry I don't have a glass."

"Yes, please. The bottle's fine."

"I'd like to express my condolences for your loss, Mrs. Kim. I know this must be a tough time for you, and I appreciate your willingness to come in and meet with us. We find that the sooner we can speak with family members in these circumstances, the more accurate their recall is." Ben walked over to the table and sat down facing Ginny.

"I will be recording our conversation, Mrs. Kim. Do you have any questions for me before we begin?" he asked.

Ginny shook her head no. She was still clutching the envelope she had brought with her. She set it down on the floor to more easily open the bottle of water. The poor woman was sitting erect, listening intently to everything Ben said. The chair had a swivel base on it, and Ginny was absently rotating back and forth.

"I'd like to begin with the break-in at your home. I know you have been cooperating with the San Marino Police Department, and I have seen the transcripts of their interviews. Could you tell me in your own words what happened that night?"

Ginny set the water bottle down; she took a deep breath and folded her hands in her lap. "My husband and I went to bed at our usual time, 11 p.m. Sometime after that, around midnight, I guess, Dave thought he heard a noise, and he got up to investigate. But before he got to the bedroom door, we heard voices and then the sound of people fighting outside our bedroom. We were too frightened to go outside, and Dave was looking for his cell phone to call the police.

"The fighting stopped before he could make the call and we were surprised to hear the voice of our daughter's former boyfriend, Billy Chu, telling us it was all right to come out.

"Billy told us a story about a death threat against us that his father had learned about in his role as the South Korean ambassador in Mexico City. The embassy tried to relay that information to U.S. officials, but the ambassador decided to call his son, who lives in Los Angeles, because he thought it would be faster."

"Is Mr. Chu a frequent contact of your family?" Ben asked.

"At one time, when he and Laurie, that's our daughter, were dating. But it's been a few years since we've seen Billy."

"Who else was there that night, Mrs. Kim?" Ben asked.

"The fellow the police arrested, Sammy Perez, and one other person who got away before any of us could identify him."

"Is it your understanding that the police are continuing to search for this individual?" Ben asked.

"Yes, but the only person who saw him is Sammy Perez, and I understand he's not cooperating."

Logan was listening intently to Ginny Kim's responses. He was familiar with her testimony and the events of that evening but was distracted by the envelope propped up against her chair. As he watched her, he couldn't help but feel that she was emotionally teetering on the edge of a cliff.

Ben continued to probe for details Ginny may have left out, unintentionally or not. "At this point, we don't have a clear linkage between the events at your home and your husband's murder. We're certain Sammy Perez and his accomplice intended to do more harm than simply breaking into your home. We found weapons in Perez's possession; it's likely that if Billy Chu had not intervened, Perez would have assaulted you and your husband. The question, Mrs. Kim, is why?"

"I have been asking myself that same question all week,"

Ginny said. "And I couldn't make sense of any of it." She paused and took a deep breath. "Until two hours ago when I received this."

Ginny bent down to retrieve the envelope on the floor and visibly shuddered. She shook her head, wearing a look of despair, and handed it to Ben.

"My husband was spying for North Korea," she said.

Ben had begun thumbing through the document and looked up abruptly, visibly shocked.

"You just learned of this?" he asked.

Ginny explained the call from Eric Wong, the brief visit with him to retrieve the envelope, and her discovery of Dave's betrayal when she read the document in her car.

"I'd like to take a break to review these materials if that's all right with you, Mrs. Kim. There's a restaurant downstairs if you'd like to take an early lunch," he suggested. They agreed to reconvene in an hour.

Chapter 45

Logan and Ben were holed up in Ben's office, each silently poring over a copy of Dave Kim's document. Meanwhile, Shelly accompanied Ginny to the Federal Cafe in the east annex, with instructions not to return until 12:30.

Dave Kim's revelations read more like a confession than a history of his relationship with the NKIS. Logan was the first to finish reading and spoke up.

"It's going to take a hell of a lot of fact-checking to verify this story. But, if it's true, the NKIS recruited Dave Kim while he was a college student in Mexico City. And, according to this," Logan said, waving the document, "Ginny Kim was entirely in the dark about the relationship."

"It makes you wonder if he's saying that to protect her," Ben said.

"But if that was the case, why would she provide us with this information?" Logan asked. "It confirms that her husband was working for North Korea. She would have to realize that she risks being implicated by revealing her husband's relationship with the NKIS."

Ben exhaled in exasperation and tossed the document down on his desk. "At some point, depending upon how cooperative she is, we may want to polygraph Ginny. But for now, let's focus on Dave Kim and his revelations here."

"It's hard to believe this all began because a North Korean intelligence officer trolling Mexican universities spotted Dave Kim as someone with the potential to immigrate legally to the U.S., start a high-tech company, and develop access to Silicon Valley," Logan said.

"And I find it hard to believe that Kim, with South Korean ties, would be attracted to the North Koreans," Ben said.

"I don't think his ties to South Korea were all that strong," Logan said. "Remember, his mother married a Mexican, and as far as we know, there was never any relationship with the South Korean relatives."

"When the Kims had Laurie, they didn't even bother teaching her Korean language or much of anything about Korean culture," Logan said.

"The way this reads, Dave Kim did this strictly for the money," Ben said.

"That's what it looks like," Logan agreed. "They gave him seed money to get his business started, and some loose tasking on high-tech intellectual property theft."

"The fact that the North Koreans are behind this operation takes it to a different level," Ben said. "I've investigated economic crimes before, and what we used to call industrial espionage is responsible for the loss of more than a billion dollars a day to the U.S. economy."

"Dave Kim probably would have continued working for the North Koreans for years, but they got greedy," Logan said. "When they found out about Laurie Kim's job at Los Alamos and asked him to recruit her to spy, he drew a line."

"According to him, over the last two years, they continued to pressure him for access to his daughter, but each time they did, he declined. Then, they began to threaten him, and he broke off contact," Ben said.

"Nobody says 'no' to the supreme leader," Logan said. "You can bet this initiative was his doing. He's desperate to get a nuke capable of reaching the U.S. If he felt Kim had access to someone who could provide this kind of information and was refusing to cooperate, he would view it as a betrayal, punishable by death."

"What do you make of the photo the North Koreans had of the Kims?" Ben asked.

"There's a lot of operational handling details we don't know about, and probably never will," Logan said. "If Kim was being met personally, he was probably tasked to provide them a photo in the event his handler couldn't meet him. The picture would be the new handler's bona fides when he and Kim met for the first time."

There was a rap on the door, and Shelly stuck her head in. "Mrs. Kim's ready whenever you are."

"Thanks, Shelly. I'll be there in a minute," Ben said.

"Do you have any specific questions for Mrs. Kim?" Ben asked.

"Based on this information, we have a better handle on why the North Koreans were behind Dave Kim's murder," Logan said. "We don't know if Roe Min-Woo was his handler, or if he was here to make sure Kim got what he deserved. He was here in alias, and he's going to be back in Mexico in an official capacity in May."

"What?" Ben asked.

"That's right," Logan said, nodding. "Roe Min-Woo has just been named the North Korean trade representative to Mexico. The Mexicans and North Koreans have been negotiating this trade office deal for months."

Ben stared at the ceiling in disbelief. "Are you telling me this lowlife is going to have diplomatic immunity in Mexico?" Ben asked.

"It looks like a sure thing," Logan said. "Our people have been tracking his status because it's a big step for Mexico to agree to this bilateral trade deal. Trade is one thing, but there's no doubt the NKIS will use the trade office as a platform to launch covert operations in the region. And the U.S. will be their prime target."

"We better get going," Ben said. "We have a lot of ground to cover."

Ben left first to make sure that Ginny was still in the interview room, and then Shelly escorted Logan to the control room.

Over the next three hours, Ben meticulously went through Dave Kim's document with Ginny. For the most part, she was cooperative but noncommittal. She claimed to be totally in the dark regarding her husband's revelations.

Logan interjected several follow-up questions throughout the interview, based upon his knowledge of NKIS modus operandi; however, Ginny Kim remained steadfast in her denial of any knowledge about her husband's clandestine relationship with the NKIS.

By 4 p.m., it was apparent that they weren't getting anywhere. Ben had gradually ratcheted up the tension in the room, implying that Ginny must have suspected something about her husband's activities after all these years. But Ginny remained unruffled, sticking to the story that her first and only insight into her husband's secret life was when she read about it that morning.

"I think that'll be all for today, Mrs. Kim. I appreciate your time, and I apologize for how long it took to get through this; your husband's document threw a monkey wrench into our schedule."

Ben pulled a name card out of his coat pocket and handed it to her. "Please call me if anything comes up that you feel might impact our investigation."

After Shelly escorted Ginny out of the office, Logan and Ben huddled for a few minutes to wrap up loose ends. The revelation that Dave Kim had butted heads with the NKIS over their desire to recruit Laurie Kim provided the most logical explanation for his murder.

Roe Min-Woo was implicated in Kim's murder despite the fact he fled the U.S. after the botched break-in at the Kim residence and was likely already back in Pyongyang at the time of the attack days later.

"Thanks for letting me participate behind the scenes," Logan said. "I sure didn't see that coming, though."

"That makes two of us," Ben said. "Let's stay in touch. You're always welcome in LA."

Chapter 46

While he was in Los Angeles, Logan had one other matter to tend to; he planned to meet with Billy Chu. Headquarters was on board with the idea; the DO had done background checks on Billy and felt that he would be a useful contact as the CI investigation at Los Alamos launched into high gear.

The Director for Operations advised his counterpart at the FBI that he wanted Logan to liaise with Billy. The FBI official agreed, asking only to be kept apprised of any new developments that could impact their criminal investigation into Dave Kim's murder and the joint CI investigation into North Korea's efforts to steal sensitive information from Los Alamos.

Headquarters also reached out to the NIS for their agreement to avoid any surprises. Realistically, Billy Chu was not a recruitment target, although he might be an excellent liaison-plus contact, someone who might go beyond his brief in providing useful off-the-record intelligence information.

Langley stipulated that the meeting with Billy be low-key. That's why Logan was on his way to Gunther Moore's tae kwon do dojang in Koreatown. When he'd reached out to the NIS officer, Billy suggested they work out together at the dojo and then find a quiet coffeehouse to talk.

Billy was already at Moore's dojo when Logan got there at 7 a.m. The former gunny sergeant was an early riser, and he had several clients who liked to come in before work to spar.

"Hey, Logan. How've you been?" Billy asked.

"Pretty good. I was in town on business and thought I'd look you up. I gather you got the okay from Seoul?"

"Yeah, we're good. I thought that's where you might be coming from," Billy said, referencing Logan's CIA affiliation.

"Let me show you where the locker room is," Billy said, leading him over to the entrance to the men's changing room. "Gunther has a dobok you can borrow," he said, pulling the white, two-piece tae kwon do uniform out of a closet. "He wasn't sure what color belt to give you," Billy said with a sly grin.

"Black," Logan said. "I mostly used Krav Maga when I was in the SEALS, but I'm a black belt in tae kwon do."

"Krav Maga?" Billy asked.

"It's a style of street fighting developed over seventy years ago for the Israeli Army. I like it because it's versatile. It incorporates some of the best techniques from several martial arts disciplines.

"Do you work out here often?" Logan asked.

"At least once a week," Billy said. "I met Gunther when I was a kid living in Kuala Lumpur. His son and I were in the same class, and Gunther taught tae kwon do after school, so I signed up. I kept it up over the years, and when I moved to LA, I reconnected with the family."

When Logan was dressed, they went into the dojo, where Gunther and several others were warming up.

"Hey, guys, this is Logan. He's visiting for a couple of days and was looking for a workout," Billy said.

"You came to the right place," Gunther said. "Welcome."

Over the next half-hour Gunther put them through a grueling warm-up incorporating stretching, planking, pull-ups, inverted sit-ups, leg lifts, and jumping rope. They took a two-minute water break and then paired off to spar. Logan was a street fighter, while Billy was more accustomed to the controlled competitive environment found at TKD tournaments.

By the time they finished thirty minutes later, they called it a draw. Both Billy and Logan scored points with powerful kicks and spinning moves that highlighted their skills. During the last ten minutes they were sparring, the others gathered around to watch the two men compete.

Later, after they'd showered and dressed, Billy suggested a coffee shop they could walk to a couple of blocks away. One lone customer wearing earbuds was working at his computer in a corner booth.

The aroma of freshly brewed coffee made Logan's mouth water. There was a selection of homemade pastries and muffins and a bowl of fresh fruit on the counter. After they had their order, they selected a booth with some privacy and sat down.

"I wanted to talk to you about North Korea," Logan said, before taking a bite out of his muffin. "I've been reading Mexico City's reporting and what the NIS has passed us. I've also been in touch with the Bureau, and I've seen the police reports of the break-in at Dave and Ginny Kim's home.

"Yesterday, I back-benched an FBI agent interviewing Ginny Kim. She didn't know I was there; I stayed in the control room. She dropped a bombshell on us." Logan shared Dave Kim's revelation that he was a North Korean agent from the time he left Mexico City up until recently.

Billy's jaw dropped; he was about to take a sip of coffee, but he set the cup back down on the table, visibly shaken by Logan's account of the interview.

"No way," he said. "Dave Kim was working for the North Koreans?"

"According to Dave's own admission, it began pretty much as a business deal. The North Koreans gave him start-up money for his business when he immigrated to the States in exchange for high-tech proprietary business intelligence.

"Years later, the NKIS found out about Laurie's job at Los Alamos and started pressuring Dave to bring her on board so they could penetrate the lab. When Dave resisted, the NKIS went after him."

"Don't I know it," Billy said ruefully. "And you know, if you saw the police reports, that I was at their house during the break-in. I didn't realize that Roe Min-Woo was there until Laurie told me her mother found their missing picture on the floor after Roe escaped."

"What do you make of the gangbanger you did a number on?"

"Sammy Perez? I think he's a hired gun the North Koreans brought on board just to kill Dave. Roe may be NKIS, but he doesn't come across as a killer."

"Why would the NKIS risk exposing him, given what's at stake? He's just been named the head of a new trade office in Mexico. If he were implicated in a murder, it could derail the trade agreement and send Mexico-North Korea diplomatic relations into a tailspin."

"I know, it doesn't make sense. What about Ginny and Laurie?" Billy asked. "Do you think they're in danger?"

"If you can believe Dave Kim's confession, it doesn't make any sense for the NKIS to go after them. The only reason they might have killed Ginny before you showed up was that she would have been a witness to the murder. They didn't want to take a chance she could identify Roe."

"What's your focus now?" Billy asked.

"We're concerned about the counterintelligence threat at the lab," Logan said. "Dave Kim's murder is proof the NKIS is dead-set on penetrating the lab. We have an active counterintelligence investigation underway and a couple of prime suspects."

Billy nodded his understanding. "Let me know if we can do anything for you," he said. "Our two services have a good relationship."

Chapter 47

Roe Min-Woo was apartment hunting in Mexico City. He and his assistant, Park Joon-Ki, who was also an NKIS operative under Ministry of Economic Relations cover, would be sharing living quarters. That was because the supreme leader enforced the same policy his grandfather instituted regarding diplomatic postings. No families were allowed to accompany North Korean diplomats serving abroad. The rationale for this was simple; the families remaining behind in North Korea were no more than hostages, an incentive to deter diplomats from defecting.

The NKIS took care of its people assigned abroad. With their combined housing allowance, Roe and Park could afford decent quarters; it wouldn't be in classy Zona Rosa, but then again, it wouldn't be in crime-ridden Morelos either. They found a modest two-bedroom apartment on Avenida Balderas, close to the city center, for $500 U.S. a month.

The lodgings came with modest furnishings. The two men didn't bring much with them from home, only clothes and a few personal effects. The administrative officer at the embassy negotiated the lease with the landlord for the NKIS operatives, and they were able to move in two days later.

Roe felt fortunate to be in Mexico; the fiasco in Los Angeles could have doomed his promising career. The bigwigs in Bureau 35 met with him twice after his return from LA to grill him on the failed operation. At one point, he was convinced the chief was going to cancel his assignment and dispatch him to a camp in the northeast, where he would remain for the rest of his days. But instead, here he was, breaking new ground in North Korea-Mexico economic relations, but better still, managing North Korea's intelligence operations in Mexico.

He was working out of the embassy for now; the ambassador had assigned him a modest office with a barely navigable anteroom for Park. It smelled musty and there was a thin layer of dust on every surface. It would do until they earned the respect of their bosses in Pyongyang, who, in time, would reward their efforts with better accommodations, or better yet, commercial office space where they could escape the watchful eye of the ambassador.

Roe and Park organized their spartan room in the embassy; most recently, it served as storage space for the ambassador's loyalty gifts to the supreme leader. Roe peeked inside a couple of cartons; boxes of Montecristo # 2 Cuban cigars selling for $450 per box of twenty-five, and Gran Patron Platinum Silver Tequila bottles going for $250 U.S. each at El Liquor Store on Orizaba.

After they were organized, Roe busied himself with two issues gnawing at him; figuring out who betrayed him in his mission to do away with Dave and Ginny Kim, and improving his son Jason's intelligence collection efforts.

Where to start? The South Koreans had it out for him ever since he defected to the North. He knew when he crossed over the border into North Korea almost thirty years ago, there could be no return. His one regret was the loss of Ha-Yoon and seeing Jason grow up. Had he known Ha-Yoon was pregnant with their son when he last saw her in Toronto, he might never have defected. Instead, he'd be going to Tim Horton's, spending loonies, and peppering his speech with "eh" every other sentence.

Maybe the Mexicans were responsible for the security breach. At one time, they were tight with the Americans, sharing intelligence in the war on drugs, but the narco-traffickers were influential in Mexico, infiltrating the highest levels of government. A mid-level Mexican police contact who talked to him over copious amounts of alcohol said the current Mexican president was doing his best to gut security cooperation between Mexico and the United States.

He concluded it was unlikely the Americans knew

anything about the attempted Kim hit until Dave Kim called 911. Then it dawned on him. What if the South Koreans were talking to the Mexicans? He racked his brain. There may have been some indiscretions on his part during previous trips to Mexico City. He recalled one raucous outing when he'd consumed too much alcohol and passed out in the arms of a Mexican prostitute. When he awoke alone in the morning with a hangover that felt like a pile driver in his brain, he worried about what he might have done or said.

The NKIS operative decided to put his ruminations aside temporarily. He would have to be more discreet from now on, especially since he was in Mexico full-time. He was likely to come under greater scrutiny from the National Intelligence Center and the hostile foreign intelligence agencies with a presence in Mexico. They would be trying their best to undermine or even recruit him.

Roe turned on the computer and logged into his secure account. There was a new message from Jason. It looked as though the young nuclear engineer had put some effort into answering the questions Roe gave him before his trip to California. His information about Technical Area-55 would get the supreme leader's attention. Los Alamos was the only national laboratory in the U.S. currently producing plutonium pits used as the first stage of a two-stage process to ignite a thermonuclear weapon.

As he read through Jason's report, Roe wondered if his son's heart was in the right place. There was a dutiful, almost passive tone to the information. However, Jason did go beyond the requirements his father gave him, including full bios on several more of the lab's scientists.

As Roe scanned the bios, one name caught his attention—Laurie Kim. She must be Dave and Ginny Kim's daughter, the scientist his NKIS predecessors had tasked Dave Kim to recruit as a penetration of the lab.

And then it hit him. At their meeting in Albuquerque, Jason mentioned that he had a new girlfriend named Laurie, whose family was South Korean. He hadn't put two and two together at the time, but Jason's girlfriend was Dave and Ginny Kim's daughter.

Although his hand hadn't pulled the trigger, he was, in part, responsible for Dave Kim's murder. If Jason ever learned of his role in the operation, it would destroy their relationship. Not only would Jason's trust in him be irrevocably damaged, but his son would at the same time likely sever his secret ties to North Korea.

Chapter 48

Logan was wrapping up a briefing on his trip to Los Angeles for Martina and Peter. Dave Kim's posthumous revelation that he was a long-time spy for North Korea set off shock waves amongst security and intelligence officials from Los Angeles to Washington, D.C., not to mention many Fortune 500 companies in corporate America.

The Bureau and Intelligence Community agencies were ramping up internal investigations that would result in damage assessments outlining how bad this national security violation was likely to be. Although Kim was a private citizen working mainly in the private sector, he had, over time, consulted on many state and federal information technology projects.

State and federal agencies and private companies would spend the next weeks and months searching their records for any signs of a cyber breach. Employees would fritter away untold numbers of hours poring through files and digital records to better understand Dave Kim's perfidy.

"I'm always shocked when something like this happens," Martina said. "Dave Kim looked like he had it all. Lovely family, professionally respected and well-liked, successful in his business. Why would someone like that commit espionage?" she asked.

"We don't have enough information now to know how Dave Kim was spying or what information he provided his handlers. We may never know if he had an ulterior motive or if, as he said in the beginning, it was about the money," Logan said.

"You're right; we may never know," Peter said. "If he was spying for North Korea for thirty years, that's a long time."

"I doubt he was actively engaged in espionage for thirty years," Logan said. "But you never know. If this is all true, the most likely scenario is that he was a sleeper agent, activated at some point when the NKIS needed something from him.

"It's not uncommon in operations involving illegals for the NKIS to leave them alone for decades while building their cover for status. These people blend into the woodwork and make every effort to keep a low profile; they prefer not to stand out. Illegals want to be 'the family next door.' And Kim may not even fit the traditional definition of an illegal, given his uncertain past."

"Well, I guess that wraps up our investigation into Ginny and Laurie Kim," Martina said.

"Whoa, not so fast," Logan said. "Dave Kim was a self-professed spy for North Korea. Are you going to take his word that he was the only one in on this?"

Martina looked flustered. "What do you mean?"

"I think it's still an open question as to Ginny and Laurie's involvement with the NKIS. There's so much we don't know. Don't you find it hard to believe Ginny Kim lived with this man for over thirty years and didn't have a clue he was spying for North Korea? I'm not saying it's impossible; there are many espionage cases where the spouse was clueless about the other's spying activities. I just think we need to keep all options in play," Logan said.

"Ginny was completely credible during her interview. She was grieving the loss of her husband and seemed genuinely taken aback by his confession. On the other hand, she's had thirty years to perfect her story."

"So what are you saying?" Martina asked. "It sounds like you're not sure."

"I just think we need to be objective. The FBI is willing to keep an eye on her for the time being. If they develop additional collateral, we may want to consider putting her on the box."

"Polygraph?" Peter asked.

"Yes," Logan said. "It's not perfect, but if you have an experienced polygrapher conducting the test, he can develop additional information."

"What do you think we should do about Laurie?" Martina asked.

"She's still in LA, right?" Logan asked.

"Yes, she took a week of bereavement leave. HR talked to Laurie yesterday and told her to take as long as she needs. She was thinking about bringing her mom back with her to stay for a while."

"What about Ginny's job? Isn't she a math teacher?" Peter asked.

"She's a math professor at UCLA," Logan said. "When she and her husband were here a couple of weeks ago, Dave told me all of her classes are virtual because of COVID. So, she can work from anywhere.

"If she does come here, we should think about asking the Bureau to beef up their coverage on Laurie's apartment. We might want to consider an audio op," Logan said. "We could pick up something if Laurie and her mom get careless talking in the apartment. I don't think Laurie knows we're looking at her."

"Doesn't Laurie have a roommate?" Peter asked.

"Yes," Martina said. "If I remember correctly, the roommate has been working remotely from home and decided to visit her sister in Florida for a month. I think she left last week."

"That'll make it easier to get in and bug Laurie's apartment if we decide to go that route," Logan said. "You know the FISA warrants don't come into play because Laurie and her mom are U.S. citizens," Logan reminded them. "The Bureau already has surveillance warrants in place for both Laurie and her mom. Say the word, and I'll give Anthony a call. Depending on Paul's availability, we could probably get it done in the next couple of days before Laurie returns."

"Who's Paul?" Martina asked.

"That's Anthony's tech. He's the one that installed the bug in Jason Lee's place."

"Right, I forgot. Go ahead and give him a call," Martina said. "I'm still not convinced Laurie is involved in this, but I also don't know her that well. As for the mom, I feel totally in the dark; we don't know a lot about her, but as you said, if she and Laurie spend a lot of time talking in the apartment, we may learn something useful."

When Logan got back to his office, he called Anthony and relayed Martina's request to install an audio bug in Laurie's apartment.

"We can do that tomorrow," Anthony said. "Paul has been playing with a new audio surveillance program that allows you to activate the target's mobile phone microphone remotely. It has to have an iPhone operating system, though. The nice thing about it is you don't have to access the phone physically. You can install the software remotely."

"She has an iPhone," Logan said. "I saw Laurie using it when I ran into her a couple of weeks ago at a Pueblo festival."

"Okay, work directly with Paul. I'll let him know you'll be in touch."

"Do you think we need to do a hardwire tap too as a backup, just in case something happens with the phone?"

"It's a little more complicated. What do you know about Laurie's living situation?" Anthony asked.

"She's out of town for a few more days, and her roommate is in Florida for a month. Our HR people said Laurie plans to have her mom stay with her for a few weeks, so she's not alone."

"I'm okay with it; we've already got the warrants in place. Work it out with Paul; I'd like you to go with him if you can. I'm going to be out of town for a few days, but you can reach me on my cell if you need me."

Chapter 49

Jason Lee walked in a daze from Norman Chen's office to his lab. His boss had just dropped a bombshell on him. Los Alamos and the Savannah River National Laboratory were moving forward with a multi-year plan to increase plutonium pit production to eighty pits a year, and he was being tapped to participate in that effort.

Years before, the National Nuclear Security Administration delayed implementing a federal mandate to increase Los Alamos' pit production to thirty pits a year because of ecological concerns. Late last year, they concluded that a 2008 Environmental Impact Statement was sufficient to resume production and that no further environmental studies were necessary.

"Jason, I know you were just getting going with your study of alternate fuels for space power generators," his boss had said. "But with the renovated Chemistry and Metallurgy Research Replacement Facility opening by the end of the year, your background will be invaluable."

"I don't know what to say," Jason said. His head was reeling as he thought about the implications of this change in focus. The first thing that came to mind was the celebration that would take place in Pyongyang when the NKIS learned he would be directly involved in the U.S. nuclear weapons program.

"I've taken the liberty of raising this with the facility director. When he saw your resume, he was thrilled to be getting you. We have had Canadian scientists at the lab in the past. Given our unique relationship with Canada, your clearance should be more than satisfactory," Chen said.

"We'll run this up the flagpole with HR and Security,

but I'm reasonably sure you can plan on moving over there by next week. What do you say?"

Part of him wanted to push back. Working on nuclear weapons would undoubtedly complicate his life. On the other hand, the professional challenge was unique. He would be working at one of only two laboratories in the U.S., indeed, the world, dedicated to maintaining the health and longevity of the U.S. nuclear stockpile. How could he say no?

"Thanks for considering me, Norm. I was just starting to feel at home here, but it's a fantastic opportunity. Of course, it's a yes."

Later that evening, after he got home from work, Jason fired up his laptop and sent a message via the secure messaging application to his father.

"It looks like your hard work is about to pay off. I've just been reassigned to the Chemistry and Metallurgy Research Replacement Facility at Los Alamos. I'll be working with a team responsible for producing replacement plutonium pits for the U.S. nuclear stockpile. The assignment isn't official until the Human Resources and Security people give it their blessing. Assuming they do, I could start as early as next week."

The newest member of the plutonium pit production team felt mixed emotions as he hit the send button. It would undoubtedly be a game-changer if he began sending the NKIS highly classified information about the nuclear stockpile. He needed to find out what level of access he would have in this new position. For now, he was just giving the NKIS a heads-up.

Jason checked the time; it was 6 p.m. Pyongyang was fifteen hours ahead of Los Alamos time, so his father would probably just be getting into work. Then he remembered that the new North Korean Trade Office in Mexico City was supposed to open by the end of April. Maybe his dad had already relocated; he hadn't heard from him in a couple of weeks.

He was about to shut down his computer and make

dinner when a new message popped up; it was from his father.

> *"Thank you for your email. Congratulations. That is excellent news indeed. Our people will be thrilled with your new responsibilities. You may even get a message from the Supreme Leader.*
>
> *"I relocated to Mexico City last week. My assistant and I have already found a place to live, and we are getting our workspace organized. Before that, I was on a foreign business trip for several days and am only now catching up on my correspondence. I look forward to receiving an update from you soon."*

Jason logged off the computer and began making dinner. He was already wondering how HR and Security would receive the news about his proposed transfer. He tried his best to keep a low profile and had no reason to believe that anyone suspected him of being anything other than a new lab employee with a bright future ahead of him.

Early the following day, Logan, Peter, and Martina were huddled in Martina's office reviewing copies of the email exchange between Jason and his father, sent over by secure email, courtesy of Anthony Brown.

"I don't see how we can let him take that position," Martina argued. "He has the potential to do severe damage to our national security."

"It's a double-edged sword," Logan said. "If we disapprove his transfer, red flags will go up everywhere. His boss will question the decision, and the North Koreans may suspect he's been compromised since he's already told them it's up to Security to approve the transfer. If we support the transfer, we're putting ourselves at greater risk.

"I've got an idea," Logan said. "When we did the technical installation on Jason's computer, Paul told me he was working on a new software capability where he could intercept a transmitted message before it reached its intended destination, read it, and then release it. It would be perfect for this kind of situation."

"Wait a minute," Peter said. "You're telling me a hacker can pull a transmitted email off the Internet after it's released, read it, and then put it back out there?"

"Yep, according to Paul," Logan said.

"How would you envision using that scenario?" Martina asked.

"We would be able to intercept any email containing information that crosses the line. Something we are not prepared to let the North Koreans see. My sense from what we've seen from Jason so far is that he's not that gung-ho about spying for the NKIS. He hasn't provided them with anything that damaging, but I'll bet his father will start pressuring him for more. And when he does, we need to be ready to take him down."

Chapter 50

Laurie Kim exited I-210 near East Etiwanda Creek, merging onto I-15 north toward Barstow. She and her mother were on their way back to Los Alamos in Ginny's car. Ginny had suggested they drive rather than fly as a way to unwind following a nerve-wracking week.

The Los Angeles Coroner's Office released Dave's body to them two days ago, and Ginny arranged for him to be cremated at James Brothers Mortuary in Pasadena. There was no religious service. Given the violent circumstances surrounding his death, Ginny didn't have the strength to endure more than a simple funeral with her and Laurie in attendance. Perhaps in six months, she would invite Dave's friends and colleagues to a memorial service in his honor.

Ginny tucked the decorative rosewood cremation urn into a back corner in her closet to deal with later. Unlike one of her university colleagues, Ramona, whose husband's remains were on display atop the fireplace mantle, Ginny preferred not to be reminded every day of Dave's death. Ginny was embarrassed by Ramona's tendency to address her husband in passing and invite visitors to greet the deceased with a wave and a "hi" as they walked through the living room.

"Are you in a hurry to get back to work, sweetie?" Ginny asked.

"Not really. We could drive through and be there in twelve hours, but what's the point? I'm in no big rush. I told my boss I was going to take a week off. Do you feel like visiting some of the scenic places along the way? Maybe it will take our minds off of ..." Laurie's voice drifted off.

"Dad?" Ginny asked.

"Yeah." Laurie was quiet for a minute.

"Let's drive through the Mojave National Preserve . Why don't you search day trips and see what comes up?" Laurie suggested.

Ginny was silent for a moment as she searched the National Park Service website. "Here's a one-hour detour that looks like fun. We can get off of I-15 in Baker and get back on somewhere around Primm, Nevada." She listed the highlights of the drive from the website—cinder cones, lava flows, the Kelso Dunes, and the Providence Mountains.

Later as they gained elevation near Cima, Arizona, both were struck by the size of the Joshua trees, spiny desert plants named after the eponymous Old Testament prophet by Mormon settlers who began inhabiting the area in the mid-1800s.

Laurie and Ginny decided to overnight in Flagstaff. They called ahead and found a room at the Hotel Little America, a delightful residence located on a 500-acre tract of land covered in Ponderosa pine trees. Before dinner, they ordered a bottle of wine from room service and, bundled up in fleeces to ward off the chill, sat on the deck outside their room overlooking the emerald-green forest.

A family with three small children played at the nearby playground; the children giggled and ran along the edge of the woods when the mother called them to supper. After they left, the only sound came from two great horned owls trading staccato hoots from the heights of distant lofty pines.

Ginny was the first to break the silence.

"He did it to protect me," she said as she poured herself another glass of wine.

"Who did what?" Laurie asked, a confused look on her face.

"Your father." Ginny sighed heavily and shook her head.

Laurie turned to face her mother head-on. For some reason, a feeling of anxiety was building in her chest. She dreaded what her mother was about to say, but she needed to know.

"What did he do, Mom?"

Ginny's lips were pursed; a bitter shadow came over her face as she stared off into the distance. She seemed reluctant to speak, but then she exhaled forcefully and began to talk.

"When your father and I were students in Mexico City, we met and became friends with Eric Wong."

"Wait. That's the same guy you went to see the other day? The one who gave you Dad's envelope?"

"Yes."

"I thought you said he was a silent partner in the business. I got the impression he was someone Dad met after you immigrated to the U.S."

"No. Eric's the one who convinced us we should try to get U.S. citizenship. With your father's computer background and my Ph.D. in math, we stood a good chance of getting green cards.

"Eric was always throwing money around, and he and your father began talking about going into business together. After we got to Los Angeles, your father and I went through a difficult period. He was busy getting his business up and running and was never home. Eric was still living in Mexico, but he frequently traveled to LA."

Ginny took a long sip of wine and looked at Laurie, her eyes begging forgiveness. "I was lonely. We hadn't made any friends yet, and Eric was the only person I knew. We became lovers. As we became close, I discovered that he was connected to North Korea."

Laurie gasped, her hand covering her mouth as Ginny shook her head ever so slightly. Laurie didn't trust herself to speak but finally asked, "What kind of connection?"

"He was a North Korean agent, sent to Mexico to recruit people who would immigrate to the U.S." Her mother spat the words out with venom. "He didn't come right out and say it when we first met; it was only after we became lovers that he confided in me.

"By then, Eric had poured hundreds of thousands of dollars into the business; your father was in over his head. Eric eventually told him about the North Korean connection, and he was forced to cooperate or lose everything.

"Eventually, Dave came around to Eric's way of thinking and began providing sensitive information to North Korea."

"Did Dad know about your affair?" Laurie asked.

"I never told him," Ginny said. "And he never said anything to me. But I feel in my heart that he knew."

"How would he know?"

Ginny turned away, and her lips trembled as she looked back into her daughter's eyes.

"After you were born, he realized that you didn't look anything like him."

Laurie was confused. "What...?"

"You looked just like his silent partner. Eric Wong is your real father."

Laurie emitted a moan that could have come from a wounded animal as she stared at her mother in horror. She felt as though her entire life had been a lie because her real father was a secret agent of the North Korean Intelligence Service. Everything she had worked for was at risk.

Chapter 51

Logan and Zahir dropped Cooper off at the sports field behind Chamisa Elementary School and parked the car. They strolled over to the home team sidelines, where the boy's mini lacrosse team was doing warmup drills, and set up their folding chairs next to a group of parents they knew from other school activities.

Cooper had expressed interest in playing lacrosse after seeing a game on TV, and his enthusiasm had not wavered since the first day of practice. He was on the mini lacrosse travel team and had already started a couple of games playing attack.

The Alexanders had always excelled at sports. Several professional football teams scouted Logan out of college, and although he wasn't Cooper's biological father, they shared the same gene pool. Logan's brother, Cooper, was a standout high school football player before enlisting in the Army as a Ranger.

Despite his best intentions to stay focused on Cooper's game, Logan's mind drifted to the Los Alamos counterintelligence investigation. Never in his wildest dreams did he imagine such a complex, all-consuming operation landing in his lap. There were times he felt he was juggling way too many balls at once, and the slightest misstep could bring them all tumbling down.

At Los Alamos, Jason Lee had transferred to the Chemistry and Metallurgy Replacement Facility, prompting real-time monitoring of his personal email account. Laurie and Ginny Kim were back from Los Angeles, but audio transcripts of their conversations revealed little except for an inexplicable level of tension between the two women. It was almost as though they were in the middle of a major blow-up.

The mystery behind Dave Kim's confession to espionage for North Korea was going nowhere at present. Did Ginny Kim have direct knowledge of his involvement with North Korea? Who recruited him, and even more importantly, who was handling him all those years?

And Roe Min-Woo was spotted on the diplomatic circuit in Mexico City. Ambassador Chu's man from the NIS reported that Roe kept a low profile, made the rounds amongst relevant Mexican officials, and liaised with diplomats from China, Russia, Cuba, Laos, and Vietnam.

"Ouch," Logan said, pretending to be hurt. Zahir had just punched him in the arm. "What was that for?"

"I've been trying to get your attention. You said you were going to leave work at the office," she whispered fiercely. "Cooper just scored a goal, and you didn't even notice."

Logan wore a sheepish grin. "Sorry. A lot's happening, and I feel I have to stay on top of it all."

After the game, they took Cooper out for pizza. From there, Cooper and Zahir went to a paintball birthday party for one of Cooper's classmates. While they were away, Logan planned to take his dog for a run in White Rock Canyon.

It was perfect running weather. When Logan reached the trailhead, he removed Trooper's leash and let him run free. He loped ahead, sniffing the profusion of wildflowers. Early prickly pear cactus blooms were out, and blue wildflowers and lilies wove an artist's tapestry over the slopes leading to the canyon floor.

As he jogged down the trail, Logan's thoughts turned to the law enforcement investigation into the break-in at Dave and Ginny Kim's home. Sammy Perez was still being held at the Los Angeles County Men's Central Jail. He'd had a hearing at the Central Arraignment Court at which the judge denied his request for bail.

In yet another stroke of bad luck for Sammy, he got into a fight with an inmate, a rival gangbanger, whose buddies smuggled in a switchblade for him, which he used to carve up the misshapen Filipino's already disfigured face.

Things were not going well for Tony Perez either. He was arrested by the Los Angeles County Sheriff's office as a prime suspect in the murders of Dave Kim and his co-worker. A combination of diligent detective work and a bit of luck had led them to Perez.

In the days following the murders, detectives visited every commercial establishment on Pershing Square facing the parking garage entrance where Dave Kim and his associate were murdered. One, a Wells Fargo Bank ATM, was equipped with security cameras that captured the parking garage entrance.

There was very little foot traffic in and out of the parking garage on the night of the murders, and they immediately became suspicious of Perez. However, he had not been positively identified at that point.

During the autopsy of Dave Kim's corpse, a bullet was retrieved from his body. Forensics analysis linked the round to a weapon believed to have been used in a Los Angeles gang murder several years earlier in which the Asian Hoods were implicated.

It took weeks of detective work, but the police eventually pulled every record they had on the Asian Hoods, comparing individual gang members' mug shots with the footage from the bank ATM. They were able to positively ID Tony Perez as the man departing the parking garage at the time of Dave Kim's murder. It wasn't an open-and-shut case because much of the evidence was circumstantial. That said, Tony didn't have a credible alibi for being in the garage on the evening of Kim's murder. LAPD had its work cut out for them if their murder charge was going to stick.

Logan heard Trooper barking up ahead. He rounded a bend and spotted Laurie and Ginny Kim standing by the edge of the trail forty yards away. They were in the midst of a heated discussion and had not yet seen him. Suddenly Laurie slapped her mother, who stepped back to ward off the blow. She lost her footing and fell over backward, sliding several feet before crashing into a boulder with a sickening thud.

Trooper slid down the incline and circled the inert form. The German shepherd poked his nose into Ginny's face, whimpering, but she was unresponsive. Laurie clambered down the slope to assist her unresponsive mother.

"Mom, I didn't mean it. I'm sorry," she wailed.

She looked at Logan, despair written across her features. "I didn't mean it," she whispered.

Logan reached the stricken woman. He had seen his share of war injuries in Afghanistan, and he knew the moment he examined Ginny Kim that she had likely suffered a traumatic injury. Logan was careful not to move her as he searched for a pulse. It was weak.

"Call 911," he said to Laurie.

She tried frantically punching in the numbers over and over, but cellular service was weak. She raced to higher ground and was finally able to reach 911. Laurie described the emergency to the dispatcher, and within twenty minutes, EMTs from Los Alamos were on the scene. They stabilized Ginny, but decided to call in a helicopter to transport her to a trauma unit in Albuquerque because of the severity of her injury. Ginny remained unconscious and her pulse was irregular.

When the helicopter arrived, Laurie hopped aboard to accompany her mother for the short flight to the city. She held her hand as they lifted off. Laurie was not a particularly religious person, but she found herself praying to God that her mother would survive.

Chapter 52

Roe Min-Woo's communications with Bureau 35 were entering a delicate phase on two fronts. A faction within the unit supported Eric Wong, a longtime NKIS illegal working in Los Angeles. Roe discovered that Wong first met the Kims in Mexico City and recruited them to immigrate to the U.S. to engage in intellectual property procurement.

Over time, Bureau 35 demanded more from Wong and the Kims, especially after Laurie Kim started working at Los Alamos. An increasingly militant element within Bureau 35 was urging leadership to engage in sabotage or disruption operations at U.S. national labs; there were even those who would detonate a nuclear device on U.S. soil if they could manage it.

Roe's boss belonged to this latter clique. And, although Roe himself was ambivalent about visiting this kind of horror on the Americans, he felt obliged to support his boss's position lest he fall out of favor. Eric Wong had lost his clout; with Dave and Ginny Kim out of the picture, Eric would have to reinvent himself, maybe even lie low for a while.

That left Jason as the only one with the kind of access to realize the supreme leader's goal of dealing a nuclear blow to America. How could Roe motivate Jason to do more? He sensed that his son did not share his own loyalty to the North. But Roe was also perceptive enough to recognize that Jason wanted to have a relationship with him and would do almost anything to make that happen.

At this stage of his development, Jason would benefit from more personal contact. It was unfortunate, given Roe's recent brush with law enforcement, that it was unsafe for him to travel to the U.S. And although Jason appeared to have the trust of security officials at the lab, given his new responsibilities, it would be too alerting for him to travel abroad.

There were rumors within Bureau 35 of a super-secret operation on the West Coast involving a sensitive asset recruited by Eric Wong code-named Nova. No one he talked to knew anything about him. Roe wondered if the powers that be would consider having Jason meet with Nova for rapport building.

Jason's new position in the Plutonium Pit Production Facility gave him access to critical national security information, access that could undermine America's goal of stabilizing and modernizing its nuclear arsenal, a pivotal deterrent to America's enemies. His position was such that Bureau 35 might consider exposing a sensitive asset to him if it would advance the case.

According to Jason's intelligence, Los Alamos P4, located in Technical Area-55, would receive an infusion of $4 billion over the next six years to modernize the facility and replace aging equipment. The best estimates were that these investments would put Los Alamos on target to produce thirty new pits per year within seven years. That and the Savannah River Lab's new pit production capability would increase U.S. pit manufacturing to eighty units a year.

Once these new pits began to roll off the assembly line, Los Alamos would start replacing the aging pits in the arsenal. With almost 6,000 nuclear weapons in the U.S. inventory, Los Alamos and eventually Savannah River would have their work cut out for them. New pit production, of necessity, would become a permanent feature of the U.S. nuclear weapons program.

During his last trip to Pyongyang, Roe accompanied scientists to the Yongbyon Nuclear Scientific Research Center, north of the capital, where he posed a hypothetical question. Hypothetical, because he could not reveal to them that North Korea already had an asset working at Los Alamos.

"Suppose you had a penetration of the U.S. nuclear program. If you could have that agent do one thing that would set the American program back, what would it be?" he asked.

One scientist spoke up almost immediately. "You could take a page from the American's own efforts to sabotage Iran's nuclear program several years ago. If your person were in the position to do so, they could corrupt the supply chain, either by inserting degraded parts or materials into it."

Yet another suggested that if the asset had access to pit storage areas, they could do something as simple as manipulating the humidity controls in these areas to promote pit corrosion, thus degrading the operability of the weapons over time.

"I would seriously think about cyber sabotage," another opined. "If your asset had access to the lab's computer systems, we could devise a program that would allow us to manipulate command and control during the manufacturing phase that could cause a catastrophic failure or, at a minimum, a malfunction at a critical moment."

One offbeat suggestion involved commandeering a transport vehicle loaded with fissile material and detonating it at a central location on Los Alamos' property. It was hard to estimate how destructive the explosion would be, given all the unknowns.

When they finished brainstorming, he thanked them for their suggestions. "Without your knowledge and close support, we would be incapable of even dreaming that we might penetrate the inner sanctum of America's national laboratories. We may never be able to remove America's threat to the Motherland entirely, but we can make it harder for them."

Following his visit to Yongbyon, Roe reported to the chief of Bureau 35 and his two deputies. He reiterated the scientists' recommendations and suggested they consider how to leverage their current access.

"Do you think your son is ready for this?" the chief asked, cocking an eye. "He's only been in the job for a few months, and from what I've seen, much of what he's given us looks like open-source material, information you can get online or from academic journals."

Roe did his best to conceal his alarm. He could feel himself sweating. Jason could be his ticket to a bigger job in the bureau. If leadership had doubts about Jason's worth, he needed to quash them now without appearing too defensive.

"I believe it's his nature to be cautious. He's an academic, and espionage is new to him. I'm confident he will respond positively to any task we give him, although it's too bad that he's on his own." Roe uttered this last sentence with his heart in his throat. He couldn't come right out and say that he was aware of an unnamed sensitive asset who might be tapped to motivate his son. He didn't need to know that information, and any hint that he did could be his undoing.

The chief inclined his head ever so slightly towards his deputies. There was an almost imperceptible shake of the head in response. "Well, it will have to do for now," he said.

"The supreme leader is anxious to make a statement. Ever since the failed summit with the previous U.S. president, he has wanted to make a grand gesture. We could destroy Los Alamos, and the Americans will provide their own delivery vehicle." He roared with laughter; after a slight pause, the others joined in.

Chapter 53

Jason was daydreaming about Laurie Kim. He was running in the mountains just west of Los Alamos with the Santa Fe Trail Runners. He had become a regular on their weekend runs and was now familiar with many of the area's running and hiking trails.

Laurie would typically be leading the pack, but she had a lot on her plate at present; first, her father was brutally murdered, and now her mother was badly injured in a freak accident on one of the nearby hiking trails. He missed being with Laurie, the challenging runs in the rugged backcountry, eating out, and their more intimate quiet time together.

He decided to stop by her place after his run to see if she needed anything. He didn't even know if she was still in town. She had gone to Los Angeles on bereavement leave to be with her mother right after her dad died and brought her mom back with her, but then her mother's accident happened, and she had not been back to work.

He rang her doorbell and waited a minute, but it seemed as though no one was home. He was about to turn away when the door slowly opened, and she stood there, mute. She looked terrible. Her face was pale and tear-streaked, and her hair hung limply to her shoulders. Her slender frame was thinner than usual.

"Hi," she said, her voice barely a whisper.

"I was going to call, but I decided just to come over," he said. "Can I come in?"

She opened the door wider for him to step inside. The apartment was a mess. It was dark, adding to the gloomy atmosphere. Laurie walked over and curled up on the couch, clutching a throw for comfort. He shivered as he sat down beside her. She usually kept the temperature around seventy-five degrees, but it felt like sixty right now. He took her icy hands in his and began to rub them. They were stiff and unfeeling.

They sat like this for several minutes, neither of them talking. Laurie shifted positions and laid her head against his chest. And then she began to speak, telling him everything.

Afterward, Jason struggled to find something to say. His initial reaction to her revelations was one of dismay. He wondered if her parents were aware of his North Korea connection. And Eric Wong had the same kind of job as his father; he was an NKIS officer. Did any of these people know about him? Or, more to the point, did Laurie?

"This must have been a terrible shock for you," Jason said, soothing her hair. "To find out your parents were both spies, and then to have your dad die and your mom get hurt. Do the authorities know?"

"I told Logan. Thank God he took his dog for a walk the day my mother got hurt. If he hadn't been there, I'm not sure I could have handled it. The Sheriff's Office brought in a helicopter to take her out of the canyon. While we were waiting for them to come, I told him the whole story."

"What did he say?" Jason asked.

"He said it was probably a good thing that I told him everything. My mother gave a copy of Dad's confession to the FBI in Los Angeles. If the lab has any questions about my loyalty, my willingness to come forward could save my job.

"It's been too much to absorb in such a short time," Laurie said, sitting up and brushing back her hair. "Dad murdered, Mom's accident, North Korea." She threw her hands out in exasperation. "Nothing hurts more than losing a parent, but finding out that your mother had a lover and he's your biological father..." Her voice trailed off, and she began to sniffle.

Jason wrapped his arms around her as she rocked back and forth in distress. Eventually, she was cried out; she slumped against him, moaning and wiping away her tears.

When she was more composed, Jason offered to fix her something to eat.

"I haven't done any shopping," she said. "I doubt if there's enough in the fridge to put together a meal."

"Why don't you get cleaned up? I'll run to the store and get something for dinner. I should be back in thirty minutes."

Jason drove to the nearest grocery store and bought enough food for dinner and some breakfast essentials. As he was shopping, he couldn't stop thinking about everything Laurie said. One thing that had him worried was the security guy, Logan Alexander.

Since Laurie told Logan everything about her parents, North Korea was no doubt on his radar. But you didn't have to be a rocket scientist to know Kim Jong-Un was trying to perfect a nuclear bomb and reliable delivery system. Logan was probably well aware of the North Korean threat.

He wondered if Logan was investigating Laurie. If so, there was a good chance he would also be scrutinizing her friends and colleagues. Jason wasn't too concerned Security would have focused on him. The young scientist kept a low profile, and there was no reason for Logan to suspect him of anything.

Still, it wouldn't hurt to get Laurie's take on her exposure and the possible fallout for anyone else at work.

By the time he got back to the apartment, Laurie had freshened up and straightened the living room and kitchen. Her color was better, and with her hair washed and pulled back, she almost looked herself.

Jason put away the groceries and started working on dinner. He poured Laurie a glass of wine and sat down beside her as he waited for the oven to heat up.

"Do you think Security is going to start investigating everyone, given what happened with your parents?" he asked.

"I don't know. The North Koreans killed my father because he refused to give them any information about me and the lab. If anything, he was trying to protect me. He might have taken money initially to start his business, but he drew the line at sensitive national security information. I can't say the same for my mother. I suspect she's trying to recruit me to spy for North Korea."

"That's what I'm worried about," Jason said. "I wonder if they'll suspect me because I'm South Korean."

"Why would they suspect you?" she asked.

Jason pursed his lips and remained silent. He couldn't tell Laurie that he was already spying for North Korea.

Chapter 54

Logan poured through his Roe Min-Woo file. There was a definite uptick in clandestine communications over the last few weeks from the NKIS officer to his son, imploring the latter to provide more and better information. The confusing thing to Logan was Jason's apparent reluctance to cross the line into real espionage. Jason was giving his father little more than open-source information he could just as easily pull off the Web.

Sure, Jason was in clandestine communication with a North Korean intelligence officer. That was a known fact, reason enough for him to lose his job, if not his freedom. Convicted spies typically receive lengthy prison sentences, and if their espionage damages U.S. national security sufficiently, they might never again see the light of day.

A plan was forming in Logan's head, one that would be a tough sell to Headquarters, not to mention the FBI, Martina, and the director of Los Alamos. He wanted to turn Jason Lee against his father and let the CIA take over his covert communications system, feeding Roe Min- Woo disinformation that would send North Korea's nuclear program back to the dark ages. Logan planned to use Roe's actions against the Kim family to drive a wedge between Roe and his son.

Surprisingly, within a week, Logan received the green light to move forward with his plan. Headquarters spelled out the usual caveats—frequent updates, regular coordination with the FBI, no threats, no coercion, etc. He had free rein to run the operation as he saw fit. He called Jason Tuesday afternoon and asked him to come to his office.

"Can you tell me what this is about?" Jason asked.

"I'd rather not discuss it on the phone," Logan said.

"See you in fifteen minutes?" He asked.

Jason knocked on Logan's door a short time later. Logan could tell the young scientist was nervous. He was fidgety and avoided making direct eye contact.

"Thanks for coming in, Jason," Logan said. "I think you probably know what this is about."

"My transfer to the pit production operation?" Jason asked.

"Not exactly," Logan said. "It has more to do with your extracurricular activities."

Jason appeared confused. "What ...?"

Logan decided not to mince words. "It's over, Jason. We know about your father and your contacts with him."

Jason slumped in his chair, leaning forward; he held his head between his hands and stared at the floor.

"You're not going to have a career at Los Alamos, and unless you cooperate with us to derail North Korea's plan to steal U.S. nuclear secrets, you could be looking at a lengthy prison sentence for espionage."

"I didn't give him anything classified," Jason protested. "I just wanted to make him feel like I was trying. I never planned to give him anything sensitive."

"You must have realized that meeting a North Korean agent secretly in the U.S. and communicating with him covertly was wrong, even if the information you provided wasn't that sensitive," Logan said.

"He might be your father, but he was grooming you to steal sensitive technology for one of our worst enemies."

Jason remained silent, his breathing shallow.

Logan half-expected Jason to push back harder than he had. He as much as admitted to working for his father. But that didn't mean he was going to be cooperative. Logan decided to play his ace in the hole, Laurie Kim.

"Did you know that your father engineered the attack against the Kims?" Logan asked.

Jason's head jerked up. "What?"

"Yes. He used the same William Gardner alias he gave you when you met him in Albuquerque a few months ago.

He broke into the Kims' house in Los Angeles with a gangster, intent on killing Dave and Ginny Kim, but the police showed up before he could kill them. Your father got away, but the gangster, a guy named Sammy Perez, is in jail awaiting trial."

"That's not possible," Jason said. "My father would never hurt anyone."

Logan rifled through his Roe Min-Woo file and pulled out copies of the flight manifest and round-trip tickets to Los Angeles from Mexico City. He splayed the documents across the top of his desk.

"Take a look. We believe your father arrived a few days early to case the Kims' home, and he returned to Mexico City shortly after the break-in."

Jason got up and perused the documents. "He told me he was on a business trip," he said. He returned to his chair and sat down, a dejected look on his face.

"Jason, I know you grew up without a father, but no matter what he has told you, Roe Min-Woo is not a nice guy. He would kill Dave Kim in cold blood because he refused to give the NKIS access to Laurie Kim."

At the mention of Laurie's name, Jason grimaced. "Does Laurie know about this?" He asked.

"What? That Roe Min-Woo is your father and is behind her father's murder? That you're working for him?" Logan asked.

Jason winced. "I didn't know any of that. I would never do anything to hurt Laurie or her family." His eyes pleaded for understanding.

"Didn't her father die after the break-in at their house?" Jason asked. "My father wasn't even in the States then, was he?" He got back up and looked at the days of his father's travel to and from Los Angeles.

"You're right," Logan said. "But authorities found a wire transfer to Sammy Perez the night of the break-in. We have a record of that transfer being initiated from your father's alias cell phone. Roe Min-Woo may not have pulled the trigger, but he might as well have.

"But to answer your question, no, Laurie doesn't know about your connection to Roe and the NKIS."

"What do you want from me?" Jason asked.

"Your cooperation," Logan said. "I want to debrief you on your relationship with the NKIS, beginning with the very first time your father told you about his work with them and everything that's happened since then.

"I also want to take over your clandestine communications with your father. It will be tricky because he may ask questions I don't know the answer to. I'll need your help making sure he doesn't suspect anything."

"What are my options?" Jason asked.

"If you refuse to cooperate, an FBI special agent will come in and arrest you; you'll be charged with espionage. You would probably go to jail right away because the court would consider you a flight risk. Los Alamos could terminate your contract with cause, although they might decide to put you on unpaid administrative leave pending the trial outcome," Logan said.

"On the other hand, if you cooperate, I'll set you up in a safe house, so you won't have to worry about living expenses. You won't have access to communications or be able to leave the premises. You will be under guard twenty-four hours a day, seven days a week."

"How long would this go on?" Jason asked.

"I don't know, two weeks, a month? As long as it takes to play out."

"What happens after that?"

"Given your cooperation, the CIA would recommend no formal charges be pressed. The Department of Energy would probably terminate your employment with the recommendation that you be expelled from the U.S. The State Department would revoke your visa, and you would not be permitted to travel to the U.S. in the future.

"The CIA would help you concoct a cover story for why you terminated your employment at Los Alamos. We would help you get resettled back in Canada or elsewhere outside of the U.S. We would not make public your relationship with the NKIS, and you would be free to seek employment in academia or elsewhere outside of the U.S. You will never be able to work on any sensitive, classified projects."

"Can I think about this?" Jason asked, a strained look on his face.

"You have five minutes to make up your mind."

Chapter 55

With Jason's surrender, the operational tempo picked up immediately. The FBI rented a safe house in the hills outside of Santa Fe. The CIA brought in a retired couple from the Office of Security to manage the place, oversee security, and take care of cooking and housekeeping chores. Nathan and Carla Riley had made a second career as contractors doing one-off gigs like this one.

Jason's colleagues, including Laurie Kim, were advised that Jason had contracted COVID-19, was hospitalized at the University of New Mexico Hospital in Albuquerque on a ventilator, and could not receive visitors or take calls.

Logan was sure this scenario would withstand scrutiny from even the most sophisticated intelligence service. The Health Insurance Portability and Accountability Act (HIPAA) would guarantee no prying eyes would access Jason's medical records.

Since no one in Jason's orbit, except for his mother, was in contact with Roe Min-Woo, Logan was confident the ruse would work. The longer the operation played out, though, the more difficult it would become to sustain the lie. Optimally, they would wrap this up in a couple of weeks.

Headquarters dispatched a staff operations officer and a Korean-speaking analyst from the Counter Proliferation Center to help Logan manage communications with Roe. Logan considered bringing the South Koreans in on the operation but decided the fewer people who knew about it, the better. Logan and his counterparts were operating out of a safe house thirty minutes outside of Los Alamos.

Valerie Rhee, the analyst, and Logan were discussing operational goals over coffee at the safe house. Ken Long, the staff operations officer, set up secure communications with Headquarters and Jason Lee's computer for messages to Roe Min-Woo.

"I want to be proactive in our messages to Roe," Logan said. "At the same time, we need to maintain the persona of Jason Lee, so Roe doesn't become suspicious."

"I think Jason's assignment to the pit production program gives us an opening to be more aggressive. It's a new job, with different access and an area the North Koreans are interested in," Valerie said. "We have plenty of feed material that goes beyond the quality of information Jason has been providing the NKIS. It would seem natural, given his new access, that he would begin providing better information."

"I'm good with that," Logan said. "I also want there to be a consistent tone to the messages that say, 'Hey, I'm out here all alone, and I'm not sure what I'm supposed to be doing.' We'll draw them out on their requirements, but better yet, maybe they'll respond by sending a handler, Roe himself, to boost Jason's confidence."

"I saw FBI reporting last week that Eric Wong has gone missing," Valerie said.

"The Bureau went out to interview him after Dave Kim's murder. At the time, they didn't know Wong was Kim's recruiting officer. They never did find him. Ginny Kim probably warned him to get out of Dodge before she had her accident."

"Do you think Roe would risk coming back to the States after all that's happened?" Valerie asked.

"Hard to say," Logan said. "There hasn't been any public information linking Roe to the break-in at the Kims' house nor Dave Kim's murder."

Ken poked his head into the kitchen where Logan and Valerie were talking. "We're all set up in here with secure comms to Headquarters. I've also gone over Jason's laptop; we can send and receive messages whenever you're ready. Jason has been spoofing the location through a VPN to look like he's in Germany. Are you good with that?"

"Yes. We don't want to change anything Jason was

doing. Roe could become suspicious and break off communications."

"What are the chances Roe will try to call Jason?" Ken asked.

"He's pretty disciplined about Opsec," Logan said. "I don't expect him to call, but we'll let it go to voicemail if he does. We can probably get away with that once or twice.

"Roe is in Mexico City, which is an hour ahead of us. During the week, Jason was emailing his father after work, usually around eight or nine o'clock. The weekend was more flexible, sometimes in the morning, sometimes in the afternoon."

"Do you want to send out something today?" Valerie asked.

"Yes. Let's do a piece on the pit production work and end it with a request for new requirements from Pyongyang."

Valerie and Ken went into the dining room to check the email and work on their first message to Roe. Logan picked up his secure phone to call the other safe house.

"Hello?"

"Hey, Nathan. It's Logan. How'd it go last night?"

"It was quiet. Your boy pretty much kept to himself. He wanted to go for a run this morning. There's nobody out here within five miles. He did ten miles round trip; I followed him in the Jeep, and he behaved."

"Do you need anything?" Logan asked.

"No, thanks, we're good for now."

"All right, I'll check in with you later this afternoon. Say hi to Carla for me."

"Will do, ten-four."

He spent the next hour working on a situation report for Headquarters which he gave to Ken to send via secure communications. It was a little before noon, and he decided to call Anthony Brown to provide him with an operational status report.

The ASAC picked up the phone on the first ring. "Logan, thanks for checking in. How are things going?"

"So far, so good," Logan said. "It's been mostly

housekeeping, up until now. We've got our comms up and running, and we're ready to send our first message to Roe this evening."

"That sounds promising. Are you having any issues with Jason?" Anthony asked.

"No. Nathan and Carla are old hands at this. Plus, Jason isn't stupid. He knows what's at risk if he doesn't cooperate. It's still early, though. He's bound to get antsy if this goes on for too long. Nathan took him out for a run this morning."

"Let me know if we can do anything for you."

Chapter 56

News of Jason Lee's transfer to the Los Alamos pit production facility provoked a sensation in the upper reaches of the NKIS leadership. Within hours, it percolated up to the office of the supreme leader himself.

There was consensus amongst Kim's advisors that Lee's access provided the opportunity to do precisely what their boss desired; make a bold statement that would seriously damage America's nuclear capability, or worse yet, launch its economy into a tailspin.

The chief of Bureau 35 wanted to be front and center in this effort. There were plans to brief the operation to the supreme leader in the coming days, and he personally hoped to report to Kim on their project. He chafed when the NKIS director told him that Bureau 35 would be back-benching him at the meeting with Kim.

Many people were chary of getting too close to Kim because if something went awry and he began looking for scapegoats, there would be no place to hide. But Roe's boss was an experienced bureaucrat who had fought many skirmishes within the North Korean bureaucracy. He might be battle-scarred, but he was not battle-weary.

The chief was also rethinking his initial reluctance to activate the sensitive agent code-named Nova for this operation. Roe no doubt had the closest relationship to Lee, given their familial ties, but it was too dangerous for Roe to travel to the U.S. on the heels of his recent close call there.

To further complicate matters, Lee, being a novice in espionage, was too inexperienced to be left to his own devices. The time to strike the U.S. was now, since North Korea might never again have Lee's level of access to the U.S.

nuclear program. This operation deserved the best shot at success.

The supreme leader was personally briefed on agent Nova. Nova had proven his worth time and time again, and committing him to this risky endeavor would not be taken lightly. If Nova were compromised, it would be a blow to the service's intelligence capabilities. But if he were to succeed, there would be much to celebrate in the halls of Residence No. 55, North Korea's presidential palace.

A flurry of activity preceded the briefing for the supreme leader. The NKIS team and nuclear scientists met until late in the evening the day before the meeting with Kim to go over their talking points. Many of the salient operational details were left out because there were so many unknowns about conditions on the ground and the actual physical access Lee had to plutonium stores.

The final plan proposed the theft of enough weapons-grade plutonium over several months to build a nuclear bomb, about ten pounds of plutonium 239. Lee would store the plutonium in a rented garage near Los Alamos. He would also be responsible for outfitting the garage with the requisite machine shop equipment to build the bomb.

During this phase of the operation, it would be essential to recruit a competent and discreet technical person to perform the hands-on construction of the bomb. Lee, with his physics background, would handle the more esoteric aspects of the bomb's design.

Although it would be more complicated, the physicists recommended an implosion device to achieve maximum destruction. The fission of ten pounds of plutonium 239 would have the same destructive energy as 20,000 tons of TNT. The bomb did not have to be delivered via ballistic missile; a U-Haul rental truck parked in Lafayette Square in downtown Washington, D.C., would incinerate the city center.

On the day of the briefing, the NKIS director's office advised the chief of Bureau 35 that he would have to brief Kim, as the NKIS director was indisposed. He was having an inexplicable bout of diarrhea and could not stray far from the toilet.

Some within the NKIS speculated that the chief of Bureau 35 had orchestrated the service chief's intestinal disposition by tampering with his food the night before. But there was no evidence to support these rumors. Thus, the bureau chief led the briefers to the presidential palace to meet with the supreme leader.

The briefing team gathered at Residence No. 55 early on the morning of the briefing. The air seemed to crackle with electricity. The operation, code-named Supreme Threat, was perhaps the most sophisticated plan the service had ever put forth against the Americans.

The chief of Bureau 35, the senior deputy of the NKIS, and two nuclear scientists from Yongbyon were the briefers. Kim, his sister, and the minister of defense were the only other senior government officials present.

From the beginning, Kim peppered the presenters with questions. He wanted to know what role Nova would play, how difficult it would be to acquire the plutonium 239, whether or not Lee had the skills to build an implosion bomb, and how they would locate a competent technician to work alongside the scientist. But more than anything, Kim wanted an assessment of the havoc the bomb would wreck.

On this latter point, the scientists were most clear. Within fifteen seconds of detonation, thousands of residents from ground zero to a radius of a half-mile out would die. Thousands more would sustain life-threatening injuries. The blast would destroy buildings at ground zero and heavily damage structures within a mile. The electrical grid would no longer function as critical substations were decimated, and relays in neighboring states were affected.

Within hours of the initial explosion, alpha and beta particles of radioactive dust thrown into the atmosphere would begin to settle back to earth. The range of radioactive fallout would depend upon wind conditions at the time and the speed with which citizens found appropriate shelter. No doubt, hundreds of thousands would be impacted by radioactive fallout alone.

There were no economists on the briefing team; however, the NKIS researched the economic modeling done by several American think tanks. They concluded that the financial toll from a nuclear detonation would be staggering, trillions of dollars due to loss of lives alone and hundreds of billions of dollars in property losses.

The supreme leader kept nodding his head in satisfaction as the briefers ticked off each point in this doomsday scenario. When they finished, Kim huddled briefly with his sister and the minister of defense. At one point, he roared with laughter.

Standing, he motioned that the meeting was over. As he walked out of the room, the supreme leader uttered only two words.

"Do it."

Chapter 57

Roe Min-Woo was at his desk when the message from Bureau 35 arrived.

"Here you go," Park said, handing him the reading file.

The message from his boss was double-wrapped in two envelopes, meaning it was Top Secret. The embassy was not authorized to retain information classified higher than Secret. He would have to read the file, take a few cryptic notes and destroy it before he locked up for the night. Roe pulled the two-page cable out of the envelopes and began to read.

"We briefed the supreme leader yesterday morning regarding developments at Los Alamos. As a result, we will be commencing with Operation Supreme Threat immediately ...."

Roe scanned the message quickly and then read it a second time more thoroughly. As he set it back down on the desk, his hand trembled.

"What is it, boss?" Park asked. He sat down opposite Roe and looked at him with concern. Roe's face had turned ashen, his forehead creased with worry lines.

"Headquarters wants my son to build a nuclear fission device and detonate it in Washington, D.C.," he said.

Park stared at Roe, eyes agape. It took him a moment to compose himself. "Is that even possible?" he asked.

"Yes. In his new job Chul-Moo has access to plutonium 239. Having access and being able to steal ten pounds of it are two different things. I am sure Los Alamos has rigorous security safeguards, because it's their worst nightmare for any of this material to go missing."

"Let's say he can get away with it. Does he have the ability to build a nuclear bomb?" Park asked.

"After his assignment to Los Alamos, I did some reading on the U.S. nuclear weapons program. One report I read was about three graduate students with no special training in physics. The government wanted to know if a layperson could build an atomic bomb. These three created a crude but functioning weapon, using available schematics and information taken from the Internet.

"I have no doubt my son could accomplish this. He does have a Ph.D. in physics, and he's an intelligent person. I don't see any problem with him designing the weapon. The hard part will be acquiring the fissile material and finding a trustworthy technical person to pull it all together."

The two men were silent for a moment as they contemplated the enormity of the operation. Finally, Roe spoke.

"The chief raised the possibility of activating Nova to guide Chul-Moo through this process. I don't know the true identity of Nova, but it's unlikely he can waltz into Los Alamos and be in regular contact with Chul-Moo," he said.

"It's too dangerous," Park replied. "From what we've seen in Chul-Moo's reporting, the security at Los Alamos is very tight. It's unlikely Nova would be able to play a hands-on role in the operation. I don't know anything about his background that would suggest he could gain access to the lab."

"I agree," Roe said. "At most, he could be a sounding board for Chul-Moo as he advances through the various phases of the operation. I feel bad that I cannot be there to guide him through this."

"You shouldn't," Park said. "You can't travel to the States so soon after what happened in Los Angeles. The authorities there have an ongoing homicide investigation into the murder of Dave Kim. We don't know what that Filipino gangster you were dealing with, Perez, has said to the police.

"I think you have to assume the worst-case scenario," Park said. "We know from intelligence reporting that the Americans use torture in their interrogations. They will be able to make Perez talk if he knows something."

"He had virtually no clue as to my true identity," Roe said. "At the most, he might have seen the license plate on the rental car and given that to the police. They would be able to link it to my alias information and possibly track me to Mexico City.

"The Mexicans have never given any indication they suspect that I'm intel. Of course, they probably know that we use our trade offices as cover for intelligence operations abroad. I'm not naive enough to think they'll look the other way."

"Getting back to the question of Nova, how exactly do you envision his participation?" Park asked.

"I think Headquarters would handle his communications out of Bureau 35," Roe said. "All I know is that Nova is somewhere on the West Coast. His mission is highly compartmented; less than a handful of people even know of his existence. Headquarters may decide it's too risky to involve him in this operation.

"You know that if we succeed in detonating a nuclear device in Washington, it changes everything?" Roe asked.

"We've been at war with the Americans for seventy years," Park replied.

"But this is different," Roe replied. "If the Americans figure out that North Korea is behind the attack, they will come after us with a vengeance such as we have never seen before. It could be the end of our world."

Park shuddered involuntarily. "Far be it from me to question the judgment of the supreme leader," he said. "But there must be something else we could do at Los Alamos that is more subtle yet still has the potential to degrade America's nuclear weapons stockpile."

Roe moved closer to Park and whispered in his ear. "You may think such things, but never say them out loud," he said in a soft voice. "Especially here; this is an official government installation, and the walls have ears. Heaven forbid someone should hear you questioning the supreme leader's judgment."

The two men pulled apart and stared at each other

without speaking. The air was thick, and the walls felt as though they were closing in on them. Both understood they were embarking upon a dangerous mission—one which could drastically change the world and their lives.

Chapter 58

Logan was meeting with Valerie and Ken when the message from Bureau 35 arrived in Jason's in-box. It took Valerie fifteen minutes to translate the document from Korean to English and print a copy. She checked her translation for accuracy and then wordlessly handed the message to Logan.

The subject line was "Operation Supreme Threat." As Logan read through Valerie's notes, he could hardly believe his eyes. In it, Bureau 35 directed Jason to steal enough plutonium 239 to build a nuclear weapon and set it off in Washington, D.C. The NKIS gave a roughly six-month time frame to steal the fissile material, construct the bomb, and detonate it. It was nothing less than nuclear terrorism. According to the author, the operation was briefed to the supreme leader, and he wholly endorsed it.

"These guys are out of their fucking minds," Logan said. "Fortunately for us, Jason Lee is never going to set foot anywhere near Los Alamos again."

"What did you think about Bureau 35's proposal to have their asset meet with Jason?" Valerie asked.

"Nova? They know Jason is out of his depth and most likely unprepared to take on an operation like this. It's one thing for him to provide the NKIS unclassified papers you can find on the Los Alamos website, and quite another to blow up the capital of the only superpower on earth."

"What do you think we should do?" Ken asked.

"I don't see much point in dragging this out," Logan said. "I don't have enough confidence in Jason to use him as bait so that we can nail them stealing the plutonium. The fact they are actively plotting a nuclear terrorist attack against the U.S. is enough to prosecute them on terrorism charges.

"We've got to get a message to Headquarters ASAP," Logan said. "We'll tell them we want to ambush Nova if he attempts to establish contact with Jason. The Bureau should be front and center on the arrest, and when the shit hits the fan, they'll be the ones talking to the press.

"I also want to propose an operation against Roe Min-Woo in Mexico City. He has diplomatic immunity there now, which complicates things. But we want him extradited to the U.S. to stand trial on nuclear terrorism charges. The Mexicans probably wouldn't publicly violate diplomatic protocols with North Korea, but maybe we can persuade them to look the other way if we pick him up on the street and bring him into the U.S. black."

The message from Bureau 35 gave Jason instructions for arranging a meeting with Nova. Before responding to the NKIS message, the CIA field team needed Headquarters' operational approvals to move forward. The plan to capture Roe Min-Woo in Mexico City had more moving parts to it. Logan volunteered to lead the team responsible for picking him up.

Logan and Valerie pulled the message together before lunch and sent it Top Secret Immediate precedence to Headquarters. They had a reply back before the close of business. The Seventh Floor agreed with the field team's proposal. Arresting the North Korean agent code-named Nova posed little risk. However, the Office of General Counsel raised concerns about political blowback if Mexico reacted poorly to the kidnapping of a foreign diplomat on their turf.

Within a day, Mexico City weighed in with a plan to begin surveilling Roe Min-Woo to determine his patterns of activity. The Mexicans had kept an eye on him during North Korea's negotiations to set up a trade office. They knew where his office and apartment were, that he had an assistant named Park, and that he liked to frequent bars and prostitutes in his free time.

The American ambassador was briefed on the proposal.

A retired Marine two-star, he was supportive of the Agency's mission. He ran it up the flagpole in D.C.; both the National Security Council and State Department were cautiously supportive. No one wanted to get into a pissing contest with the Mexicans, but this was too important to ignore.

If North Korea felt it could run operations of this magnitude against the homeland from a neighboring country, what else might they try? This operation had to be killed before it gained any more traction. It would send an unmistakable message to the North Korean regime—don't fuck with Uncle Sam.

Logan called for a meeting with Anthony Brown. Martina and Peter were there too.

"Holy shit," Anthony said when Logan briefed them on the details of the North Korean plan. He held up his hand, thumb and forefinger an inch apart. "We came this close to Armageddon. If the North Koreans pulled this off, it would make 9/11 look like a picnic.

"I got a call from the Director's office this morning with a heads-up this was coming my way. What's the game plan?" Anthony asked.

Logan filled him in on their recent activity. "We got a green light from Headquarters to reach out to Nova. We'll send him a covert message from Jason's computer this afternoon. If he agrees to a meeting in Albuquerque, we'll try to schedule it next week. How do you envision the arrest going down?"

"We'll get adjoining rooms at the hotel, and I'll have the arresting team next door. Are you planning to have Jason in the room?" he asked.

"I don't know that it buys us anything," Logan said. "If we can convince Jason to cooperate, we could record the meeting and have additional evidence to use against Nova when his case goes to trial. But he's a little bit of a wild card. What if he screws it up?

"I know Jason's scared. He hasn't made a fuss about being detained, and he knows he's going back to Canada when this is all over. If he cooperates, it could help his situation, particularly if the Canadians decide to get involved."

"Worst-case scenario, we don't get anything useful to use in our prosecution of Nova. I'm still going to have agents with guns next door, who will detain Mr. Nova," Anthony said.

Everyone agreed Valerie should reach out to Nova using the contact information Bureau 35 provided. They set the meeting four days from today, giving the team ample time to get everything in place. In the interim, Logan had Headquarters' and Mexico City's approval to move forward with Roe's capture and rendition. He was leaving for Mexico City in two days.

Chapter 59

Logan and a team of three Agency paramilitary officers were huddled in a black Chevrolet Suburban with tinted windows a half-mile from Roe Min-Woo's apartment on Avenida Balderas. All of the team members had served combat tours in Iraq or Afghanistan. They traveled to Mexico City separately by air on alias tourist passports, stayed in different hotels around the city, and would not set foot in the American Embassy to better maintain a low profile.

Their local contact had brought them handheld two-way radios synched to the frequency the surveillance team would be using so that they could monitor their comms for real-time reporting on Roe's movements. He also provided them with three days of surveillance reports on Roe's activities around town, weapons, and body armor.

The Mexican officer targeting Roe was recently recruited by the CIA and was working clandestinely behind the scenes with the Agency. He was considered a unilateral penetration of the local service and took an oath not to report his activities on the CIA's behalf to his bosses in the Mexican government.

The Americans spent a day and a half casing the area around Roe's neighborhood. They rented bicycles and went out separately to check out pedestrian and vehicular traffic. They specifically wanted to get a feel for what the streets looked like in the early evening hours when they anticipated snatching Roe.

This evening's plan called for the Mexican officer to invite Roe out for drinks at a bar near Roe's neighborhood. From the surveillance team's reporting, they knew the routes Roe favored to and from his apartment and had identified several spots along the way from there to the bar where they could safely intercept him.

Meanwhile, they would be evaluating the lighting conditions and the number of people on the street to decide which spot was best suited to approach their target. Once they received word from the surveillance team that Roe was on the move, they would only have minutes to decide where to snatch him.

When they got him off the street, Roe would be gagged and bound. A hood would be placed over his head, and he would be moved to the SUV's cargo area, where Logan would inject him with a light sedative to keep him calm. They would cover him with a tarp, lest a pedestrian or someone in a vehicle spot the inert form and become curious. This precaution was probably unnecessary because the tinted windows did an excellent job of concealing the interior of the SUV.

The snatch team did a dry run the previous evening of the route to the private airfield just north of Mexico City from which they were flying. A small, seven-person Agency jet would be waiting for them there. The plane would be parked in a hangar where Roe could be loaded onboard out of sight of prying eyes; he would be strapped into his seat for the four-and-a-half-hour flight to southern Virginia.

It was nine o'clock when the team got word that Roe had departed his apartment. He was by himself, walking one of the routes the surveillance team had identified. The radio crackled, and the surveillance team leader spoke up.

"Subject is on the move. He took a right outside the apartment building and walked south on Avenida Oaxaca, passing the Fuente de Cibeles." The voice paused.

"Wait a minute. He just went into a tobacco shop."

Logan could hear background chatter as the team deployed around Roe pulled back. The team leader put out one surveillant to go into the store to see what their target was up to and another to cover the rear of the store, lest the wily North Korean try to escape out the back.

"Okay, he just exited the tobacco store," the surveillant

who followed Roe inside reported. "He's walking south on Medellin and just passed the Moshi Moshi takeout-delivery restaurant."

"Does he seem surveillance-conscious?" Logan asked. He was following their target's route on a map on his lap, squinting to make out the names of the streets despite the bright light his tactical flashlight was emitting.

"He's not rubbernecking or taking long looks," the team leader said.

"Can you describe what he's wearing?" Logan asked.

"Yes. The subject is wearing a short-sleeved red golf shirt, brown khaki pants, and black loafers. He's smoking as he walks.

"He took a right on Medellin and is turning onto Colima. It looks like he is going to cut through an open-air street market. It's dark in there. At this hour, everyone has closed up for the night.

"Let's move," Logan said.

They had been following the surveillance team leader's vehicle a block and a half back, better to stay out of sight. Now they sped up and pulled around him. They turned onto Colima, a tree-lined street that snaked through a mixed commercial-residential neighborhood. They were coming up on an elementary school with an outdoor swimming pool when they spotted Roe fifty yards ahead of them walking on the sidewalk.

Cars lined both sides of the street; in front of the school, separating the sidewalk from the road, there was a three-foot mesh fence. Logan scanned both sides of the street, looking for danger. Two boys a block away were kicking a soccer ball in the street, while across from them, an elderly gentleman lounged on his doorstep smoking.

"Let's go," Logan said.

Two team members exited the car, vaulted the fence, and began walking towards Roe. They were armed with Glock semi-automatic handguns and were wearing light Kevlar body armor under their shirts. It was unlikely Roe would be armed, but it was better to be prepared in the event he was.

The next couple of minutes would be tricky. There were casuals in the area who might interfere if they noticed what was happening, or worse yet, could alert the police. Logan had covered the two license plates temporarily to make it harder to identify the vehicle.

The car sped up, passed Roe, and stopped forty feet in front of him. There was no fence along this section of the sidewalk. Logan slid out of the vehicle, slipped between two parked cars, and walked towards the North Korean.

Chapter 60

Roe sensed something was off kilter; he had been on edge all week. He and Park got drunk the night they received the message from Bureau 35 outlining plans to set off a nuclear device in Washington, a bomb that would be built and detonated by his son. After their initial reaction, they couldn't talk about it at work. No one else at the embassy was briefed on Operation Supreme Threat, not even the ambassador; there was no plan for him to be read in.

Truthfully, Roe was shaken by the details. This attack would go down as one of the most brutal acts of infamy in history. It had the potential to decimate the U.S. economy, take out the entire federal government, and turn the capital of America into a nuclear wasteland.

But history had shown the Americans to be resilient. Every time they were confronted with adversity, they rallied and beat it down. They spent ten years tracking down Osama Bin Laden in retaliation for the 9/11 attack on the World Trade Center. What would they do to North Korea? He shuddered at the thought.

He heard footsteps behind him. Turning, he saw two men, young, athletic types striding towards him. He had seen the SUV with tinted windows drive by but thought nothing of it. Suburbans with tinted windows were popular in the Federal District. But then he heard the car door slam and seconds later saw a third man walking towards him.

Alarm bells went off in his brain; it was a trap. He swallowed anxiously and glanced back again. The two men behind him had picked up the pace. Usually, taking on three guys would not have fazed him; he had a black belt in tae kwon do, after all. But there was something about the way these men carried themselves that screamed special forces. All of these thoughts went through his brain in a split second.

He decided to make a run for it. He had just passed Valentin Zamora Elementary School, behind which there was an open-air market. If he managed to get there, he might be able to elude them. He broke into a run, making a beeline for the market. He heard the pounding of feet behind him. He could tell that they had fanned out and were chasing him from different angles. Who were these people, and why were they after him?

The exertion of running was catching up with him; his breathing was labored, and his heart was pounding. The excessive drinking, smoking, and whoring over the years had taken a toll on his fitness; he hadn't realized how soft he had become.

He thought of screaming for help but immediately dismissed it. If only he could get to his mobile phone and make an emergency call, but there was no time. He could feel them breathing down his neck. Suddenly the man who was in the SUV in front of the school was there. A pistol in his hand was pointed at Roe's head.

The other two men came up behind him and stopped. They also had weapons drawn and pointed at him. His situation was dire. He might be able to take out one of the men with a round-house kick to the head, but there was no telling what the other two would do. He did the sensible thing; he put his hands up in the air.

"Roe Min-Woo?" The man from the car asked.

The man spoke to him in English; he sounded American, and he used his name. Who were these guys? CIA? What did they want with him? There was ample press coverage about the new trade office, and the CIA undoubtedly knew that the NKIS used these facilities as cover for their intelligence officers. It crossed his mind that the Mexicans were probably working with the Americans. How else would they have known where to find him tonight?

"Who are you?" Roe asked. "What do you want with me?"

Logan studied the man in front of him. He was smaller than expected from the photos he had seen. Logan had watched him make the mental calculation, "fight or flight," when he tried to get away from them in front of the school. And even now, Logan sensed Roe was weighing his chances of taking on the three of them, although the odds were stacked against him. Fortunately, he didn't appear armed; the last thing they needed was to get into a gunfight in the middle of Mexico City.

"We want to talk to you," Logan said.

"I'm a diplomat," Roe responded with bluster. "My country is a signatory to the Vienna Convention on Diplomatic Relations. You have no right to detain me."

"I know the Vienna Convention has to do with diplomatic relations, including diplomatic immunity," Logan said. "I'm not sure it was meant for North Korean intelligence officers," he added, taking a swipe at the North Korean. Of course, he knew it did. All of the signatories to the Geneva Convention used their immunities to cover bona fide diplomats and their intelligence people working abroad.

"Look, we can do this the easy way or the hard way. It's up to you. We don't want to hurt you, but if you resist, we'll use force," Logan said. He could see that the man was sweating profusely.

Roe nodded his head uncertainly. He started to lower his arms, but Logan gestured sharply with his pistol, and he raised them again.

"What do you want me to do?" he asked.

"Keep your hands in the air," Logan said. He gestured to one of the other men who was standing by. After handing his weapon to his buddy for safekeeping, the man frisked Roe for weapons but found none. He confiscated Roe's wallet, cell phone, and keys to the apartment and placed them in a bag.

Roe resisted when they began to put on the zip-tie handcuffs, and two of them had to muscle him into the restraints, hands behind his back. He protested when they affixed tape to his mouth, but they couldn't take a chance that he would shout out.

The team got Roe into the Suburban without incident. He struggled when they put a bag over his head and again when two of the men held him down as Logan administered the sedative. Eventually, he stopped flailing around and settled into a restive sleep. The old man sitting on his stoop stood up and looked their way. He turned abruptly and went into his house.

"Let's get out of here," Logan said. While they were driving to the airfield, he retrieved Roe's cell phone and pasted a message into the text application that Valerie had written for him. The message was short, mentioning an operational opportunity that had come up at the last minute. He promised to elaborate in the morning. Logan entered Park's cell phone number, retrieved from intercepts, and hit send.

Logan's watch showed that they had only been on the ground for ten minutes. It seemed like an hour. As they sped out of the Federal District towards the airfield north of town, he breathed a sigh of relief. They wouldn't be entirely in the clear until they departed Mexican airspace. But this had been the hard part, capturing Roe without setting off alarms from Mexico City to Pyongyang.

Chapter 61

Severe weather over the Gulf of Mexico buffeted their small jet, even at thirty thousand feet. Air traffic control tried routing them around the storms, but the scorching temperatures in the Gulf of Mexico were producing more moisture and cloud formations, hence more significant turbulence.

Three of the rendition team members and their prisoner were the sole passengers aboard the Agency aircraft; the pilot and steward were the only other people on board. The fourth team member stayed behind for an extra day to return the SUV and brief their inside contact.

The weather cleared north of Miami, and they had a smooth ride into a small private airport in southern Virginia. The Agency had a facility there where Roe would be securely held and debriefed.

Careful attention to detail would keep Roe in the dark about his whereabouts; nothing in his room or the outside exercise area would indicate that he was in the United States, let alone Virginia. Roe probably suspected that he was in the hands of the CIA, but they would not confirm that for him.

The aircraft's main cabin was blacked out with shades on the windows pulled down. People had made the mistake in the past of letting captives look out the window in flight, only to have them glimpse an identifiable geographic formation, a body of water, or a man-made structure that gave away their location.

When they landed, Roe was again hooded and led to a van for the short ride to his new quarters. While Roe was being processed, Logan paid a courtesy call to the facility night manager. They chatted briefly, and then Logan and the rest of the team went in search of their rooms to crash.

The following day after breakfast, Logan met briefly with the officer in charge of the installation, after which he steered Logan to an empty office with a secure phone where he would be able to work. The other two members of the team were already on the road back to Langley.

By now, Headquarters would have heard that Roe was in hand; they would be deploying a debriefing team to meet with him over the next several days or weeks. The seventh floor would appreciate Logan's first-hand account of how it all went down. He called the ADDO's office; Greg answered the phone himself on the first ring.

"Greg?"

"Logan. Good to hear from you. Where are you, down south?"

"Yes, we got here after midnight. They did a good job taking care of us. Everyone got some shut-eye, and I'm getting ready to write my report. I thought I'd give you a quick rundown before I start writing. The other two guys are already on their way home."

"You guys did an exceptional job, Logan. From what I heard, everything went as planned."

"It was pretty smooth. Our friends in Mexico City took care of us. Without their support, I doubt we could have pulled it off.

"Their guy set up a meeting with Roe, which got him out on the street. They put surveillance on him; I've got to hand it to their surveillance team—very professional, discreet, and easy to work with.

"It was a little touch-and-go when we first confronted Roe. He ran, and we had to chase him down. Fortunately, it was dark, and there was hardly anyone outside. He didn't put up much of a fight. I know he was thinking about it, but he got winded just running fifty yards. So much for being a party animal.

"Do you know when the debriefing team is getting here?" Logan asked.

"They're on their way. I imagine they'll be there before

lunch. Are you planning to sit in on their debriefings?" Greg asked.

"Initially. I want to be back at Los Alamos when the Nova operation goes down. Have you heard anything from the team there?"

"Yes. Nova didn't agree to meet right away. He said he had a conflict and would have to delay a couple of days. I don't know if that's a stalling strategy on his part or if he does have other commitments."

"This could be a problem," Logan said. "When Bureau 35 finds out Roe has gone missing, they might call off Nova. We need to come up with an explanation for why he's disappeared. We sent a message on Roe's cell phone to Park before leaving Mexico with a vague reference to an operational opportunity and a promise to follow up in the morning. We didn't want Park to freak out when he found out Roe didn't make it home last night."

"Good thinking. What do you have in mind?" Greg asked.

"Let's have Valerie send a message to Park in Mexico City from Roe saying he has to go off the grid for a couple of days because of a hot operational lead. Say that his Mexican police contact has a commie friend close to the president who wants to help North Korea. This guy's family has a hacienda in Toluca, and they're going down there to meet."

"That might work," Greg said. "Does Roe have that level of autonomy? When I was working North Korean targets a few years ago, it was almost impossible to get anyone out alone; they were required to go out in pairs."

"His bosses trust him," Logan said. "They let him go to Albuquerque to seal the deal with Jason and to LA to handle the Dave and Ginny Kim operation. I don't think they'll question a trip out of town for a couple of days, especially if it's to recruit someone positioned to influence the president of Mexico."

"We want to apprehend Nova," Greg said. "That's the important thing right now. I know our techs are good at spoofing the location of an outgoing email message, but I'm not sure if they can mirror the IP address to make it look like it's coming from Roe."

"Ken's very competent, and Valerie has spent enough time reading Roe's emails to Jason to have a feel for his writing style. Fortunately, Roe copied his assistant on all of his emails to Jason so that Jason would have a backup contact if something happened to him.

"I'll reach out to Valerie and Ken as soon as we're done and ask them to write a message from Roe to Park along those lines for my review ASAP. It's morning in Mexico City, and Park's going to be wondering where his boss is."

Chapter 62

Billy Chu re-read the classified message from Mexico City with increasing bewilderment. The NIS chief running the Mexican official with ties to Roe Min-Woo reported that Roe was a no-show for a planned get-together yesterday. Repeated calls to Roe's cell phone went unanswered, he added.

When pressed, the Mexican asset admitted he was cooperating with the Americans, giving them information similar to what he was sharing with South Korea. His American contact had asked him to invite Roe out for drinks to gain insights into how North Korean intelligence officers comport themselves on the street. Was Roe surveillance-conscious, did the North Korean do surveillance detection runs, did he employ disguises or use multiple modes of transportation?

The Mexican said he did not know for sure but presumed the Americans had people on the ground tracking Roe's movements from his apartment to the bar where they were supposed to have drinks. When he later reached out to his American contact, the latter said they had seen Roe on the street but backed off when he approached the bar. So they assumed he had gone inside as planned.

Separately, the asset told his handler that a fugitive from the U.S., Eric Wong, who years ago had been on CNI's radar when he was living in Mexico City, was now holed up in Guadalajara. Apparently Wong was wanted for questioning by the FBI in connection with the murder of a U.S. citizen. The Mexican government didn't want a flap with the Americans, but they didn't plan to move against Wong unless the

U.S. Embassy officially asked them to.

Billy was under the impression the NIS had an agreement with the U.S. to share intelligence on North Korean issues, particularly Dave Kim's murder and the counterintelligence problem at Los Alamos. His meeting with Logan Alexander in Los Angeles left no doubt in his mind that the CIA wanted to work together.

Yet here it was only a couple of weeks later; if you could believe the reporting coming out of the South Korean Embassy in Mexico City, the CIA had horned in on a source recruited by his counterpart there, so that they could unilaterally target Roe Min-Woo.

The CIA's end-run to get at Roe was uncalled for. If not for the South Koreans' intelligence on Roe and Lee's relationship, the Americans would still be laboring under the false impression that security at Los Alamos was rock-solid.

He wondered if the CIA had picked Roe up and cold-pitched him to defect to the U.S. It would no doubt be a tough sell. Roe left a secure life in South Korea for the uncertainty of residence in the north. By all appearances, he didn't defect because of ideology; he did it out of love for his North Korean family. An offer of asylum in the U.S. might not be that appealing.

Billy was curious to know if the NKIS operated under the same guidelines as other intelligence agencies. For example, if a hostile intelligence service pitched an NIS officer, he was required to report the pitch to Headquarters. In all likelihood, if he were serving abroad, he would be recalled, and the CI center would initiate a comprehensive counterintelligence investigation.

The presumption was that the officer had displayed some vulnerability that led the hostile service to conclude they had a good chance of recruiting or blackmailing him. Sometimes in these cases, although not always, the investigators recommended termination of employment. Spying was a risky business. Was this what was in store for Roe?

Instinctively he wanted to reach out to Logan and ask him what was going on. Why had he decided to go it alone?

The problem was the CIA was the big dog on the block. Even though the NIS provided the original lead information on Roe Min-Woo and Jason Lee, the South Koreans were the junior partner in this relationship. It would be arrogant of him to call the CIA out for leaving the NIS in the dark.

Billy decided to go for a run to clear his head. He stopped by his secretary's desk on the way out.

"Susan, I've got some personal things to take care of. Tell the boss I'll be back in about an hour."

"She has a lunch meeting with the Chamber of Commerce. So you'll probably be back before her," she said with a wink.

Billy drove home, changed into his running gear, and was back outside in minutes. Running in Koreatown was a different experience than the competitive running he and Laurie did at UCLA. Since he'd been here, he had gone on several runs with the Koreatown Run Club. They were a fun bunch, and copious amounts of beer were always involved.

One of his favorites was a five-mile loop that began at a local brew pub and wound through a changing landscape of seedy and upscale areas before circling back to the brewery. The KRC usually did this run on a Thursday night, leaving plenty of time after the workout for craft beers and socializing.

This afternoon as he set out, Billy's mind was still on the Roe Min-Woo operation. He was so preoccupied he failed to notice the three gangbangers trolling the neighborhood in a restored Pontiac GTO. They sped past him and pulled over next to an alleyway.

Billy looked up just in time to see a gun pointed at his chest. The man holding the weapon looked Filipino. He gestured toward the alley, and the other two hoods followed them in.

"What do you want?" Billy asked. "I don't have any money on me."

"We don't want your money, asshole," the man with the gun said. "You're Billy Chu, the asshole that fucked up Sammy and Tony's lives." He spat the words out, eyes shooting darts at Billy.

Billy was momentarily confused. And then it hit him; these must be gangbangers from the Asian Hoods. "How did you find me?" He asked.

"I'll ask the questions," the leader snarled. "But for your information, the LA Times reporter who covered the Kim murder case identified you as the person who saved the Kims the night of the break-in.

"You're the one who screwed over our buddies; they're looking at life without parole thanks to you. Now you're going to pay."

"What's going on in here?" A worker from the corner restaurant had stepped into the alley to empty a trash barrel. The distraction was all Billy needed to spring into action.

Billy launched himself at the hood with a jarring kick to the groin. He went down hard, wailing in agony from the intense pain spreading through his loins. Billy whirled, delivering a roundhouse kick to one man's head and smashing his clenched fist into the other man's nose. It was over in seconds.

Billy was breathing heavily from the adrenaline surge and the exertion. He retrieved the gun while the three gangbangers continued to writhe on the ground. Billy looked at the stunned restaurant employee, standing by the open back door to the restaurant. The trash barrel had slipped from his hands, and garbage was strewn all over the ground.

"Don't just stand there," Billy yelled. "Call the police."

Chapter 63

Laurie Kim had been trying to reach Jason on his cell for several days. However, it wasn't until she contacted his boss at the pit production facility that she learned Jason had been hospitalized in Albuquerque with COVID-19.

Jason's boss didn't have any more information other than his case was severe, and he was on a ventilator in the intensive care unit. However, when Laurie spoke with Human Resources, she learned they had contacted Jason's mother in Toronto, and she was aware of the situation. Dr. Lee was trying to navigate the travel restrictions between Canada and the U.S. and hoped to visit him post-haste.

"Does that mean only family can visit him?" Laurie asked.

"You'll have to check with the hospital, Laurie," the HR officer said. "We don't know. We had another case a few months back; the employee was in the same situation, and not even his wife could get in to see him until they transferred him out of the ICU."

Laurie called the hospital looking for an update on Jason's condition, but the nurse she spoke with cited patient health information privacy under the HIPAA rules. "I'm sorry, Ms. Kim, our hands are tied. Unless you are next of kin, I can't tell you anything."

Laurie was depressed. Her father had died a violent death, and her mother was in the ICU. Now, the person she felt closest to was on a ventilator in the ICU, and she couldn't even hold his hand. She regretted pushing him away. The only other person she had been that intimate with was Billy, but that was years ago. They would always be friends, but the spark she felt for him in college was no longer alive.

Later that evening, Laurie was enjoying a glass of wine at home when the phone rang. It was Billy.

"Hi," he said. "I was thinking about you today and wondering how you're doing."

Laurie sighed. "It's been difficult. First Dad, and then Mom's accident."

"Of course, I know what happened with your dad, but I never did get the full story about your mom. Something about a hiking accident? Wasn't she staying with you in Los Alamos?"

Laurie told him the whole story; her mother's revelations about spying for North Korea, her affair with Eric Wong, that Wong was her biological father, and the altercation with her mother, which ended in her near-fatal accident.

Billy listened to Laurie's account without interrupting. However, the revelations about Ginny Kim's espionage career and her accident left him in shock. There were so many questions he wanted to ask. He'd known the Kims for years; nothing in his interactions with them could have prepared him for this.

He cleared his throat. "I don't know what to say. That's a lot to absorb. How are you holding up? Is anyone helping you get through this? Maybe Jason?"

"Jason has COVID," she said. "He's on a ventilator in the ICU at the University of New Mexico Hospital in Albuquerque."

"What?" Billy exclaimed. "When did this happen?"

"I just found out. I saw Jason right after Mom's accident; he stopped by to check up on me, and we talked. I was busy dealing with everything, and I haven't seen him since." She was silent for a moment.

"I told him a little while back that I wanted to cool things off. He was getting too serious, and I'm just not ready for that now."

"Sounds familiar," Billy said.

Laurie was silent for a moment and then burst out laughing. It took her a moment to catch her breath. "Whew," she said. "I guess I deserved that."

She thought back to their time together at UCLA. She and Billy had fallen for each other, but Billy had fallen hard. She broke up with him just after graduation, with the same lame excuse she gave Jason. She knew herself well enough to admit that she had commitment issues.

"One last thing," Billy said. "I had a pretty hairy run-in with three gangbangers from the Asian Hoods."

"I thought the Perez brothers were in jail," Laurie said.

"They are, and it looks like they're going away for a very long time. But their buddies came out looking for revenge." He told her about the confrontation in Koreatown and his good fortune.

"If that guy from the restaurant hadn't come into the alley when he did, I'm not sure it would have turned out that way. That split-second distraction probably saved my life."

Laurie gasped. She couldn't bear the thought that someone else she cared for might die.

"I'll give you a call next week to see how you're doing," Billy said. "Take care."

Billy hung up, a thoughtful expression on his face. He felt Laurie's pain. They had been together the entire time they were at UCLA. But he was distracted by her revelation that Jason Lee was in the ICU with COVID. Was it just a coincidence that both Jason and his father were incommunicado at the same time?

According to Laurie, Jason went into the ICU just a couple of days ago. That would have been about the same time that Roe Min-Woo went off the grid if the reporting from Mexico City was accurate. Billy had an intelligence officer's instincts, and his intuition told him that there was something fishy going on.

Maybe Bureau 35 got wind of the FBI and CIA's investigation and decided to pull them out before there was a flap. Instead of one ailing in the ICU in Albuquerque and the other chasing a promising agent candidate in Mexico City, Jason and Roe could be on their way to Pyongyang.

Or just maybe the CIA's hand was behind all of this. There was a certain finesse to the way this was playing out.

But why? Why would the CIA take the NKIS officer and his agent out of play? How long would it be before Pyongyang found out and responded?

Chapter 64

Logan was back at Los Alamos, following a full day with the debriefing team and Roe. He was bringing Peter and Martina up to date on his meetings with the NKIS officer.

"Roe's going to be a tough nut to crack," Logan said. "He was combative most of the time I was in the room. Plus, he's feeling disoriented, not knowing exactly where he is or who we are."

"So you brought him in black?" Peter asked.

"Yeah. The whole time we were moving. He probably suspects he's in the U.S., and he's already asked me once if we're the CIA. So I doubt either one of those would come as a surprise to him.

"Koreans are hardcore, especially if they're from the North. The usual rules don't apply to him, though, since he's originally from the South. Still, I'll bet the NKIS teaches their recruits how to deal with interrogations. Roe is probably more afraid of what will happen to him back home if word gets out that he talked than anything we could do to him."

"Will you do that to get him to cooperate?" Martina asked. "Use enhanced interrogation techniques?"

"No, nothing like that. We want to turn him, get him to cooperate with us, maybe even turn him back against the NKIS, although they may never trust him again if they suspect he was in our custody. We might be able to use Jason as leverage. If we tell Roe that he and Jason will be locked up for a very long time if they don't come clean, that may be enough to bring him over."

"And if he doesn't?" Martina asked.

"It'll be up to the FBI and DOJ. Conspiracy to commit a

terrorist act against the United States is a big deal. And in Roe's case, his involvement in the attempt against Dave and Ginny Kim is a punishable crime."

"So what's next?" Peter asked.

"I need to get together with my team and find out where we are with the NKIS agent that's supposed to meet with Jason. The longer that meeting is delayed, the riskier it becomes."

"Why is that?" Martina asked.

"For one thing, we can't keep Roe for more than a day or two without the embassy in Mexico City reporting him missing. They don't want to send that message back to Pyongyang because, in a sense, it reflects poorly on the ambassador. North Korea's leadership goes ballistic when one of its diplomats goes off the radar.

"Their first thought is defection, and of course, they're worried about anything sensitive the defector reveals to their enemies—state secrets, plans, and intentions. But, just as bad, or maybe worse, is the public relations nightmare of having a senior government official turn on the regime. It makes the supreme leader look weak."

"You suggested there was more," Peter said, getting out of his chair to stretch.

"Right," Logan said. "It's the question of how long we can play out the story about Jason's absence. We put that out there mainly for local consumption because we had to get him off the street, and there was no other reasonable explanation for his going missing. His colleagues and friends would start asking questions.

"We didn't need that for Pyongyang or Mexico City because we took over Jason's computer, so for all Bureau 35 or his father know, Jason is on the other end, not the CIA. The downside of that ploy is if word gets back to Pyongyang somehow that Jason is on a ventilator in the hospital, they're going to wonder who's been answering the mail."

"What's your best-case scenario?" Martina asked.

"Best case is Nova reaches out to Jason in the next twenty-four hours. If he shows up, and we're able to intercept him, that will be a coup. We'll have three of their intelligence people under wraps, and we will have foiled a significant threat to U.S. national security.

"One more thing that came up while I was away. The CNI asset who's cooperating with us told his case officer that Eric Wong, who was on CNI's radar when he was living in Mexico, is back and is hiding out in Guadalajara. I don't know if we can get the Mexicans to extradite Wong to the U.S. They're probably not happy about how the Roe rendition went. You can only go to the well so many times before it dries up."

"Isn't that the truth," Peter said. "Thanks for the update, Logan. Do you need help with anything?"

"Thanks, Peter, but I'm good for now."

Logan headed over to the safe house he was sharing with Valerie and Ken.

"Want some coffee? I just made it." Ken was pouring himself a cup and held up the pot.

"I could use some," Logan said. "I didn't get much shut-eye last night."

Ken reached into the cabinet over the counter and pulled out two more coffee mugs. He poured coffee for Logan and Valerie, and then the three of them sat down at the kitchen table.

"How's everything going?" Logan asked.

"Quiet," Valerie said. "Everyone's waiting for Nova to say when he's available to meet Jason."

"When was the last time you checked Jason's messages?" Logan asked.

"An hour ago." She logged onto Jason's computer and navigated to the secure messaging browser again.

"We've got something," she said. "It's from Nova." It took five minutes for her to work out the translation, which she then handed to Logan. He took it from her and began reading; when he was finished, he looked up, eyes flashing.

"He wants to meet tomorrow afternoon, 4 p.m. at the Crowne Plaza Albuquerque on University Boulevard Northeast. Jason's supposed to use the house phone and ask for J. Colada." Logan pounded his fist on the tabletop. "That's what I'm saying. Game on."

Logan made a secure call to Anthony Brown to advise him that the Nova operation was on for the next day.

"I've already reached out to the Special Agent in Charge of the Albuquerque Division to brief him in general terms on the operation," Anthony said. "It's his turf, so he's going to want his people involved."

The men agreed to meet at the ops center Anthony was setting up in one of the rooms at the Crowne Plaza tomorrow at 2 p.m.

Chapter 65

Logan spent the morning writing up his meetings with the debriefing team and Roe, and separately outlining the ops plan for the afternoon takedown of Nova. Everyone agreed Jason should remain in the safe house and not go to the hotel; it was too risky for him to be seen in public.

A couple of hours before the meeting, Anthony's people got Nova's room number and a key card from the front desk; then, they occupied a vacant room across the hall to use as a command post. It was now 3 p.m., and Logan, along with two FBI agents, was waiting for 4 o'clock. According to the hotel registration records, J. Colada used the hotel's mobile check-in/mobile key feature the night before; he secured the room with a Platinum American Express card in the name of J. Colada.

The men took turns eyeing the peephole to see if there was any activity in the hallway. A room service trolley trundling down the hall caused a moment of excitement, but it continued past them. There was some foot traffic, but for the most part, it was quiet. They decided to wait past the meeting time, just in case Nova was running late.

At 4:15, the three men crossed the hall, and the agent in charge rapped on the door. Logan tensed. He didn't know what to expect, but this arrest was going to put a dent in North Korea's covert operations in the United States.

"FBI, open up," the agent said. He and his partner had weapons drawn and stood to one side of the door as a precaution. They waited, listening intently, but there was no sound from within.

"This is the FBI," the agent repeated. "Come out with your hands up."

Still, it was quiet on the other side of the door. The agent in charge nodded to his partner, who slid the room key up to the keypad and held it for a second until he got a flashing green light.

The two agents flung open the door and rushed inside, sweeping their weapons left and right.

"FBI, don't move," they shouted as they stormed the room. It was empty, and there were no signs that anyone was staying there. One of the agents checked the bathroom while the other looked in the closet and under the bed. The fourth-floor balcony was also unoccupied.

"What the hell?" Logan said, a perplexed look on his face. "The message from Nova was unambiguous. Four o'clock today at the Crowne Plaza. He's registered here and checked in yesterday."

"That's one of the problems I have with all this remote/mobile stuff," the lead agent said. "You never get the chance to set eyes on the person coming in carrying their bags."

"Yeah, for all we know, J. Colada may not even be Nova. Maybe he's a cutout."

"We should get out of here on the off-chance Nova is the real deal and got held up; he still might make the meeting."

"Good idea," Logan said. They returned to the command post and contacted the agent surveilling the hotel lobby.

"The target was a no-show. Anything going on in the lobby?" the lead agent asked.

"Negative. It's quiet down here."

"Okay, thanks. We're going to remain in the command post for a few hours and then pack it up."

"Roger that. Over and out."

"If you guys don't mind, I'm going to head back to Los Alamos and see if something came up," Logan said. "Maybe Nova got spooked. If something happened, he might reach out to Jason."

On his way back to Los Alamos, Logan replayed everything in his mind. Their plan was sound, but they didn't control one key element crucial to its success—Nova.

Anything could have happened to him. Maybe he slipped in the shower and broke his leg. Or perhaps he never planned to show up in the first place.

When Logan got back to the safe house, the first thing he did was to ask Valerie to check for any new messages from Nova.

"I just checked ten minutes ago and there wasn't anything. What happened?" she asked.

"He was a no-show," Logan replied. "Let's go back and review the message traffic to see if we missed anything."

Valerie, Ken, and Logan spent the next hour rifling through any communications dealing with Nova or his trip to Albuquerque. Nothing jumped out. Nova was supposed to meet at the Crowne Plaza today at 4 o'clock, come hell or high water.

"I need to go over to the other safe house and check in on Jason. Maybe he's got some ideas." He called Nathan Riley's cell phone, but it went to voicemail.

"Hey, Nathan, it's Logan. I'm coming your way. I should be there in about twenty minutes. I need to talk to our houseguest." Nathan must have taken Jason on one of his runs.

When Logan got to the safe house, it was already twilight; the Rileys hadn't turned on the outside lights yet. Nathan's car wasn't parked in the driveway where it usually was. Logan rapped on the door a few times, but no one answered. He let himself in and turned on a light.

"Nathan, Carla, Jason. Anybody home?"

He searched the house top to bottom but could find no one. He tried Nathan's phone again and heard it ringing upstairs; he discovered it stuffed under a mattress in Nathan and Carla's bedroom.

What the hell was going on? When he searched the garage, he found out why Nathan wasn't answering his phone. He and Carla were tied up and sat slouched against one wall. They jerked awake as Logan came in. He stooped down to untie their hands and feet and help them up.

"What the hell happened?" Logan asked.

"It was this little Asian woman. Showed up here around

one o'clock with some cockamamie story about being lost. Then she pulled out a gun. We tried to talk her out of it, but she paid no mind. Jason helped her tie us up, and then they left together."

"Did she say where they were going?" Logan asked.

"Not a clue. She didn't seem to be the type to do something like this. She even apologized before they took off."

Logan had an idea who it was, but he had to know for sure. He remembered that the door to the house was equipped with a wireless doorbell camera. He handed Nathan his phone to pull up the video and found himself staring at the smiling face of Laurie Kim.

Chapter 66

Laurie and Jason were nowhere to be found. Within a day, they erased their social media accounts, canceled their credit cards, and ditched their cell phones. It was as though they had dropped off the face of the Earth.

The FBI launched an intensive search for the two fugitives throughout the Southwest, extending as far west as California. Anthony Brown was leading the effort from Santa Fe, given the North Korea case was in his jurisdiction.

Logan was furious over Jason's escape and blamed himself for failing to double-down on security at the safehouse to ensure this kind of thing didn't happen.

When he returned to Los Alamos, Logan suggested Headquarters and the TDY team dismantle the two safe houses. However, doing so didn't mean they were giving up on their investigation, because the North Korean nuclear threat remained real. Headquarters concurred with Logan's recommendation and ordered Valerie and Ken to wrap it up and return to Washington to continue their work.

"Right now, the most important thing we can do is run Jason and Laurie to ground," Logan said as he drove Valerie and Ken to the airport for their flight back to Dulles.

"As far as I'm concerned, apprehending those two would be a twofer," Valerie said. "I have a gut feeling that Laurie Kim is Nova; the evidence points to it. She's the personification of a North Korean illegal, playing the role effectively throughout her adult life."

"How do you think she found out we had Jason?" Logan asked.

"She probably has her own commo system," Valerie said. "She knew Jason couldn't make the Nova meeting if he were hospitalized and on a ventilator. She reported that back to Bureau 35, and they realized Jason wasn't corresponding with them; it was us. So they told her to cancel the meeting."

"Meanwhile, Laurie took the initiative to find out where Jason was," Ken said. "It was a long shot, but it paid off. She used GPS to locate his cell phone. It's not that hard; there are all kinds of commercial software programs capable of doing that. There weren't many other houses nearby, so it was easy for her to figure out where he was."

"But we had Jason's phone," Logan countered. "Even if she could have done that, it would have pointed her to our safe house."

"There was that one time," Ken said, looking sheepish. "Remember, early on, I took the phone over there so he could show us his log-on password and dismantle the biometrics log-on. Afterwards, I plugged it in to charge, but forgot it when I left. It was there overnight. We know he didn't use it during that time because I changed the password after he logged on. She could have found him then. That's all I can think of."

"I'm pretty sure by now Bureau 35 is aware that we are onto Operation Supreme Threat and Nova," Valerie said as Logan pulled up to the departures lane at Albuquerque International. "The last message we had from them was the one with the particulars for meeting Nova, and that was a week ago. They've shut down communications with Jason."

"Let's back up a second. I'm curious about Bureau 35's decision to go with a hotel meeting, if we truly suspect Laurie is Nova," Logan said. "Is it possible her handlers didn't know Jason and Laurie were dating? They had a romantic relationship and could meet anywhere without arousing suspicion. I suspect Roe was aware of their relationship, but I don't know if he reported it to his Headquarters."

"It was probably precautionary," Ken said. "The North Koreans know we are technically capable and may have suspected we had audio coverage in her apartment, but it's hard to pull off in a hotel, especially when it's a short-fuse requirement. So doing the hotel meeting was their best shot." He paused a moment. "Or maybe we're barking up the wrong tree. Maybe Laurie isn't Nova."

Logan pulled up opposite Valerie and Ken's departure gate. "Thanks for everything. I didn't know how this was all going to end when we started. We still have some serious loose ends to tidy up, but I think we did some good work here. Stay in touch." On his way back to Los Alamos, Logan called Anthony. He picked up on the first ring.

"Brown here."

"Anthony? Logan. Do you have time for a beer after work? I'm on my way back to the lab from Albuquerque, and I thought I'd swing by."

"What are you, about an hour out?"

"Yeah, I'm just leaving the airport."

"Okay, you remember the alehouse we went to last time?" Anthony asked.

"Yes, the one with the frosted mugs."

"That's the one. And, Logan, there have been some developments; we have a lot to discuss."

An hour later, Logan pulled into the Green Room Ale House's crowded parking lot. He'd been thinking about Anthony's comment all the way there and was anxious to hear what he had to say. He spotted the FBI agent waiting for him in a booth by a couple of pool tables where two good old boys were trash-talking each other over a friendly game of pool.

"Sorry I couldn't get better seats," Anthony said, nodding slightly towards the men playing pool. "They're busy tonight."

"No problem," Logan said, sliding into the booth. They ordered beers and relaxed for a moment. Logan broke the silence.

"You got my attention on the phone. What developments?"

"We found Laurie Kim's car in a self-parking garage at Caesar's Palace in Las Vegas. It was left there two days ago. Security footage showed Laurie and Jason arriving and getting picked up by a taxi outside."

"Were you able to track the taxi?" Logan asked.

"Video caught the license plate, and we were able to find the cabbie, who said he dropped them off at the Greyhound transit terminal in Las Vegas."

"Any idea where they went?" Logan asked.

"They purchased one-way tickets to LA online. Greyhound runs eight trips daily from Las Vegas to LA. We're not sure which bus they took, because the tickets were purchased under another name.

"Also, it seems they took some steps to disguise their appearance, hats, and sunglasses. We thought we lost them, but here's where it gets interesting."

Logan gripped his mug in anticipation. The good old boys were whooping it up, and a live band was setting up on the other side of the room.

"We got a call this afternoon from the FBI Division in LA. Earlier in the day, they received a call from a boat charter company in Marina Del Rey. A couple matching the description of our suspects and one other person chartered a bareboat catamaran with plans to sail it one-way to Cabo San Lucas. Laurie and Jason used the same identification they had on their Greyhound tickets. The captain is a guy by the name of Aaron Fowler from LA. We're still trying to run down his particulars," Anthony said.

"The Coast Guard spotted the catamaran yesterday afternoon about thirty nautical miles offshore, just north of Ensenada. The boat was not under sail and appeared to be drifting. They called out and got no response, so they boarded and found no one there. The gas tank was empty."

"That's bizarre," Logan exclaimed. "What do they think happened?"

"The Coast Guard has been checking up and down the coast with aircraft and other Coast Guard vessels, but so far nothing. There were no Mayday calls in that area over the last forty-eight hours and no apparent reason for abandoning ship. The weather has been perfect. The Coast Guard is beginning to suspect, and I agree with them, foul play."

"How do three people just disappear off of a sailboat?" Logan asked. "But my big question is, who the hell is Aaron Fowler?"

Chapter 67

It had been a week since Laurie Kim, Jason Lee, and Aaron Fowler disappeared off the coast of California. Search planes and vessels spent days scouring hundreds of square miles of open water for any signs of the missing fugitives. Finally, the Coast Guard called off their search at dusk on the seventh day.

Logan was TDY to the Agency facility in southern Virginia when he got the news. He was participating in the Roe debriefings, and they were beginning to make some progress. The Agency had yet to advise Roe that Jason was missing, lest it cause a setback in the progress they were making. At some point, though, they would have to tell him what they knew.

Logan had a headache. They allowed Roe to smoke during the debriefings because it relaxed him, but eight hours of inhaling secondhand smoke gave Logan brain fog. Nonetheless, there was an exciting development in today's debriefings; it emerged as they were wrapping things up for the day. Logan asked Roe if he knew much if anything about Dave Kim's recruitment.

"Yes, it was a fellow by the name of Eric Wong, who went into business with Kim and ended up recruiting his wife too," Roe said.

"I thought Bureau 35 kept his identity close-hold," Logan said. "How did you come to know about him?"

"I heard about it after Dave Kim's murder. Eric Wong disappeared, and Bureau 35 asked us to be on the lookout for him in case he showed up in Mexico."

"Was Wong doing anything else in LA besides handling the Kims?" Logan asked.

"Yes, he was managing an important case for the front office."

"What was it about?" Logan asked.

"It was a sensitive asset only he and a few other people knew about. I didn't know the person."

"Was there a case file or code name they used to refer to this asset?" Logan asked.

"Yes. Bureau 35 referred to him as Nova."

"Nova?" Logan's pulse raced.

That night, Logan put together a proposal for his travel to Mexico to meet with Eric Wong. According to embassy reporting Wong was hiding out in Guadalajara. There were sensitive negotiations between CNI and the FBI over Wong's possible extradition to the U.S. for questioning, but talks had hit a snag with the Mexican Department of Justice. Logan felt time was of the essence and there was probably a lot Wong could tell them. His immediate goal was to get Wong to reveal the identity of Nova before he disappeared.

It was a long shot as to whether Wong would be cooperative. He was comfortable in Mexico, having spent so many years there when he was younger. But the problem for him was the Mexicans could extradite him to the States if the U.S. applied enough pressure.

A day later, Logan was on a flight to Guadalajara. Wong didn't know they would be meeting; it would be a cold approach. Before he left, Logan asked the surveillance team from Mexico City to surveil Wong in Guadalajara for a couple of days to get a sense of his patterns of activity. When Logan checked into his hotel, the surveillance chief dropped off a package of photos and surveillance reports.

After a shower and a change of clothes, Logan sat down to review the material. One photo, taken with a telephoto lens, showed two people sitting on an outside verandah. He recognized Wong from the file the FBI put together in LA. But it was the second person who got his attention. The man's head was turned, almost as if to pose for the camera. The sunlight caused him to squint, and he was in the process of tilting a bottle of beer to his lips. Logan's breathing slowed, and he brought the photo closer to his face as he looked into the eyes of Billy Chu.

It took a day, but the employee who leased the sailboat charter out of Marina Del Rey to Laurie Kim and Jason Lee confirmed that Billy Chu, also known as Aaron Fowler, was the third person in the party. After that, things moved quickly. The U.S. ambassador demarched the Mexican government to extradite Billy Chu as a person of interest in the disappearance of Laurie Kim and Jason Lee. He also asked the authorities to detain Eric Wong for questioning by the FBI.

Because Billy was assigned to the South Korean consulate in LA., he did not enjoy diplomatic immunity in the United States; only personnel assigned to the embassy in Washington did. After some wrangling, the Mexican government agreed, and the FBI arrested Billy at Eric Wong's residence without incident. A U.S. marshal accompanied Billy back to LA for questioning. Special Agent Ben Conroy from the Bureau's Los Angeles Division conducted the interview.

Confronted with proof that he was on the boat with Laurie and Jason, Billy confessed to their murder and his long-time espionage career for North Korea. Eric Wong had recruited him when he was at UCLA, and Eric told his lover, Ginny Kim, about the relationship with Billy after her husband was murdered.

"Ginny told Laurie when they went hiking in Los Alamos that I was involved with the North Koreans. That's what led to their argument and Ginny's accident," Billy said.

"At first, Laurie didn't want to reach out to me, but she thought I would be able to introduce her to Eric. I found out from her that Jason supposedly was hospitalized with COVID just as I was being directed to meet with him to discuss a sensitive operation coming out of Bureau 35. I knew then that the operation was compromised because Jason couldn't be communicating with me if he were truly incapacitated.

"Laurie never spied for North Korea, and she felt betrayed by everyone she's ever loved. She felt Jason was being set up by his father and would do anything to free him. She wanted to meet Eric because she thought he could help clear Jason's name. Laurie knew I had been around boats all my life and had a captain's license for offshore sailing. It was her idea to sail to Cabo when I told her Eric was in Mexico.

"Eric told me he was going to Guadalajara before he left. Later I found out that you knew he was in Mexico and were considering extradition. I knew it was risky, but given what happened on the boat I needed to talk to him."

"So, what happened when you got out there on the water?" Ben asked.

"We were about ten miles offshore and got into a huge argument. Laurie was screaming and threatening to expose me to the police. She said she was going to ruin my life. Later that night, she and Jason got wasted drinking wine. I couldn't see myself spending the rest of my life behind bars; she made it clear she would do anything to clear Jason's name, so I shot them both. Afterwards, I wrapped the bodies in a tarp, weighed it down with a spare anchor, and tossed them overboard." He heaved a deep sigh and looked down at the table.

"Before dawn I brought the boat close to shore, set it on autopilot to take it due west, and swam ashore. At that point, I figured it was all over, so I decided to run for it."

"I have one more question for you, right now Mr. Chu," Ben said. "What made you decide to spy for North Korea?"

"That's the demon I'm still searching for," was all Billy said.

THE END

Epilogue

Billy Chu's confession and trial six months later resulted in his conviction for espionage and the murders of Laurie Kim and Jason Lee. California is one of eleven states in the U.S. with the death penalty; however, it has been ten years since a convicted felon in the state has been executed. Although he is cooperating with the Intelligence Community from his prison cell, Billy Chu will likely spend the rest of his natural life behind bars.

Eric Wong remained in police custody in Guadalajara for two weeks. Following his interview with FBI agents there, the U.S. sought extradition to the U.S., where he is now facing espionage charges.

Roe Min-Woo defected to the U.S. following his rendition from Mexico and cooperation with the CIA. His revelations about Bureau 35, the North Korean Intelligence Service, and North Korea's nuclear program provided invaluable insights into North Korea's plans and intentions against the U.S. He was inconsolable over the death of his son and has been resettled in an undisclosed foreign location.

Martina Rodriguez and Peter Hanlon continue to fight the good fight every day at Los Alamos. Their security program has become a model for counterintelligence programs at the national labs nationwide.

Logan Alexander will finish his tour at Los Alamos, where he is training a new counterintelligence officer, following Congress's authorization of a permanent position at the lab. Given his exceptional accomplishments exposing secret North Korean operatives and derailing a North Korean plot to set off a nuclear device in Washington, he is expected to be named to a senior position at the CIA. Zahir and Cooper are looking forward to having him around the house more often.

The CIA is conducting damage assessments and reevaluating their intelligence relationship with South Korea. Billy Chu's access to sensitive CIA intelligence reporting over the short time he was posted to the South Korean Consulate in LA may have seriously compromised sources and methods.

After the president of the United States was briefed on North Korea's failed operation, code-named Supreme Threat, he asked Congress to earmark additional funds to beef up the Intelligence Community's efforts against the North Korea nuclear threat. He gave the directors of the relevant intelligence agencies two months to formulate operational recommendations to neutralize Kim's nuclear ambitions once and for all. At this writing, the Intelligence Community is weighing its options.

Laurie Kim's and Jason Lee's bodies were never recovered.

GLOSSARY

ADDO	Associate Deputy Director for Operations
ASAC	Assistant Special Agent in Charge
CBP	Customs and Border Patrol
CI	Counter Intelligence
CIA	Central Intelligence Agency
CINT	Center for Integrated Nanotechnologies
CNI	Mexican Intelligence Agency
CPC	Counter Proliferation Center
CSIS	Canadian Security Intelligence Service
DDO	Deputy Director for Operations
DO	Directorate of Operations
DOD	Department of Defense
DOE	Department of Energy
DOJ	Department of Justice
FBI	Federal Bureau of Investigation
FISA	Foreign Intelligence Surveillance Act
IAEA	International Atomic Energy Agency
LEGATTFBI	Legal Attache (Assigned Overseas)
LUMOS	Lab for Ultrafast Materials and Optical Science
MFA	Ministry of Foreign Affairs
NCIC	National Counter Intelligence Center
NIS	National Intelligence Service (South Korea)
NKIS	North Korean Intelligence Service
NNSA	National Nuclear Security Administration
NPA	National Police Agency (South Korea)
NR Division	National Resources Division (CIA Domestic Office)
NSA	National Security Agency
OSS	Office of Strategic Services (Predecessor organization to CIA)

OST	Office of Secure Transportation
RCMP	Royal Canadian Mounted Police
ROK	Republic of Korea / South Korea
SAC	Special Agent in Charge
SPO	Security Police Officer
TSD	Transportation and Safeguards Division

CPSIA information can be obtained
at www.ICGtesting.com
Printed in the USA
BVHW070953071021
618410BV00006B/57

9 780988 440098